PRAISE FOR
THE DETECTIVE HELEN GRACE THRILLERS

"It's almost always cause for skepticism when a book's jacket copy promises an ingenious new variety of serial killer, but amazingly enough it's true of M. J. Arlidge's gripping debut. . . . His story is honest to us and to itself, and boy, do the pages fly by."
                                                                —*USA Today*

"A fast-paced, twisting police procedural and thriller sure to become another bestseller."
                                                —The Huffington Post

"I couldn't turn the pages fast enough."

                        —#1 *New York Times* bestselling author Tami Hoag

"There are so many things about this novel that are expertly pulled off . . . a dark, edgy thriller."   —*New York Times* bestselling author Will Lavender

"What a great premise! . . . A fresh and brilliant departure from the stock serial killer tale. And Helen Grace is one of the greatest heroes to come along in years."   —*New York Times* bestselling author Jeffery Deaver

"Exciting. . . . Readers will root for this admirable if flawed heroine every step of the way."   —*Publishers Weekly*

"Pure, gripping entertainment."   —Crime by the Book

"M. J. Arlidge has created a genuinely fresh heroine in Helen Grace. . . . He spares us none of the dark details, weaving them together into a tapestry that chills to the bone."   —*Daily Mail* (UK)

Also by M. J. Arlidge

Detective Helen Grace Thrillers

Eeny Meeny
Pop Goes the Weasel
The Doll's House
Liar Liar

LITTLE BOY BLUE

A DETECTIVE HELEN GRACE THRILLER

M. J. ARLIDGE

BERKLEY

NEW YORK

BERKLEY
An imprint of Penguin Random House LLC
375 Hudson Street, New York, New York 10014

Copyright © 2016 by M. J. Arlidge
Excerpt from *Eeny Meeny* copyright © 2014 by M. J. Arlidge
Penguin supports copyright. Copyright fuels creativity, encourages diverse voices,
promotes free speech, and creates a vibrant culture. Thank you for buying an authorized
edition of this book and for complying with copyright laws by not reproducing, scanning, or
distributing any part of it in any form without permission. You are supporting writers and
allowing Penguin to continue to publish books for every reader.

BERKLEY is a registered trademark and the B colophon is a trademark of
Penguin Random House LLC.

Title page art © Geoffrey Kuchera/Shutterstock Images

Library of Congress Cataloging-in-Publication Data

Names: Arlidge, M. J., author
Title: Little boy blue / M. J. Arlidge.
Description: Berkley trade paperback edition. | New York City: Berkley,
2016. | Series: A Helen Grace thriller; 5
Identifiers: LCCN 2016012507 (print) | LCCN 2016018593 (ebook) | ISBN
9781101991374 (softcover) | ISBN 9781101991381 (ebook)
Subjects: LCSH: Policewomen—Fiction. | Women detectives—Fiction. | Serial
murder investigation—Fiction. | BISAC: FICTION / Suspense. | FICTION /
Thrillers. | GSAFD: Suspense fiction. | Mystery fiction.
Classification: LCC PR6051.R55 L58 2016 (print) | LCC PR6051.R55 (ebook) |
DDC 823/.914—dc23
LC record available at https://lccn.loc.gov/2016012507

Penguin Group (UK) trade paperback edition / March 2016
Berkley trade paperback edition / October 2016

PRINTED IN THE UNITED STATES OF AMERICA
10 9 8 7 6 5 4 3 2 1

Cover photo by David Lichtneker / Arcangel Images
Cover design by Colleen Reinhart

LITTLE BOY BLUE

1

He looked like a falling angel. His muscular body, naked save for a pair of silver wings, was suspended in midair, turning back and forth on the heavy chain that bound him to the ceiling. His fingers groped downward, straining for the key that would effect his release, but it remained tantalizingly out of reach. He was at the mercy of his captor and she circled him now, debating where to strike next. His chest? His genitals? The soles of his feet?

A crowd had gathered to watch, but *he* didn't linger. He was bored by the spectacle—had seen it countless times before—and moved on quickly, hoping to find something else to distract him. He always came to the Annual Ball—it was the highlight of the S&M calendar on the South Coast—but he suspected this year would be his last. It wasn't simply that he kept running into exes who he'd rather avoid; it was more that the scene had become so *familiar*. What had once seemed outrageous and thrilling now felt empty and contrived. The same people doing the same old things and wallowing in the attention.

Perhaps he just wasn't in the right mood tonight. Since he'd split up with David, he'd been in such a deep funk that nothing seemed to give him any pleasure. He'd come here more in hope than in expectation, and already he could feel the disappointment and self-disgust welling up inside him. Everybody else seemed to be having a good time—and there was certainly no shortage of offers from fellow revelers—so what was wrong with him? Why was he incapable of dealing with the fact that he was alone?

He pushed his way to the bar and ordered a double Jameson, then scanned the scene as the barman obliged. Men, women and others who were somewhere in between paraded themselves on the dance floors and podiums—a seething mass of humanity crammed within the basement club's crumbling walls. This was their night and they were all in their Sunday best—rubber-spiked dominators, padlocked virgins, sluts who blossom into swans and, of course, the obligatory gimps. All trying so hard.

As he turned back to the bar in disgust, he saw him. Framed by the frenzied crowds, he appeared as a fixed point—an image of utter stillness amid the chaos, coolly surveying the clubbers in front of him. Was it a "him"? It was hard to say. The dark leather mask covered everything but the eyes, and the matching suit revealed only a sleek, androgynous figure. Running his eyes over the concealed body in search of clues, he suddenly realized that the object of his attention was looking straight at him. Embarrassed, he turned away. Seconds later, however, curiosity got the better of him and he stole another glance.

The person was still staring at him. This time he didn't turn away. Their eyes remained glued to each other's for ten seconds or more, before the figure suddenly turned and walked away, heading toward the darker, more discreet areas of the club.

Now he didn't hesitate, following him past the bar, past the dance floor, past the chained angel and on toward the back rooms—heavily in demand tonight as private spaces for brief, fevered liaisons. He could feel his excitement growing and as he picked up the pace, his eyes took in the contours of the person ahead of him. Was it his imagination or was there something familiar about the shape of the body? Was this someone known to him, someone he'd met in the course of work or play? Or was this a total stranger who'd singled him out for special attention? It was an intriguing question.

The figure had come to a halt now, standing alone in a small, dingy room ahead. In any other situation, caution would have made him hesitate. But not tonight. Not now. So, entering the room, he marched directly toward the expectant figure, pushing the door firmly shut behind him.

2

The piercing scream was long and loud. Her eyes darted left just in time to see the source of the noise—a startled vixen darting into the undergrowth—but she didn't break stride, diving ever deeper into the forest. Whatever happened now, she had to keep going.

Her lungs burned and her muscles ached, but on she went, braving the low branches and the fallen logs, praying her luck would hold. It was nearly midnight and there was not a soul around to help her should she fall, but she was so close now.

The trees were thinning out, the foliage was less dense and seconds later she broke cover—a svelte, hooded figure darting across the vast expanse of Southampton Common. She was closing in fast on the cemetery that marked the western edge of the park, and though her body was protesting bitterly, she lurched forward once more. In a few seconds she was there, slapping the cemetery gates hard before wrenching up her sleeve to arrest her stopwatch. Forty-eight minutes and fifteen seconds—a new personal best.

Breathing heavily, Helen Grace pulled back her hood and turned her face to the night. The moon was nearly full, the sky cloudless, and the gentle breeze that rippled over her was crisp and refreshing. Her heart was beating out a furious rhythm, the sweat creeping down her cheeks, but she found herself smiling, happy to have shaved half a minute off her time, pleased that she had the moon at least to bear witness to her triumph. She had never pushed herself this hard before, but it had been worth it.

Dropping to the ground, she began to stretch. She knew she made an odd sight—a lone female contorting herself in the shadow of a decaying cemetery—and that many would have chastised her for being here so late at night. But it was part of her routine now and she never felt any fear or anxiety in this place. She reveled in the isolation and solitude—somehow being alone made it feel like *her* space.

Her life had been so troubled and complex, so fraught with incident and danger, that there were very few places where she truly felt at peace. But here, a tiny, anonymous figure dwarfed by the immense darkness of the deserted common, she felt relaxed and happy. More than that, she felt free.

3

He couldn't move a muscle.

Conversation had been brief and they had moved quickly to the main event. A chair had been pulled out into the middle of the room and he had been pushed down roughly onto it. He knew not to say anything—the beauty of these encounters was that they were mysterious, anonymous and secret. Careless talk ruined the moment, but not here—something about this one just felt right.

He sat back and allowed himself to be bound. His captor had come prepared, wrapping thick ribbon around his ankles, tethering them to the chair legs. The material felt smooth and comforting against his skin and he exhaled deeply—he was so used to being in control, to being the one thinking, planning, doing, that it was gratifying to switch off for once. It had been a long time since anyone had taken him in hand and he suddenly realized how excited he was at the prospect.

Next it was his arms, pushed gently behind his back, then secured to the chair with leather straps. He could smell the tang of the cured hide—it was a smell that had intrigued him since he had been a boy, and its aroma was pleasantly familiar. He closed his eyes now—it was more enjoyable if you couldn't see what was coming—and braced himself for what was ahead.

The next stage was more complicated, but no less tender. Wet sheets were carefully unfurled and steadily applied, from the ankle up. As the minutes passed, the moisture began to evaporate, and the sheets tightened, sticking close to his skin. Before long he couldn't move anything below his waist—a strange but not unpleasant sensation. Moments later, he was bound to the chest, his lover for the night carefully finishing the job by securing the upper sheet with heavy-duty duct tape, winding it round and round his broad shoulders, coming to a halt just beneath his Adam's apple.

He opened his eyes and looked at his captor. The atmosphere in the room was thick with expectation—there were many different ways this could play out: some consensual, some less so. Each had its merits and he wondered which one he, or she, would choose.

Neither spoke. The silence between them was punctured only by the distant thump of the Euro pop currently deafening those on the dance floor. But the sound seemed a long way away, as if they were in a different universe, locked together in this moment.

Still his captor made no move to punish or pleasure him and for the first time he felt a flash of frustration—everyone likes to be teased, but there are limits. He could feel the beginnings of an erection straining against its constraints, and he was keen not to let it go to waste.

"Come on, then," he said softly. "Don't make me wait. It's been a long time since I had any love."

He closed his eyes again and waited. What would come first? A slap? A blow? A caress? For a moment nothing happened; then suddenly he felt something brush against his cheek. His lover had moved in close—he could feel his breath on the side of his face, could hear his cracked lips parting.

"This isn't about love," his captor whispered. "This is about *hate*."

His eyes shot open, but it was too late. His captor was already winding the duct tape over his chin, his mouth . . . He tried to scream, but his tongue was forced back down by the sticky, bitter adhesive. Now the tape was covering his cheeks, flattening his nose. Moments later, the tape passed over his eyes and everything went black.

4

Helen stared out into the darkness beyond. She was back in her flat, showered and swathed in a towel, sitting by the casement window that looked out onto the street. The adrenaline and endorphins of earlier had dissipated, replaced by a relaxed, contented calm. She had no need for sleep—she wanted to enjoy this moment a little first—so she'd taken up her customary position in front of the window, her vantage point on the world beyond.

It was at times like this that Helen thought she was making a go of her life. The old demons still lurked within, but her use of pain as a way of controlling her emotions had eased off of late, as she'd learned to push her body in other ways. She wasn't there yet—would she ever be?—but she was on the right track. Sometimes she suppressed the feelings of hope this engendered in her, for fear of being disappointed; at other times she gave in to them.

Tonight was one of those moments when she allowed herself a little happiness.

Cradling her mug of tea, she looked down on the street below. She was a night owl and this was one of her favorite times, when the world seemed quiet, yet full of mystery and promise—the dark before the dawn. Living high up, she was shielded from view and could watch undetected as the night creatures went about their business. Southampton had always been a bustling, vibrant city and around midnight the streets regularly filled with workers, students, ships' crews, tourists and more, as the pubs emptied out. Helen enjoyed watching the human dramas that played out below—lovers falling out and reconciling, best friends declaring their mutual affection for each other, a woman in floods of tears on her mobile phone, an elderly couple holding hands on their way home to bed. Helen liked to climb inside their lives, imagining what would happen next for them, what highs and lows still lay ahead.

Later still, when the streets thinned out, you saw the really interesting sights—the night birds who were up at the darkest point of the day. Sometimes these sights tugged at your heart—the homeless, vulnerable and miserably drunk plowing their lonely furrows through the city. Other times they made you sit up—fights between drunken boys, the sight of a junkie prowling the derelict building opposite, a noisy domestic incident spilling out onto the streets. Other times they made Helen laugh—fresher students pushing one another around in "borrowed" Sainsbury's trolleys, clueless as to where they were or how they would find their way back to their digs.

All human life passed before her and Helen drank it in, enjoying the feeling of quiet omniscience that her elevated view gave her. Sometimes she chided herself for her voyeurism, but more often than not, she gave in to it, wallowing in the "company" it afforded her. On occasion, it did make her wonder whether any of the night stalkers were aware they were being watched, and if so, whether they would care. And occasionally, in her darker, more paranoid moments, it made her wonder whether somebody might in turn be watching *her*.

5

The panic shears lay on the floor, untouched. The heavy-duty scissors were specifically designed to cut through clothing, tape, even leather—but they wouldn't be used. There would be no deliverance tonight.

The chair had toppled over as the panicking victim attempted to wrestle himself free of his bonds. He made a strange sight now, bucking pointlessly on the floor as his fear grew and his breath shortened. He was making no headway in loosening his restraints and the end could not be far away now. Standing over him, his attacker looked on, wondering what the eventual cause of death would be. Overheating? Asphyxiation? Cardiac arrest? It was impossible to say and the uncertainty was quietly thrilling.

His victim's movements were slowing now and the leather-clad figure moved away. There was nothing to be gained by enjoying the show, especially when some sexed-up freak might burst in at any minute. His work here was done.

Turning away, he walked calmly toward the door. Would they get it? Would they realize what they were dealing with? Only time would tell, but whatever happened, there was one thing that the police, the public and the freaks out there *wouldn't* be able to ignore: the lovingly bound figure lying on the floor nearby, twitching slowly to a standstill as death claimed him.

6

Where was he?

The same question had spun round Sally's head for hours. She'd tried to go to sleep, but had given up, first flicking on the radio, then later switching on the light to read. But the words wouldn't go in and she'd reach the end of the page none the wiser. In the end she'd stopped trying altogether, turning the light off to lie awake in darkness. She was a worrier—she knew that—prone to seeing misfortune around every corner. But surely she had a right to be worried. Paul was "working late" again.

A few weeks ago, this wouldn't have been a cause for concern. Paul was ambitious, hardworking and committed—his fierce work ethic had often meant him returning to cold dinners during the course of their twenty-year marriage. But then once, three weeks ago, she'd had to contact him urgently, following a call from his mother. Unable to reach him on his mobile, she'd called his PA, only to be told he'd left the office at five p.m. sharp. The hands of the kitchen clock pointed mockingly to eight p.m. as Sally hung up in shock. Her mind had immediately filled with possible scenarios— an accident, an affair—but she'd tried to quell her anxiety and when he returned home safe and sound later that night, she said nothing.

But when he next called to say he'd be home late, she plucked up courage and visited him in person. She'd gone to the office armed with excuses, but they proved unnecessary, as he wasn't there. He'd left early again. Had she successfully hidden her distress from his PA? She thought so, but she couldn't tell. Perhaps his PA already knew. They say the wife is always the last to find out.

Was Paul the kind of man to have an affair? Instinctively, Sally thought not. Her husband was an old-school Catholic who'd promised to honor his marriage vows and meant it. Their marriage, their family life, had been a happy, prosperous one. Moreover, Sally had kept her looks and her figure, despite the birth of the twins, and she was sure Paul still found her attractive, even if their lovemaking was more sporadic these days. No, instinctively she rebelled against the thought that he would give his love to someone else. But isn't that what every scorned wife believes until the extent of her husband's duplicity is revealed?

The minutes crawled by. What was he up to so late at night? Whom was he with? On numerous occasions during the last few days, she'd resolved to have it out with him. But she could never find the right words, and besides, what if she was wrong? Perhaps Paul was planning a surprise for her? Wouldn't he be devastated to be accused of betraying her?

The truth was that Sally was scared. One question can unravel a life. So though she lay awake, groping for the correct way to bring it up, she knew that she would never ask the question. Not because she didn't want to know. But because of what she might find out if she did.

7

It was nearly two a.m. and the seventh floor was as quiet as the grave. DS Charlie Brooks stifled a yawn as she leafed through the cold-case files on her desk. She was exhausted—the twin pressures of her recent promotion and motherhood taking their toll—but she was determined to give these cases the attention they deserved. They were unsolved murders going back ten, fifteen years—cases that were colder than cold—but the victims were all someone's daughter, mother, father or son, and those left behind craved answers as keenly now as they had at the time of initial bereavement. There was so much going on during the daily grind that it was only at night, when peace finally descended on Southampton Central, that Charlie could get to grips with these cases. This was just one of the extra duties required of her now that she'd made the leap from detective constable to detective sergeant, and she was determined not to be found wanting.

She had Helen Grace to thank for her elevation. Although Helen already had DS Sanderson to act as her deputy, she'd demanded that Charlie be promoted following her good work on the Ethan Harris case. Helen had met resistance from those who worried that the chain of command would be compromised, but in the end Helen had got her way, convincing enough of the people who mattered that Charlie deserved promotion.

DC Charlie Brooks had thus become DS Charlene Brooks. Nobody called her that, of course—she would always be Charlie to everyone at Southampton Central—but it still felt good when she heard her full name read out at the investiture ceremony. Helen was on hand that day, giving Charlie a discreet wink as she walked back to her place among the other deserving officers, trying to suppress a broad grin from breaking out over her face.

Afterward she'd wanted to take Helen out, to say thank you to her personally, but Helen wouldn't have it—ushering her instead to the Crown and Two Chairmen for the traditional "wetting" of the new sergeant's head. Was this to avoid any charges of favoritism, or simply because she wasn't comfortable accepting Charlie's thanks? It was hard to say and in any event, the booze-up that followed had been a good one. The whole team had turned up and everyone, with the possible exception of Sanderson, had gone out of their way to tell Charlie how pleased they were. Given the dark days she'd endured getting to this point, Charlie had been profoundly grateful for the vote of confidence they'd given her that night.

Charlie was so wrapped up in her recollections—dim memories of a very drunken, late-night karaoke session with DC McAndrew now surfacing—that she jumped when she looked up to see the duty sergeant standing over her.

"Sorry, miles away," she apologized, turning to face him.

"Justice never sleeps, eh?" he replied with his trademark wink. "This just came in. Thought you'd want to see it straightaway."

The piece of paper he handed her was scant on details—a suspected murder with no victim ID and no named witness—but there was something that immediately leaped out at her. Listed at the top of the incident sheet was the address—one she'd never been to but which was notorious in Southampton.

The Torture Rooms.

8

Helen walked toward the chaos. The club had been packed to the rafters and the partygoers now spilled onto the street, ushered there by the harassed bouncers. It was an arresting sight—a dozen police officers in their high-visibility jackets drowning in a sea of PVC, chain mail and naked flesh. In different circumstances it would have made Helen smile, but the fear and shock on the faces of those present banished any such thoughts. Many of the clubbers lingered outside despite the management's attempts to move them on, clinging to one another as they speculated about the night's events.

Flashing her warrant card, Helen pushed through the throng toward the entrance. The uniformed officer gave her an awkward nod, embarrassed to be found standing guard over a notorious S&M club, then heaved open the vast leather doors that kept its members in and the world's prying eyes out. Helen had never visited the Torture Rooms, and as she stepped across the threshold, she was immediately struck by the gaping staircase that descended in front of her. Deep crimson from floor to ceiling, flanked by walls studded with ingenious instruments of torture, it looked like the entrance to hell.

Helen descended quickly, clinging to the rail to avoid slipping on the stairs, which were uneven, sticky and cast in shadow. The club was composed of a series of brick-arched vaults and Helen made her way to the largest of them now. An hour or two earlier, this had been a scene of wild abandon, but it was deserted now, save for Charlie, DC McAndrew and a number of junior officers. Only the smell lingered: sweat, spilled lager, perfume and more besides— a sweet, pungent cocktail that was at odds with the lifeless feel of the club.

"Sorry to have called you so late. Or early. I'm not sure which it is."

Charlie had spotted Helen and was walking toward her.

"No problem," Helen replied warmly. "What have we got?"

"Lover boy over there found the body," Charlie answered.

She indicated a pale, blond youth who was giving his statement to McAndrew. The police blanket he'd been given couldn't completely conceal his skimpy LAPD outfit and he tugged nervously at it now, seemingly embarrassed by the presence of genuine police officers.

"He and a friend were looking for somewhere to be intimate. They barged into one of the back rooms and found our victim. We've separated the pair of them, but their accounts tally. They swear blind they didn't go into the room—Meredith's taken samples from them to check."

"Good. Any sign of the manager?"

"DC Edwards is in the back office with Mr. Blakeman now."

"Okay. Let's do this, then, shall we?"

Charlie gestured Helen toward the back of the club and they walked in that direction.

"Any witnesses?" Helen asked.

"We've no shortage of people who want to talk, but I wouldn't call them witnesses. It was dark, noisy and crowded. Half the punters were in costumes or masks. We'll be lucky to get anything useful, and no one is saying they saw anything 'unusual.' According to the bouncers, a few punters scarpered as soon as the police turned up. We've asked Blakeman for a full list of their members, so we can try to track them down, but—"

"They're unlikely to have used their real names," Helen interjected. "And I can't see them willingly coming forward to help us. Keep on it anyway—you never know."

Charlie nodded, but Helen could tell her mind was also turning on the peculiar complications a case such as this might offer. Given the paucity of eyewitnesses, they would probably have to rely heavily on forensic evidence, CCTV and the postmortem results if they were to make any tangible progress.

Upping her pace, Helen now found herself in the company of scene-of-crime officers. They had reached the murder scene. Slipping sterile coverings onto her shoes, Helen nodded to Charlie and, bracing herself, stepped into the room beyond.

9

The small space was a hive of activity. Meredith Walker, Southampton Central's chief forensics officer, was already on her hands and knees, diligently searching the floor space. The club's owners clearly didn't spend much on cleaning and it was going to be a mammoth job for Meredith and her team to bag all the detritus. The foot traffic in this room was evidently large—Helen feared it might be easier to work out which of the club's members *hadn't* been in this room than to pin down those who had—further complicating the task that lay in front of them.

Helen caught Charlie looking at her and, putting these defeatist thoughts aside, moved cautiously forward. The victim lay in the middle of the room, bound to a metal chair with duct tape and wet sheets. Helen presumed he was a man, given the height, but it was hard to be sure. The victim's entire head was encased in silver tape, not a strand of hair or a patch of skin visible anywhere. The wet sheets clung to him, bolstering Helen's sense of the paralyzing immobility the victim must have felt. It was a horrific way to die.

There had been S&M deaths before, of course—autoeroticism and sex games gone wrong—but this one felt different. A pair of sturdy panic shears lay on the floor next to the body, circled by Meredith's team and tagged for inspection. Whoever did this, then, had the means to release the victim, but had *chosen* not to. Instead, they had left the room, closing the door behind them and walking away without once attracting anyone's attention. This was no accident, then. This was a deliberate, calculated attempt to kill.

The police photographer gave Helen the nod and she now moved forward. Slipping her gloved hand beneath the victim, she raised him from the ground. The chair wobbled a little, then righted itself, settling into position in front of her. The victim's head lolled downward, eventually coming to rest on his chest.

"Could you give us a couple of minutes, guys?" Helen said quietly, but firmly.

Meredith and her team withdrew, leaving Charlie and Helen alone with the deceased. It was time now to reveal the victim and begin the process of trying to identify him—a task that didn't require an audience.

Gripping a pair of sterile scissors, Helen snipped through the wet sheets that bound the legs and torso. She was unlikely to be able to ID him from the sight of his feet, but she wanted to release his arms and legs from their constraints. This would allow her a better line of attack on the duct tape that bound him from the chest up. She knew she could ill afford to inflict any postmortem injuries on him by hacking blindly at the tape, so though every instinct urged her to remove the tape from his eyes, nose and mouth, she resisted for now.

Patiently, Helen cut through the stiff sheets, releasing his body from its purgatory. The sheets fell away, revealing the ribbon that secured his ankles to the chair legs. Helen untied this, bagging it along with the sheets, but the body didn't respond at all. Rigor mortis was setting in—their victim looked like a man frozen in time.

Pressing on with her unpleasant task, Helen stripped off the upper sheets, passing them to a rather pale-looking Charlie. Now she slipped one scissor blade underneath the tape on his chest, sliding it over the soft leather of his suit without marking the surface. She slowed her progress as she cut upward toward his neck—every mark, every bruise on his body might provide them with vital clues, and Helen was determined not to stymie their investigation through human error.

The tape covering his throat came away easily—only his head remained covered now. Downing the scissors, Helen decided to finish the last, most delicate stage by hand. Teasing her fingers along the top of his head, she soon found what she was looking for. The end of the tape had been stuck down firmly, but with a bit of coaxing, it came free.

This was the moment of truth, then. Grasping the loose end, Helen began to unwind the tape. Slowly at first, then faster and with more confidence, until finally it fell away altogether.

The sight that greeted her took her breath away. Not because she was disgusted by the victim's waxy, lifeless face, but because she *recognized* him. This poor wretch was her friend. Her dominator.

It was Jake.

10

Helen stumbled up the stairs, her hand clamped over her mouth. She could feel the vomit rising in her throat and she needed to be *away* from this underground hell. The green EXIT light could be glimpsed up ahead and she took the final steps at speed, barreling through the exit and out into the night.

Ignoring the startled looks of the uniformed officers on guard, Helen hurried over to the chain-link fence that bordered the club and clung onto it. Her breath was short, her heart was racing and the waves of nausea just kept coming. She gulped in huge lungfuls of air, desperate to avoid drawing attention to herself, but to no avail. She vomited now, hard and loud, her stomach cramping over and over again until there was nothing left inside.

Nobody made a move to help her, so Helen remained staring at the ground, empty and drained. It *couldn't* be Jake. A small part of her was tempted to return to the crime scene, to prove to herself that she'd made a stupid mistake. But in her heart she knew it *was* him. His face was distinctive and familiar, and besides, the tattoo on his neck sealed it. The man whose company she'd paid for on numerous occasions over the years, who'd beaten her dark introspection from her many times during their S&M sessions, was dead. Jake was the only person who knew the real Helen, and his sudden death left her feeling disoriented and confused.

The last time she'd seen him, he was happy and settled. He was dating a new boyfriend, had relinquished his crush on Helen and seemed to be making a decent fist of his life. What had gone so terribly wrong that he had ended up here, in an after-hours club, falling into the clutches of a brutal and pitiless killer? Helen would have given anything to be able to turn back time, to step into that small room as Jake was being attacked and drag his assailant away.

"Are you okay?"

Helen looked up to find Charlie standing nearby, framed by the darkness. No one else would have spoken to her so informally or with such affection and it knocked the stuffing out of her now. A large part of Helen wanted to blurt out that she knew the victim, that he was a friend. But as she opened her mouth to speak, her tongue refused to obey.

"What is it, Helen? What's wrong?" Charlie persisted.

Still Helen said nothing. To admit that she knew the victim would mean confessing how they'd met. Instantly she recoiled from this—she didn't want to offer Jake up to them like this—and besides, how could she look any of her colleagues in the eye once the details of her private life were laid bare? She'd be a laughingstock, the butt of endless ribald jokes, but more than that, they would *know*. Her sessions with Jake had always been private, discreet and special—a space

27

where she could reveal her historic wounds and confront her feelings of guilt. If she opened herself up like that, she'd be exposed, humiliated and in all likelihood taken off the case—and that was something that Helen was not prepared to countenance.

"I'm fine. It was just a shock," Helen replied, straightening up.

"Not a pretty sight, was he? If you want me to handle this—"

"It's okay. I'm good now," Helen said quickly. "Let's get it over with, shall we?"

Her jaunty tone sounded forced, but Charlie didn't comment. So, swallowing down another wave of nausea and putting her best foot forward, Helen walked back toward the club's gaping entrance to perform her grim duty.

11

He slipped into bed and turned his eyes to the wall. He could tell Sally wasn't asleep—though she was pretending to be—and he wondered what she was thinking. Could she hear his heart beating sixteen to the dozen? Could she sense his excitement?

He had taken his time returning home, hoping that he would be in a calmer state of mind on his arrival. But the adrenaline coursed through him still, and even though he had taken a long shower, he felt sure the stain of the night remained on him.

He sometimes had the sense that Sally wanted to say something, as they lay together. That his increasing absence from her life had been noted, that her patience was reaching the breaking point. If he was honest, he wanted her to ask. Not just so that he could apologize and make amends for the cruel way he'd treated her. But also because he wanted to explain—to make sense of his wanton, self-destructive actions. He was playing with fire, risking every-thing and everyone he held dear, and he wanted to share this bur-den with her.

Should he seize the initiative? Tell her himself? As soon as the thought entered his head, he dismissed it. Where would he begin? What would he say? Sally was no doormat—she was an intelligent and spirited woman—why couldn't *she* tackle him on it, demand-ing an explanation for his actions?

She wouldn't, of course. Theirs was a marriage sustained by silence now. So nothing would change, while with each passing night *everything* changed. He was slowly becoming a different person—someone new and unfamiliar. It thrilled and scared him in equal measure; such was the strength of his obsession. And this was why he wanted someone to talk to him, challenge him. Because he knew instinctively that, left to his own devices, he would never, ever stop.

12

It was only seven a.m., but Emilia Garanita had been working for several hours. Journalists are often up at odd times, but crime reporters have it particularly bad—murderers, rapists and kidnappers having no respect for those who have to chronicle their deeds. Emilia was used to it and, if she was honest, rather enjoyed her lifestyle. She loved her bed as much as the next girl, but the buzz of her mobile phone in the middle of the night always presaged something exciting, something new.

She had been called at four a.m. by PC Alan Stark, a tame officer who was happy to accept cash payments for information. There had been a murder during the night—an unusual one—which was why Emilia was now ensconced with him in a transport café near the Torture Rooms, huddled over a bacon sandwich.

"Did you see the body?" Emilia asked, cutting to the chase.

"No, but I spoke to a mate in SOC and they gave me chapter and verse. This place is something else."

"Meaning?"

"It's a fetish club and tonight was their 'Annual Ball.' So they were all out in force—poofs, dykes, gimps, devils, angels—"

"Did you recognize anyone?"

"I'm sure they were all there." He laughed grimly. "City councillors, BBC folk, vicars, but you can bet your bottom dollar they scarpered before CID turned up. Those that did hang about were wearing masks, helmets and such, so—"

"Did you pick up anyone with a criminal record?"

"We're still processing them."

"And who owns it—the club, I mean?"

"Pass. But the manager—if that's what you can call him—is talking to CID now. Sean Blakeman."

Emilia wrote the name down.

"Tell me about the victim."

"White guy in his early forties. Tied to a chair, before having his head taped up from chin to crown. I'm guessing the poor bastard suffocated."

He continued to describe the scene, giving what details he could about the victim and the clientele of the club. Emilia was only half listening, writing his testimony down in her crisp, efficient shorthand, her mind already spooling forward to the story she would write. Sex, murder, torture, titillation—this case was kinky with a capital *K* and would go down a storm with her editor. It had everything going for it, and the icing on the cake was Stark's confirmation that the case would be handled by Emilia's erstwhile friend, now nemesis.

DI Helen Grace.

13

Helen walked briskly along the corridor, her heart sinking lower with each step. She'd been up all night, heading straight from the crime scene back to the incident room. She'd secretly hoped that the team might have made some quick progress, but in reality she knew it was too early for that—the peculiarities of this crime meant that they would have to be patient. Eyewitness reports were thin on the ground, and with no surveillance systems in the club, they would have to garner amateur shots from mobile phones and piece together some kind of timeline. This might yield something, and of course, Meredith was still working her team hard on the forensics. Meanwhile, there was one very valuable piece of evidence that was as yet untapped—Jake's body.

Helen reached the mortuary doors and buzzed herself in quickly. If she hesitated, she would lose her nerve and turn back.

Jim Grieves, the pathologist, turned as Helen now approached. He didn't offer much of a greeting and Helen was glad of it. She hadn't the mental capacity or emotional strength for small talk. She just wanted to get this over with.

"He's a Caucasian male, late thirties to early forties, with a keen interest in body art, piercing and masochism. Lots of old injuries associated with the use of restraints, including a fractured wrist sustained a few years ago and a dislocated ankle that has never fully healed. Some evidence of STDs and I also found historic semen residue—not his own—on parts of his clothing."

Helen nodded but said nothing—it was upsetting to hear her friend dissected in such a cold, clinical way.

"We've done preliminary bloods—alcohol, ketamine and a small amount of cocaine, but that's not what killed him. He died of asphyxia. You can tell by the petechial hemorrhages on his cheeks and eyelids and also the cyanosis, which is what gives his face that blue discoloration. There are no bruises or marks on his torso, so we can assume that the duct tape around his head was sufficiently tight to cut off oxygen to his airways and that his killer had no need to apply any pressure to his throat or neck. The bleeding and bruising to his lips suggest that he was trying to bite his way through the tape when he lost consciousness."

Helen shut her eyes, overwhelmed by the horror of Jake's predicament.

"He suffered severe dehydration thanks to a massive rise in his body temperature, which eventually led to a cardiac arrest, but he wouldn't have known much about it. His brain was starved of oxygen—it was this that killed him rather than anything that came after."

"How long?"

Helen's voice sounded brittle and tight.

"Four to five minutes to lose consciousness, a little longer to die."

"Would he have known what was happening?"

"Until he blacked out. Perhaps that was the point. There was no attempt to torture or harm him physically, even though he was at his killer's mercy. Which might suggest your attacker wanted his victim to be cognizant of what was happening, to *feel* his helplessness as his oxygen failed."

Helen nodded, but said nothing in response. She was riven with emotion—anger, despair, sickness—as Grieves laid bare the brutal details of Jake's death. *Did* his assailant stick around to watch him die? Was being there at the point of death important to him? Beneath her fierce outrage, Helen now felt something else stirring—fear. Fear that the darkness was descending once more.

"Anything else? We're light on hard evidence at the moment," Helen went on.

"Given the environment his body was found in, his clothing is surprisingly clean. I did find some fresh saliva on his cheek and right ear, however. I doubt it's his own, given the position of it."

"Can we fast-track the analysis?" Helen said quickly. "We need something concrete we can work with—"

"I'll do what I can, but I've got three other cadavers to process and everyone wants things yesterday, don't they?" Grieves grumbled.

"Thank you, Jim. Quick as you can, please."

Helen squeezed his arm and turned on her heel. Grieves opened his mouth to protest, but he was too slow. Helen was already gone.

14

Helen walked back to her Kawasaki, lost in thought. Barring one occasion, she had only ever encountered Jake in his professional guise. They had met at his flat, where the lighting was dim and conversation kept to a minimum. Over time they had got to know each other better, but they were still playing roles during their sessions and Helen now realized how little she knew her friend. She had certainly never seen him as she had this morning—naked and unadorned, under the powerful glare of the mortuary lights.

She'd remembered that he had an eagle's head tattooed on his neck, but had never asked him what it signified. She knew he didn't speak to his parents, but had never asked who they were or where Jake had been brought up. She knew he had an eye for the boys as well as the girls, but didn't know which came first or whether he was looking for the same things as everyone else—commitment, security, a family. She wished now that she had asked more questions of someone she considered a true friend.

He had in the past thought of her as more than that. During the Ben Foster case, Jake had taken to following Helen—such was the level of his romantic obsession with her. She had put a stop to that, cutting off their relationship for a while, and to her surprise it had worked. When they had last met, by chance in a city center bar, he'd been seriously dating a guy he'd recently met. He seemed happy and together, so much so that when he texted Helen a few months later, asking if she wanted to resume their sessions, she'd been sorely tempted. In the end, caution had won out, however, and she'd made alternative arrangements, keen to avoid messy emotional entanglements. But she still often thought of him.

Could the boyfriend be involved? It would be interesting to find out the status of their relationship and whether he frequented the Torture Rooms too. Had their romance been one long seduction, building up to this savage murder? It was tempting to head round to Jake's flat now, tear it apart in the hunt for concrete leads, but to do so without an official ID of the victim would be foolish in the extreme. It was agonizing to have to wait—it felt like she was deliberately letting his killer off the hook—but she knew Jake had been picked up for drug offenses previously and that, once his tissue samples had been processed, his identity would be swiftly established.

Then the investigation would begin in earnest. The thought cheered and chilled Helen in equal measure. She knew her team would leave no stone unturned in their hunt for Jake's killer, but what might their interrogation of Jake's life mean for her? Had he kept records of their meetings? Any tokens of her? Had she left her mark on him? It was over two years since she'd used his services, but it was very possible that gaining justice for Jake would result in her exposure.

Part of her wanted to run from this, but her better part knew she had to run *toward* it. Whatever the possible consequences for her, she had to find his killer. She owed that—and a whole lot more—to her old friend. So, climbing onto her bike, she fired up the engine and kicked away the brake. Her heart was thumping and she felt sick to her stomach, but there was no point delaying the inevitable, so, pulling back the throttle, she sped away from the mortuary in the direction of Southampton Central.

15

Detective Superintendent Jonathan Gardam stood by his office window, looking out at the world. It was not the finest view Southampton had to offer, but it afforded him a discreet vantage point on the station's car park below.

Helen Grace had just arrived and was now dismounting her bike. She was a creature of habit, always choosing the same spot, always removing her helmet and leathers in the same precise order. Whether this was driven by logic or superstition, Gardam couldn't tell. He knew that her passion for motorbikes was a legacy of her childhood—in one unguarded moment she had confessed to stealing mopeds as a teenager—but beyond that, he knew little. The inner workings of her mind were as much a mystery to him as they always had been.

So he watched her from afar. He had a pretty good idea of her

routine now—when she went to the gym, when she went running—
and he timed his arrival at the station to coincide with hers. He
would be positioned at his window by the time she walked away
from her bike, running her fingers through her long hair to breathe
new life into it after its temporary constraint. She was always so
focused on the business in hand that she never looked up, never
clocked his face at the window. He often wondered how she would
react if she did. Would she be alarmed to see him there or would
she offer him a smile and carry on? He had pictured the situation
many times and in his head it was always the latter.

She was later than usual today, following an early-morning trip
to the mortuary. Gardam had had to delay his first meeting by half
an hour so he could be in place to receive her. It had put his PA in a
mood, but it had been worth it—Helen looked particularly beguil-
ing this morning. She was unfailingly attractive—he had always
been captivated by her Amazonian figure, pale skin and fuck-you
attitude—but as he'd got to know her better, he had seen a deeper
beauty. There was a vulnerability there that was hidden from all
except those closest to her. This fragile quality was very much in
evidence today. Pale, distracted, deep in thought, his best DI looked
utterly haunted.

Gardam pressed his fingers to the glass. As so often these days,
he wanted to reach out and comfort her. But she remained beyond
his reach. He hoped in time to change that, but for now all he
could do was watch.

16

This was better than she could possibly have imagined. She had heard the stories about the Torture Rooms before, of course, but had never had the inclination—or the bottle perhaps—to investigate further. Seeing the club now for the first time, she felt a surge of excitement—you couldn't have dreamed up a better backdrop for a gruesome murder. The moral majority out there would hoover this up, scared and titillated in equal measure.

Emilia pulled out her Nikon and got to work, snapping the exotic instruments of torture and restraint. Her time here was limited and she knew she had to work fast. Gaining access had been harder than usual—the manager and most of the bartenders had gone to ground—so she'd had to track down the security company who usually provided the muscle on the doors. The first two guys she'd contacted had told her to sling her hook, but the third one was twice divorced, with a drinker's thirst, and needed the money.

"You can have twenty minutes, but that's it. I need this job and I'm not going to get fired on your account."

Emilia had agreed, knowing that once she was in there, she could push it to half an hour. Once people have your money in their pocket, they become a bit less grand.

Having photographed the dance floor area, she headed swiftly down the corridor to the crime scene. But it was taped up and the door firmly secured. So, feigning a weak bladder, Emilia scurried back down the corridor, making her way to the small boxroom at the back that served as the club's office.

The room was nearly bare—a decrepit desk, a small filing cabinet and a naked lightbulb. Emilia got to work, but the drawers were empty, the files uninteresting, and there was little here to detain her. Emilia cursed—this visit wasn't proving quite as fruitful as she'd hoped.

As she turned to leave, her attention was caught by the photos that decorated the walls of the poky office. They were of past events—balls, fashion shows, photo shoots—that had been held in the club. They were full of exotically dressed revelers and deserved her careful attention.

"Gary, can you come in here a second?" Emilia shouted.

Moments later, he entered the office, looking flustered and annoyed.

"What're you doing in here? I said front of house and back corridor only."

"I got lost," Emilia said, smiling sweetly, "but now that I'm here, could you take a look at these?"

She gestured toward the photos on the wall. But her partner in crime was already backing off.

42

"We've been here too long as it is."

"You saw the victim, right?"

"Not exactly."

"Either you did or you didn't."

"His face was taped up, but I knew the fella from the way he was dressed. Can't tell you his name—we always used to call him 'Twinkletoes' because of the gold boots he wore—"

"Look at these photos, then, and tell me if you see him."

"No way. We need to be going—"

"You've had good money out of me—now you have to earn it. I know Sean Blakeman's mobile number," she continued, lying. "It would only take a minute for me to put you back on benefits."

Grumbling, Gary pulled some reading glasses from his top pocket. Emilia suppressed a smile as he perched the owlish glasses on the fleshy folds of his red face. He really did make a comical sight.

"There. That's the fella."

His finger was now pointing toward a figure on a podium who was dressed in gold lamé shorts and posing for the photographer. Emilia shot a look at the photo frame—"Annual Ball 2013"—and moved in for a closer look. The man in the photo was half-naked, muscular and seemingly having a very enjoyable time.

"But I've no idea who he is and you won't get anything more out of me today," the burly bouncer added.

"No need," Emilia said, straightening up. "I know exactly who he is."

Her guide was stupefied for a moment, before replying:

"Who? Who is he?"

Emilia was already walking to the door, but turned now. Smiling coyly, she answered:

"Read the paper tomorrow and you'll find out."

17

"The victim's name is Jake Elder."

Helen's voice held firm. It was the first time the full team had gathered together and she was determined not to reveal her distress to them, despite the emotions that churned inside her. She *had* to be strong.

"Forty-one years of age, he's been living in Southampton for the last fifteen years. His DNA matched samples taken following an arrest for possession of a Class B drug three years ago. He's got a couple of other charges on his file—nothing major, but we should chase them down anyway. See if he owed anyone any money, whether he was consorting with known dealers. DC Lucas, can you coordinate that?"

"Of course."

"His family have been informed and are on their way over from

Taunton now. I'll field them, but in the meantime I want us to climb inside our victim's life. Did he have a boyfriend or girlfriend? Was he invited to last night's ball by anyone? The victim had fresh saliva on his cheek—was it left there by a companion or by someone more casual? Also, it appears from his online activity that Elder was a professional dominator. Who did he meet? Who were his regular clients? Let's interrogate his phone records, e-mail, bank accounts, credit card statements . . ."

The team were busy scribbling down Helen's instructions, so she paused now to gather herself. It was strange and unsettling to be talking about Jake as if he were a total stranger, to be deliberately withholding vital information from the team. Helen took a deep breath, before continuing:

"Jake Elder lived his life online and via his phone—he is not your usual office worker. So check his Web history, the chat rooms he used, his text messages, Snapchats, his Twitter followers . . ."

"Do we think he was specifically targeted?" DS Sanderson piped up.

"Impossible to say, which is why we have to dig," Helen resumed evenly. "His killer may have a personal motive or Elder might just have been in the wrong place at the wrong time. There are numerous DNA traces at the scene of the crime—cigarette butts, items of clothing, discarded fetish gear. We'll need to run them all down, but I'd like us also to pay particular attention to the equipment our killer employed. You can't buy wet sheets and panic shears in your local Tesco's—they are specialist equipment with only one purpose. So let's contact local bondage retailers—I'd like a list of all outlets situated within a twenty-mile radius of South-ampton. Many of these operations are online only, meaning you *have* to pay with a credit card. So let's interrogate their transactions, find out who's been buying this stuff. Edwards, are you good for this?"

"It's my natural home," the handsome young officer replied, earning a few wry smiles from the rest of the team.

"Let's also make ourselves visible in the immediate environs of the club," Helen carried on, ignoring Edwards's joke. "People heading to the Torture Rooms presumably cab it, rather than taking the bus. Find out if the local cabbies saw anything. Our victim was probably killed sometime between midnight and one a.m.—we should follow up on anyone seen leaving the club around this time, particularly if they appeared distressed or agitated."

"Perhaps they stayed to party?" Lucas interjected.

"Possibly, but we've got a lot of lines to run and my instinct is that they would probably try to leave the scene before the body was discovered. But you're right—we should rule nothing out."

Helen paused, picking up a file from the desk. She was finally getting into her stride, but the most difficult part was yet to come.

"Alongside this, I want us to look at mummification."

A ripple of nervous laughter spread through the team.

"Also known as total-enclosure fetishism. It's at the extreme end of the S and M spectrum and involves somebody getting a sexual kick from being completely reliant on another for their liberty, their movement, even their life."

Visions of Jake—bound and taped—punched through Helen's mind. Flicking through her file to buy herself a moment, Helen swallowed and pressed on:

"There are many different ways to do it—straitjackets, wet sheets, bandages, rubber strips—but one thing that's crucial to every method is *trust*. You have to trust the person doing it to you or you wouldn't even start—"

"So he *knew* his attacker?" Charlie suggested.

"It's very possible. There are S and M groups who meet regularly to discuss, socialize and occasionally play. Their meets are called 'Munches.' I want us to investigate them, see what we can dig up about the scene. Have there been similar incidents that we haven't heard about? Is there anyone out there who is known for taking things too far? I don't think a head-on attack is going to work, so I'll be looking for a volunteer for undercover work."

More nervous laughter, but as Lucas jokily tried to raise Edwards's arm against his will, Sanderson stepped forward:

"I'd like to take this, unless anyone objects?" she said firmly, scanning the team for dissenters.

"Thank you," Helen replied quickly. "Run down a list of forthcoming meets and then let's discuss which ones to target."

"I'll have it for you within the hour."

"Good."

Helen paused, her ordeal nearly over, then said:

"I don't need to tell you how much coverage this murder is likely to get. So no talking out of school, no shortcuts, and any leads come *straight* to me. We do not rest until we have found Jake Elder's killer. Understood?"

The looks on the faces of the team showed that they had got the message and they now hurried off to do her bidding. Helen was aware that her tone had been a little harsh, but she was not prepared to soft-soap anyone while they still lacked any tangible leads. The investigation was starting to take shape now—the victim identified, multiple strands of inquiry set in motion—but there was one key element of this killing that remained as impenetrable and mysterious as ever.

The motive.

18

He was rooted to the spot. He knew it was coming, but even so, it was a shock. The newscaster was only relaying information that had been buzzing around Internet chat rooms for hours, but hearing it relayed in her professional monotone was still disquieting.

Nobody else in the office seemed to be paying attention to the radio bulletin, but he drank in every word: "A popular S and M club . . . appealing for witnesses . . . the victim has not yet been formally identified." He knew the victim's name, of course, but did the police too? Was their "failure" to identify him just a smoke screen as they pursued their inquiries or were they genuinely in the dark? He suddenly realized how much he needed to know.

He had been careful to conceal their connection, but who knew what they were able to access these days? Terrorism had a lot to answer for, providing the police with the perfect excuse to snoop on everything and everyone. He had never used the computer at home and had never contacted Jake via direct text, but even so, he suddenly had the unnerving feeling that he hadn't been careful enough.

The newscaster had moved on to local traffic and travel, but still he didn't move. Things seemed to be moving fast now and he was suddenly aware of how much he had to lose. Would they suspect him? Or would his middle-class exterior and respectable job shield him from suspicion? He was too far into this, too stained by his actions, for this to unravel. There were two sides to him—but they were known only to him—and that was the way it *had* to stay.

He was so deep in thought that at first he didn't notice his PA marching across the room toward him. He might have remained there for hours were it not for her sudden intrusion.

"Your ten o'clock is here," she said testily.

He didn't respond, didn't trust himself to. Instead, he gathered up his files, nodded at her and walked purposefully away toward the meeting room.

19

The silence in the room was suffocating. Helen had given Moira and Mike Elder the basic facts of their son's death, avoiding the more distressing details. She'd shouldered this unpleasant duty many times before and knew that if you hit people with too much too soon, you lose them. Assaulted by the shock, bowing under their grief, the bereaved just implode. It wasn't fair to treat them like that, and besides, it served nobody's purpose—she needed facts, not tears.

But, to Helen's surprise, Jake's parents had barely reacted at all to her carefully chosen words. Moira had shot a brief look at her husband, then joined him in staring at the floor. Their gazes remained doggedly turned in that direction, and though Helen provided a few gentle prompts, the couple stayed resolutely silent.

"We have a full team working on this. As I said, your son was discovered at a nightclub in Banister Park, and once you've formally identified him, we can make arrangements for you to visit it, if you feel that would be helpful. Relatives sometimes find that it's important to see the place where—"

"What sort of club was it?"

Mike Elder's voice was cracked and harsh. For a moment Helen wondered if it was a trick question—the news was already out there in radio bulletins and on the Internet—then pushed that thought aside. They had probably driven all the way from Taunton in silence, their minds trying to grapple with their unexpected tragedy. It was no surprise that they were still processing the details.

"It was an S and M club," Helen replied gently. There was no point dressing it up—they'd find out soon enough anyway.

Mike sniffed loudly, while his wife fiddled with the buttons on her cardigan.

"It wasn't a club he visited regularly, just somewhere he used now and then."

"I bet he did."

Now it was Helen's turn to be silent. Four words—four simple words—but they were said with such bitterness that for a moment Helen was speechless. She had encountered many emotions in the relatives' room—despair, denial, fury—but she had seldom seen such distaste. She felt anger flare in her but, aware that the eyes of the Family Liaison officer were on her, swallowed it down.

"Can I ask you what you mean by that, Mike?" she said.

"I'm sure by now you know what my son was," was the curt reply.

"Obviously we're aware that Jake worked as a professional dominator. That's one of our main lines of inquiry, to see if he might have been attacked by someone he knew through his work."

"His work," Mike repeated, shaking his head ruefully, before casting a sardonic smile at his wife.

"Can you tell me how much you knew about Jake's professional life?" Helen continued.

"Too bloody much, but nothing that would help you."

Helen was beginning to see why Jake had never got on with his parents, but resumed her questioning as patiently as she could.

"His life in Southampton, then? Did you ever visit his flat? Meet up with him?"

"This is our first visit to Southampton."

Finally, Moira had spoken.

"He moved away from Somerset when he was a young man. He threatened to come back and visit us, but . . . but he never made it."

Was the use of the word "threatened" deliberate? Helen was so bewildered by this interview that she couldn't tell.

"And you weren't tempted to visit him here?"

"It's a long way to come and we can't leave the animals," Moira replied quickly, trotting out her excuse with practiced ease.

"I see."

"Do you?" Mike Elder now said, suddenly turning to look directly at Helen. "I can tell from your tone what you're thinking, but you've got no right to look down your nose at us."

Helen stared back, refusing to break eye contact. He was right, however—Helen *was* allowing her feelings to affect her judgment and was behaving in a manner that was unprofessional and unkind.

"I've nothing but sympathy for you and your wife, believe me," she said quickly.

"That may be, but it doesn't change things. You might feel our son's 'lifestyle' was acceptable, but we didn't. I don't blame the boy entirely—we should have been tougher on him when he was small," he resumed, his wife flinching slightly as that barb landed. "But he made his choices and had to live by them. He was never interested in my opinion, but, for the avoidance of doubt, I'll give it to you anyway. I thought what he did . . . was perverted. For the life of me, I could never understand why he wanted to surround himself with degenerates and freaks—he could never explain it himself, just said it was 'who he was.' He thought we should accept him, but why should we accept something like that? He chose his path, we chose ours and, believe you me, they never met."

It was said with something approaching pride and for a moment Helen thought she might actually slap him. She had never heard someone damn his own flesh and blood in such blunt terms.

"We haven't seen him in nearly ten years and we're not going to be much help now, so let's just get this over with, shall we? I don't want to be here any more than you do."

He rose abruptly, clearly keen to get the formal identification of his son over and done with. Moira followed suit, hurrying after her departing husband.

As she left, she glanced briefly back at Helen. After her husband's harsh words, Helen had expected to see some embarrassment there, perhaps even contrition. But not a bit of it.

The look Moira now gave Helen was one of pure scorn.

20

Her fist slammed into the metal, rebounding off it violently. Without hesitating, she raised her arm again, plowing her clenched fist into the unyielding surface. This time her impact was true and the metal buckled under the assault. Wincing, Helen withdrew her hand and stepped back to survey the damage. To her shame, she saw that she had left a large dent on the unfortunate locker door—a complement to the bloody knuckles on her right hand.

She turned away, furious with herself, but angrier still with Jake's parents. They seemed so dismissive, so fixed in their view of him, yet if they had known their son *at all*, they would have known that he was kind, generous and loving. They refused to see that, remaining blinkered to the bitter end. What must it be like to live your life that way, Helen wondered, to sacrifice so much on the altar of your principles? Would it bring them happiness in the end? She suspected not.

Helen hadn't trusted herself to return to the incident room straightaway, so had been pacing the ladies' locker room ever since, trying to quell her growing anger. Helen knew that indignation and fury were sometimes positives, driving you to work harder and faster, but this wasn't like that. For the first time in years, Helen felt out of control. She hadn't slept at all, which didn't help, but still she was surprised at how upset and disoriented she was by the morning's events. She knew that, for Jake's sake, she had to find a way to contain her emotions. She couldn't run a major investigation in this state.

A sharp knocking sound made her look up. Seconds later, the door swung open and Charlie entered, clutching a thin file.

"Sorry to disturb you. I looked for you in the interview suite and Gardam's office but—"

"No problem," Helen said quickly, slipping her grazed hand into her pocket. "What have you got?"

Charlie pulled a sheet of paper from the file, but hesitated now before replying. The look on her face suggested she knew Helen was upset, and was perhaps debating whether to say anything. In the end caution won out, and dropping her eyes to the paper, she said:

"We've made a bit of progress with Elder's communications. He sometimes used texts and e-mails to set up his appointments, but his favored method of communicating with his clients was Snapchat."

"Right."

"Now, most people assume that when Snapchats disappear, they disappear for good, but actually the phone companies store them. We pulled Elder's this morning, along with his recent texts and e-mails, so we've now got pretty much every communication he sent or received in the last three months."

"And?" Helen said, hurrying Charlie to the point.

"Well, we cross-referenced them with mobile phones that were transmitting in or near the Torture Rooms on the night Jake was killed and we've got a list of about twenty numbers."

Helen took this in—their first small lead in a difficult case. As she did so, she saw Charlie's eyes flit to the dented locker, before quickly returning to Helen once more. If there was a question implied there, Charlie hid it well.

"Any links to anyone with a criminal record?"

"Not yet, but we're still processing them."

"Chase them all down," Helen replied impatiently. "Anything else?"

"One regular texter who *wasn't* in the vicinity was David Simons. He appears to have been in a serious relationship with Elder until fairly recently."

Helen said nothing, her mind flitting back to the man she'd glimpsed in a city center bar all those months ago.

"How recently?"

"Split up a couple of months back."

"Why?"

"Lack of commitment from Jake, clinginess from David— judging by their lengthy e-mails on the subject."

"Where is Simons now?"

"Los Angeles. He divides his time between the US and the UK. He's been there the last four weeks. I've been trying to get hold of him, but . . ."

"Get him over."

"Of course," Charlie replied, bristling slightly at Helen's tone.

"But I think we have to mark him off the list as a suspect, don't you?"

There was something challenging in Charlie's tone, but Helen decided not to rise to it. Instead, thanking her, she sent her on her way. Helen knew that she was being overly assertive, but the news that Jake's boyfriend was long gone had sent her mood plummeting still further. Jake had seemed so happy when they last met, but Helen was suddenly struck by how lonely his life must have been.

No lover or friend had come forward to claim him, his parents wouldn't have spat on him if he was on fire and even Helen had feigned ignorance of his identity to protect herself and her career. He had been abandoned in death by all those who should have cared for him, and that was something those who remained would have to live with for the rest of their lives.

21

"The victim lived and worked in Portswood. We're still pinning down the precise details, but it appears that he earned his living in the sex trade, working out of his flat as a professional dominator. Today we are asking anyone who's encountered Jake Elder—in whatever capacity—to get in touch and help us with our inquiries."

Emilia jotted down the details, chuckling at Gardam's careful euphemism. Everyone present knew what he meant—he was appealing to the spankers to put aside their embarrassment and come forward.

"Good luck with that," Emilia whispered to her neighbor, who raised a jaded eyebrow in response. Gardam was in cloud cuckoo land if he thought anyone in the BDSM community was going to willingly walk into a police station. A lot of them had criminal records, others had wives and families, and none of them would want to run the gauntlet of being judged by the small-minded sergeant on the front desk. Better let a killer walk free than endure that.

As Gardam continued, casually talking over his Media Liaison officer's attempt to direct proceedings, Emilia's mind began to wander. She already knew what her article would look like—she'd written it in her head on the way over—and there was little that Gardam could offer that she hadn't already been told. The real question—and the only reason she'd come to this briefing at all—was what role DI Grace would play in the proceedings. She was not someone who embraced the fourth estate, preferring to leave that to her superiors, but still her absence from the press conference was intriguing.

Emilia was pretty sure she was the only person present who knew that Helen had used Jake's services. She had stumbled on their connection during the Ella Matthews investigation and had immediately tried to use it to her advantage, threatening the unfortunate DI with exposure unless she gave her exclusive access to the investigation. Not surprisingly, Grace had fought back, calling her bluff by revealing her knowledge of Emilia's illegal surveillance techniques. It had ended in a score draw, both relieved to have emerged unscathed, but it still stuck in Emilia's craw.

She had never been a good loser and perhaps it was payback time. Helen Grace had kept her on a short leash for a while, but the boot was on the other foot now. Had Grace confessed her knowledge of the victim to her team? Was that why she wasn't present? Or had she kept her secret close? Emilia intended to find out. Journalists always love an exclusive and this story—"the copper and the bondage freak"—was going to be the best scoop she'd ever had.

22

Helen sped through the city streets, pleased to be away from the station. She found the incident room claustrophobic and unnerving—photos of a happy, carefree Jake staring down at her from the murder board—and there was little point being there just now. Charlie was chasing down Jake's clients, McAndrew was leading the house-to-house calls and, until something concrete turned up, she was better used elsewhere.

As she slid past the stationary traffic, Helen felt her mood rise. Perhaps it was the fresh air, or the satisfaction that riding her bike always gave her, or maybe it was just that she was finally *doing* something. Her interview with Jake's parents had yielded nothing, so it was good to be on the road at last, taking the lead.

Jim Grieves was still poring over Jake's body, just as Sanderson, Charlie and the team were trying to climb inside his life. The items used to imprison and kill Jake, however, were only just being examined—Meredith and her team having recently returned from the crime scene—which was why Helen's first port of call was the Police Laboratory at Woolston.

Meredith ushered Helen into the viewing area. Lying on the table in front of them were the wet sheets, the loose reel of silver duct tape and the leather restraints—their killer's weapons of choice.

"Preliminary testing on the victim's clothing and the bondage items has shown up only one source of DNA—the victim's. We'll run them again, but I wouldn't bank on anything more on that front."

Helen nodded, disappointed but not surprised.

"As for the rest of it, there's nothing particularly unusual about these items. The duct tape can be bought from any hardware store and though the wet sheets and restraints are specialist gear, they're the standard size, color and design. They were probably bought off the shelf, rather than custom-made."

"Had they been used before? Was this gear the perpetrator already owned?"

"Probably not, given the lack of DNA traces. Plus, look at this."

Meredith reached forward and picked up the leather straps, holding them up to the light. Intrigued, Helen leaned in closer.

"The hole which the buckle prong penetrated to secure the victim has been punched through cleanly. You can see the light through it."

"But the others haven't," Helen replied, running a gloved finger over the sequence of closed holes. "Which suggests that last night was the first time these straps had been used."

"Your killer could have used them before, perhaps, practiced at home—"

"But he'd have to have known exactly which hole he'd use.

And unless he correctly guessed the diameter of the victim's ankle and the chair leg, then—"

"Exactly, so let's assume they're brand-new. That might narrow the field down a little?" Meredith offered hopefully.

Thanking her, Helen pulled her mobile from her pocket and headed on her way, speed-dialing Edwards back at base.

By the time she left the building, he'd already pinged her his list of local bondage outlets. And by the time she was on her bike, they'd divided up the list—split four ways between Edwards, Helen and a couple of broad-minded DCs.

It was time to take a walk on the wild side.

23

Sanderson sat perfectly still, as the brush caressed her cheek. As soon as Helen had asked her to lead the undercover work, her mind had been turning on how best to ingratiate herself into a scene that was utterly alien to her. She was a conventional, middle-of-the-road girl and now she wondered if she was a little bit "vanilla" for the role. She was no prude, but humiliation, submission, restraint and punishment had never been part of her personal lexicon and she knew she would be on a steep learning curve. She had spent most of the day studying the scene, picking out the latest trends in the fetish world, while creating a new identity and personal history to carry into the operation.

She'd already colored her hair and purchased the necessary bondage gear and now her good friend Hannah P. was applying the finishing touches to her face. Face painting and body art seemed to be a big part of the "peacocking" that characterized a world fueled by fantasy and role-playing. If she was honest with herself, it made her feel more relaxed, concealing her true identity beneath brightly colored paint. If she could forget herself, she could more easily become her alter ego. And that was crucial for the task that lay ahead.

It was not just that she wanted to appear convincing to elicit information from those attending the "Munch" this evening. It was also a question of safety. Their perpetrator had already proved to be without mercy or scruple, proficient and artful in taking another's life. Sanderson was not easily scared—she could handle herself—but she knew she was out of her comfort zone here. This was the sharp end of the job.

Hannah had finished her work and now presented Sanderson with a mirror. Her older, more bohemian twin stared back at her. It was a good look and would serve her well tonight. Now was not a time for trepidation. If she could fashion a break in the case, it would play well with Helen. She'd always looked up to her superior, admiring her dedication, professionalism and bravery, and had felt well-placed to be her deputy. Now, though, there was competition and if she was honest, she feared that the personal connection between Helen and Charlie would hold her back. The only way to counter this was to prove to her boss that she was first among equals, the officer best suited to be her deputy. Which was why tonight was so important.

Thanking Hannah P. once more, Sanderson swept up her phone and keys before sliding her baton carefully into her suit. She was ready and there was no point putting it off. It was now or never.

24

Paul Jackson was between meetings and resentful of Charlie's intrusion. He was a manager at the Shirley branch of Santander—a position of some responsibility—and was clearly embarrassed by her presence. His eyes kept flicking to the clock, and his answers—when they came—were brief.

"So just to confirm, that phone number—07768 057374—belongs to you?"

"Yes."

"And you had your phone with you last night?"

"I think so."

"Can I ask where you were? Between the hours of ten p.m. and two a.m.?"

There was a moment's pause, before Jackson responded:

"I went for a drink after work. Watched the football. Then went home."

"Oh, right, who was playing?"

Another slight hesitation, then:

"Saints versus Watford. Easy win."

"And which pub was this?"

"The Saracen's Head, near the hospital."

"Bit out of your way, isn't it?"

"There are pubs closer to the office, but the beer's better there, so . . ."

"And you went with colleagues?"

"No, I went by myself."

"Right," Charlie replied, making a note on her pad. "And what time would you say you got home?"

"A little after midnight, I think."

"That's pretty late for a school night, isn't it?" Charlie replied, smiling.

For the first time, Jackson seemed lost for words.

"Is it usual for you to be out that late?" she continued.

"Not really, but it's not one of those pubs where they kick you out after last orders."

"Lock in, was it?"

"Something like that."

"I didn't realize they did those on Tuesday nights."

She smiled once more, but Jackson only gave her a tight grimace. He was nervous and uncomfortable and his answers were a little too stiff for Charlie's liking. There could be a perfectly innocent explanation—most people tensed up as soon as they saw a warrant card—but Charlie suspected that was not the case here. Fortunately there was one surefire way to find out.

"Your phone number has come up in our investigation into the death of Jake Elder. His body was found in the early hours of this morning at a nightclub in Banister Park. You probably heard the headlines on the radio."

Jackson nodded, but said nothing.

"A series of messages were sent to Mr. Elder from your phone. Snapchat messages organizing appointments with him—"

"I didn't send any messages."

"So you don't know Mr. Elder?"

Jackson shook his head.

"Have you ever visited the Torture Rooms?"

"No," Jackson replied quickly. "I'd never even heard of them until this morning."

"And you've never used Mr. Elder's services?"

"Of course not."

"No contact with him whatsoever?"

"No."

"Okay, then, I know you're a busy man, so I'll get out of your hair . . ."

Charlie could see the relief on Jackson's face.

"But, before I do, I would be grateful if you'd consent to provide a DNA sample. Just so we can strike your name off our list."

"Clearly my phone has been cloned or someone at your end has cocked up. As I've said, I didn't know the guy. I've never met him—"

"I know this seems intrusive, but as we've established that you were out last night and were in the vicinity of the club in question, we'll need to eliminate you from our inquiries, and believe me, this is the quickest way to do that."

"I'm not sure. I'm already late for my next meet—"

"It is your right to refuse, but we could later compel you to provide one. So what do you say? I've got a swab here. It will only take a few hours to process and that will be that. All being well, I'll never darken your door again."

Keeping up her breezy patter, Charlie pulled the swab tube from her bag. Jackson stared at her, saying nothing. Before, he'd looked angry; now he just looked empty. He seemed determined to resist, to try to pretend this wasn't happening, but Charlie had done this many times before and knew that insistent good humor often overcomes the fiercest of objections. If you give them nothing to argue with, they have nowhere to run.

Which was why, despite his unmistakable hostility, Paul Jackson now opened his mouth. Slipping the swab in, Charlie extracted the necessary skin cells and sealed them in the clear plastic tube.

"That's me done. Thank you for your time," she said, shaking Paul Jackson's hand and heading for the door.

Moments later, Charlie was out of the foyer and walking fast away from the building. As she went, she chanced a look back. Her suspicions had been raised by her interview and she wasn't surprised by what she now saw.

Paul Jackson staring right back at her through the window.

25

"I'm not a snooper, but when it's paraded under your nose, what can you do?"

DC McAndrew sighed inwardly, but smiled as she took the cup of tea being offered to her. She had been knocking on doors all afternoon, working her way up and down Jake Elder's street. Elder was not a man who got involved in community events and he was seldom seen by other homeowners during the day. So far she had amassed precious little information about Elder or his activities. Now she expected she was about to get rather too much.

She was seated in Maurice Finnan's front room. His wife had passed away some years back, but the "good room" was still spick-and-span, in keeping with the standards the dear departed Geraldine had laid down. Pristine sofas, startling white lace, a faux Persian rug—the whole room had the air of a museum piece. It was the sort of setup that made the naturally clumsy McAndrew nervous. A tea spillage here might herald the apocalypse.

"They were coming and going all hours and they weren't social calls, if you get my drift," he insinuated knowingly.

"I see. Anyone in particular catch your eye?"

"Not really," he replied. "They don't come dressed up, you know? They're just ordinary-looking people—probably lawyers, accountants and the like. I imagine that kind of thing always attracts people with a guilty conscience."

He winked at McAndrew, clearly pleased to have a young female to perform to. McAndrew sensed that Maurice was probably lonely and reminded herself not to judge him too harshly.

"Ever see Mr. Elder with any boyfriends? Girlfriends?"

"Confused, was he?" Maurice retorted. "Not really. There was a fella a few months back—tall chap, with short, chestnut hair, barrel-chested—but he didn't last long. Funny thing is I seldom saw *him*—this Jake, I mean—just his visitors going in and out. Quiet as you like during the day, but as soon as darkness fell, you'd see them traipsing up to his front door. Three, four, sometimes more in a night. Say what you like about him, he was a hard worker."

McAndrew smiled and this time it was genuine—despite his curtain twitching, verbosity and fastidiousness, Maurice had a nice sense of humor.

"I never worked out exactly what he did for them, though if you're as old as me, you can hazard a guess. It was all very discreet, but they always came and went on the hour, see? Doesn't take much imagination, does it?"

McAndrew was about to butt in, but Maurice beat her to the punch once more.

"Each to their own—that's always been my motto. But we've

all got to live around here, haven't we? Kids, pensioners, mums and dads. And you don't know who a place like that will attract. Then there's the house prices. Soon as it becomes common knowledge that you've got a brothel next door— Sorry, love, am I boring you?"

McAndrew realized her gaze had drifted out of the window toward Jake's flat. Snapping out of it, she turned to Maurice once more.

"Not at all."

"You're very sweet, but you're not a good liar and I know you're busy. Now, I did jot down a few number plates in case the police should ever get around to doing anything about it. Let me see if I can find them . . ."

He hurried over to the dresser. McAndrew thanked him, grateful that her time here hadn't been completely wasted. It was tough doing door-to-doors—"hit-and-hopes"—when you knew the real police work was going on elsewhere.

"Right, let's start at the beginning—this was from March 2013," Maurice said cheerfully, seating himself and opening his large notebook at the first page.

McAndrew sighed again. Perhaps Maurice had important information for the investigation. Perhaps he didn't. Either way, one thing was clear—she was going to be here for a long, long time.

26

"Don't tell me. Let me guess. I've got a talent for these things."

Helen said nothing. She had just spent a dispiriting couple of hours trawling industrial estates and wasn't in the mood for games. Two of the businesses on her section of the list had gone into liquidation, another had refused to talk without a lawyer and two more were dead ends, with nothing in their recent transactions that fit the bill.

"I look at you and I see . . . nipple clamps, bondage mitts and perhaps a cock cage for that special someone in your life," the bearded man drawled.

"Well, feast your eyes on this," Helen replied, flipping open her warrant card. "Is there somewhere we can talk?"

"You'll get nothing out of me without a warrant."

They were seated on cardboard boxes in the back office. In truth it was little more than a storeroom, but Steven Fincher clearly felt it was his turf and was determined to press home the advantage.

"If that's the way you want to play it, that's fine," Helen replied. "But your lack of cooperation suggests to me that you have something to hide."

"Bullshit."

"And any formal investigation of your affairs would necessarily be quite wide-ranging. I take it you're up-to-date with your tax returns, National Insurance and so on . . ."

Fincher's eyes narrowed, but he kept his counsel.

"So perhaps it would be easier all round if you just do as I ask. Do you have an up-to-date list of recent transactions?"

"Of course. This is a legitimate business."

"I'm very glad to hear it. And I take it you sell these items: wet sheets, leather restraints, duct tape?"

"Of course."

"Have you sold any of those items within the last three months? Either individually or as a package?"

Grumbling, Fincher opened a nearby box file and pulled a tea-stained ledger from it. Helen watched him closely as he ran his finger down the columns. Edwards hadn't had any joy in his search; neither had the other DCs—they were fast running out of options here.

"This *might* be it," Fincher said cautiously.

"Go on."

"Three wet sheets, blue, two tan leather restraints with gold buckles and a roll of silver duct tape."

Helen nodded, concealing the excitement rising within her. She had been deliberately vague in her description of the items so far, but Fincher had just described the murder weapons in perfect detail.

"Were they bought in store?"

"No, delivery."

"Do you know the name of the courier company who delivered them?"

"Course I bloody do. It was me."

"So you saw him?" Helen said quickly. "The person you delivered them to?"

"No. The house was derelict. But it was definitely the right address and the order form had instructions to post through the letter box if no one was at home. I never heard any more about it, so I assumed everything was okay . . ."

"How did he pay for them?" Helen asked further, her tone hard with disappointment.

"Credit card."

"And do you still have those details?"

"Sure," Fincher replied, rummaging around in another box file. "I've got the card number, the cardholder's name, and"—he pulled a transaction receipt from the box with a flourish—"I've got his home address too."

27

"Who is this? What do you want?"

Emilia suppressed a smile. It was still early in Los Angeles and David Simons sounded bleary and half awake. His cracked voice and faltering speech suggested that he'd probably been out half the night. That wasn't ideal—he might still be drunk or high and was more liable to get emotional—but the key thing was to get to him before the police did. They would have been trying to contact him, but they were spread thin over what was already shaping up to be a major investigation. Simons was a freelance cameraman, whose Web site had all the relevant contact details, and she'd had his mobile number on repeat dial since early afternoon. It had been going to voice mail for hours, but finally he had turned his phone on and she had struck gold.

"My name is Emilia Garanita. I'm a journalist."

"Is this about the film? You need to talk to someone in the publici—"

"No, it's about Jake Elder. I was wondering if you'd heard the news?"

Silence on the end. Emilia could picture the groggy Simons sitting up in bed, trying to process what he'd just heard.

"What news?" Simons eventually said.

"I'm sorry to have to tell you this . . . but Jake was killed last night."

"I don't understand. Is this a joke?"

"It's a lot to take in and you have my sincere condolences. I know you and he were very close."

Another long silence. Simons's breathing was short and erratic.

"Killed how?"

"He was murdered. At a nightclub called the Torture Rooms in Southampton. Do you know it?"

The first teaser question to see if he was going to lie to her.

"Yes, I know it. But I still don't understand. Was he involved in some kind of fight?"

"No, nothing like that."

"Was it an accident? Did something go wrong?"

Even with the line as echoing as this was, Emilia heard the wobble in David Simons's voice.

"It looks like he was murdered. And, like everybody else, we're just trying to work out why. Can I ask when you last saw him?"

"Jesus . . . I . . . This is hard to take in."

"I know and I'm sorry to be the bearer of such dreadful news. But I thought you'd want to know straightaway."

"Why? Who are you?"

"I work for a newspaper here, but I also knew Jake. Given how close you were to him, I thought you'd want to be told."

Another long silence.

"Now, I'm sure you'll want to get back here, but that'll probably mean you missing out on some work, not to mention the cost of the flight from LA, so I was going to suggest that we pick up your expenses."

"I'm not sure . . ."

"And all I'd want in return is ten minutes of your time now. What do you say?"

The deal was already done—she could sense he wanted to talk, wanted to find out more about what had happened to his ex. Emilia made all the right noises, adopting a consoling tone and offering her condolences, all the while reveling in the doublespeak of it all. She said she was sorry to be the bearer of bad news, but the truth was very different.

There was something exhilarating about being the harbinger of death.

28

"I haven't seen your face before."

The man, dressed from head to toe in black leather, gripped Sanderson's chin, turning her head this way, now that, to admire her painted face.

"I'm new to town."

"And what do we call you, new-to-town?"

"Rose."

"A rose with thorns, no doubt. Come this way. I'll introduce you to the others . . ."

The burly man led Sanderson down a long corridor. The light sockets hung down from the ceiling without bulbs, and only a couple of weak wall lights rescued the pair of them from total darkness. Sanderson was pleased to feel the hard steel of her baton on her flank, as they walked farther and farther away from the light.

They soon reached another door. Her companion—who'd introduced himself as Dennis—knocked on it, and immediately a hatch in the door slid open.

"Fresh meat," Dennis said, a thin grin on his face. Moments later, the door swung open and they hurried inside. Sanderson wondered if her mobile phone would work in here, especially as they now seemed to be heading down to some kind of basement, but she didn't dare look at her phone. Dennis's eyes were glued to her.

The Munch convened minutes later. Fifteen committed sadomasochists, hunched round in a circle, enjoying the subversion and secrecy of their gathering. Normally they would have been discussing best erotic practice and comparing case notes, but today there was only one topic of conversation. Less than twenty-four hours had elapsed since Jake's death, but it had sent shock waves through the community.

Dennis sat Sanderson next to him, acting as her friend and sponsor, despite having only "known" her for a few minutes. She had contacted him via a Web site—the BrotherHood—and after a few exploratory messages he'd sent her a curt e-mail including an address and a time. She'd turned up five minutes early—time enough to check that her backup team was in place—then rang the bell for admission. Dennis had stuck close to her the whole time and Sanderson wondered if he did this to all new members or whether there was something special about her.

"Bloke I know from Bevois Mount had a similar thing happen to him," a guy who appeared to be dressed as a satyr was saying. "Took a bloke home he hardly knew. The guy taped him up and robbed him blind."

"There was a girl I knew—right vicious little bitch she was," added his female neighbor, covered head to toe in PVC, apart from webbing at the crotch. "Used to advertise for partners, but as soon as they turned up, her boyfriend and his mates set on them. Beat a couple of people half to death."

"One person you don't want to mess with is my ex," said another, to general agreement. "You get him on the wrong night, he'd kill you as soon as look at you. If he wasn't doing a two-stretch, I'd have said this was him."

"This is different, though, right?" Sanderson piped up, dismissing all these suggestions out of hand. "I think it was a hate crime."

"No," Dennis countered quickly. "If it was a hate crime, they'd have been more explicit. They'd be all over social media now talking about poofs, freaks—"

"What, then?" Sanderson countered.

"This is someone *within* the community, someone who's into Edge Play."

The thought was clearly not a welcome one and an angry debate now ensued. Sanderson said very little, glad of the cover the argument gave her. She knew Edge Play was at the extreme end of the BDSM spectrum, pushing supplicants almost to the brink of death by starving them of oxygen, but she knew little more than that and was not keen to be drawn into the discussion.

"Do you have anyone in mind?" Sanderson butted in. "You seem to know a lot about it."

The comment was directed at Dennis with just enough mischief in her tone to provoke a response.

"Well, *I* was at home," Dennis replied, pretending to bridle at the insinuation. "My mother had had a funny turn, so you can count me out."

There followed a few minutes' discussion about the welfare of Dennis's mother. Sanderson hid her frustration as best she could, waiting for a chance to steer the conversation back to where she needed it to be.

"Well, I won't be taking any risks until I know what's going on," she said, as the conversation once more hit a lull.

"Like the rough stuff, do you, honey?" chipped in the PVC enthusiast.

"Not as much as Dennis, here," she said leadingly, raising another half smile from her new friend. "Come on, you know the scene. Help a girl out who's new to town. I don't want to run into trouble the first time I hit the scene proper."

Dennis thought about it for a moment, then said:

"There was one person. Everyone likes to push things a bit, but this one was cruel. Proper messed up, in and out of therapy, drugs, pills, didn't know if it was Christmas or Tuesday half the time. I've only ever been scared once in my life . . . and that was it."

"Who was it?" Sanderson replied, keeping her voice neutral. "Don't tease us, Dennis."

He looked straight at her, then at the assembled throng, then back to Sanderson again.

"I'd love to share, but I'd need to trust you a little better first. And trust has to be *earned*, doesn't it, Rosie?" he said, as fourteen pairs of eyes turned toward Sanderson. "So why don't you tell us your story?"

"I show you mine, if you show me yours?"

"Something like that. And why not start from the very beginning," he continued, reclining in his seat. "I want to know *all* about you."

29

Helen stood on the doorstep, pulling her coat around her in an attempt to keep warm. The sun had dropped from the sky and the air temperature had dipped sharply. Helen could see her breath dance in front of her, as she pressed the doorbell for a third time.

The credit card used to purchase Jake's instruments of torture belonged to Lynn Picket, a single mum living in a council house in Totton. The first couple of rings had gone unanswered, but Helen could now hear someone coming to the door and braced herself for what was to come.

"Do I look like I use that kind of stuff?"

Helen was now in Lynn's living room, balancing on the edge of a sofa that had seen better days. It was clearly not the best time to have called round—Lynn had three children, all of whom appeared to be in varying stages of outrage, distress or meltdown—but Helen was not going to be put off by this or Lynn's blustering response. She knew bondage practitioners came in all shapes and sizes.

"Well, I don't," sniffed Lynn. "I don't have the time and I don't have the money."

"Do you have a computer, Lynn?"

"No, I bloody don't."

"Tablet?"

"I've got a Chromebook that the kids use. If you want to take a look at it, be my guest. But all they use it for is watching CBeebies. There's nothing like *this* on it," she said, looking at the list of S&M purchases Helen had given her.

"What about a smartphone?"

"Course—who doesn't? Knock yourself out."

She tossed Helen her phone. It was badly dented and the screen was cracked.

"So you're sure you didn't purchase these items?"

"I know what I have and haven't bought. Besides, I don't even know what half these things are. What's a wet sheet, for God's sake? It sounds like something I'd use to wipe my little girl's bum . . ."

"Does anyone else have access to your credit card?" Helen interrupted. "Boyfriends, family, friends . . ."

"No, I wouldn't let it out of my sight. And I certainly wouldn't trust a fella with it."

"Do you shop online?"

"Yes, I do, but not on sites like that and if you don't believe me, you can see my statements. I've got them going back three, four years, maybe more."

She bustled out of the room to get them, leaving Helen alone.

Helen flicked through her phone search history, but in truth she was going through the motions. She believed Lynn. Which meant that someone had cloned her credit card.

It was an alarming thought, suggesting a level of criminal sophistication that Helen hadn't been expecting. Their killer was clearly no amateur—he was methodical, tech savvy and adept at covering his tracks. Which made Helen wonder what his game plan was exactly—and what this elusive killer might do next.

30

Charlie's eyes were glued to the house. Paul Jackson had left the bank just as the sun was setting and Charlie had followed him. To her surprise, this proved far more difficult than usual—Jackson was on a bike, so she was constantly in danger of losing him in the busy city center traffic. But something told Charlie it would be worth the effort, so she'd stuck with it, following him all the way home. They hadn't had the results of his DNA sample back yet, but Jackson had lied to her—Charlie was sure of that—and he had clearly been rattled by her visit.

Charlie stifled a yawn and pulled the last Dorito from the bag. It was pushing midnight now—she had been here over four hours already—and so far she had little to show for her patience. Jackson had returned home, greeted his wife, then sat down to dinner in front of the TV. They had remained together until just after ten p.m., when Jackson had taken himself off upstairs. No lights came on at the front of the house, so Charlie had decided to walk round the block. The houses round here had long gardens, and by clambering onto a bin in the adjacent street, Charlie could see a light burning in a small room at the back of the house. Was it a study of some kind? Attic storage? What was he doing there?

Charlie lingered there for twenty minutes, but it was cold tonight and as the pubs began to empty, she'd abandoned her position and returned to the comparative warmth of her Renault Twingo. Minutes later, she'd been rewarded with the sight of Paul Jackson returning to the front room once more, kissing his wife good night as she headed off to bed. Jackson stayed where he was, watching the TV, but occasionally casting a glance upstairs.

Would he venture out tonight? Charlie looked at the clock. Her partner, Steve, had not been pleased when she'd called to say she wouldn't be home. She usually relieved him for Jessica's bath and bedtime, and even though he knew her job was unpredictable, he still got grumpy when she didn't show up.

She suddenly felt foolish to be stuck out here on her own, when she could be home in bed with her family. Police work was increasingly encroaching on her home life, but it was hard for it to play out any other way. She wanted to make a decent arrest, create a bit of a splash, if only to rid herself of the feeling that she was on probation. The odd look from Sanderson and a stupid sexist comment from a junior officer had been enough to make her feel as if she still had something to prove, despite her promotion.

Which was why she wasn't going anywhere yet. Even though it was well past midnight, she would give it one more hour.

31

"I knew it was time for a change. I mean, no one needs that abuse, do they?"

Sanderson was deep into her tale about a violent and neglectful boyfriend. Despite the fact that she had actually been single for nearly eighteen months, she was doing rather well, sprinkling her tale with lots of choice details.

"So what did you do, flower?" Dennis replied, his eyes still glued to her.

"I cleaned him out and moved on. He'd saved up nearly ten grand for some souped-up Mazda and I took *every* penny of it."

One of those present whistled, earning a smile from Sanderson.

"You should have seen the texts he sent. Vile, they were. I replied a few times—then when I hit the M25, I threw my phone out the window."

"A new life," the PVC enthusiast said.

"Exactly."

"And how long have you been doing *this*?" Dennis gestured at the dungeon they now sat in.

"Most of my adult life."

"Why?"

"What's the point of walking in a straight line? Life's more fun if you deviate."

"So what are you—top or bottom?"

"Bottom. I like to be disciplined."

"Then you've come to the right place."

Dennis rose now and crossed to the wall, running his finger over the heavy chains attached to the wall.

"Why don't I give you a little test-drive, then? See how you like the Southampton touch . . ."

There were low chuckles from the group, as they turned their attention from Dennis to Sanderson. Was this what they'd come to see? Maybe Dennis hadn't been joking about his "fresh meat."

"All in good time. I'd need to know *you* a little better first."

"What you see is what you get," Dennis said, opening his arms to her.

"Uh-uh," Sanderson said. "You're still holding out on me, Dennis. You were about to give me a cautionary tale before."

"That's one way of putting it," the satyr chuckled.

"You had someone in mind when you were talking," Sanderson said, ignoring the joke. "Someone I should steer clear of."

"Why are you so interested in her anyway?"

"Because she obviously got to you."

"Perhaps."

"Why won't you talk about her? Are you scared of her?"

"Of course not," Dennis responded sharply, but Sanderson didn't believe him.

"Well, then?"

Dennis hesitated. Was he intimidated by this mystery person? Or was it just not the done thing to name names?

"Her name is Samantha. She's a mid-op she-male."

"What did she do to you?" Sanderson inquired, banking the name.

"Half killed me is what she did," Dennis replied tersely.

Sanderson nodded sympathetically, but said nothing. Dennis was going to elaborate—he just needed a moment to collect himself.

"She put me in hog ties and a deprivation hood. You shouldn't wear those things for more than an hour unless you want to go gaga, but she left me in it for five. I was panicking, couldn't breathe, but she just seemed to enjoy it. She abused me, told me I deserved it—she even laughed at one point."

Dennis's voice shook as he said it. He was no longer the cheeky figure of fun he purported to be. It was clear that he had genuinely thought he was going to die during the experience.

"Is she likely to have gone to the Annual Ball?" Sanderson asked.

"Never missed it."

"And where do you normally find her? Where does she live?"

"Well, that's the million-dollar question, isn't it?"

"Do you know?"

"Maybe I do; maybe I don't. But I think I've said more than enough already. I've got no love for Samantha, believe me, but I've got even less love for the police. So I think it's time you were going."

As he said it, fourteen pairs of eyes swiveled toward her. Sanderson opened her mouth to respond, but Dennis quickly went on:

"You're going to have to work on your act a little, *Rose*. The look of terror in your eyes when I suggested a bit of slap and tickle was a dead giveaway. Missionary all the way with you, is it?"

Now he was looking at her with open hostility. The atmosphere had suddenly turned and Sanderson wanted to be out of this basement as quickly as possible. She had overplayed her hand, pushed too hard. There was nothing to do now but retreat, so Sanderson stood up and scurried toward the exit, watched all the way by thirty accusing eyes.

32

"I won't be able to come here again."

Angelique looked up, pausing momentarily.

"Something wrong?"

"It's just work," Helen replied. "I'm going to be abroad a lot, so . . ."

Helen wasn't a liar by nature and it showed. Fortunately this was not an environment in which awkward questions were likely to be raised.

"Let's make it a good one, then," Angelique replied. "Something to remember me by?"

The slender dominatrix moved forward, taking Helen's wrist in her hand.

"No restraints tonight," Helen said firmly.

Angelique paused. The look on her face suggested to Helen that there was much that could be said. Angelique was well-known on the S&M scene and had presumably heard about Jake's murder. Had she known Helen a little better, she might have raised it—it had clearly rattled people—but they barely knew each other, so whatever it was, it would remain unsaid. Helen had visited Angelique on a handful of occasions in the last three months. She had tried to wean herself off her habit, but when the need became too great, she had sought paid companionship. This time she had sought out female company, hoping it would remove any sexual attraction from the equation—this had been her undoing on more than one occasion before.

Overall it had worked pretty well and Helen was glad to be able to use her services when the need arose. But she knew this would be her last visit. She would have to absent herself from this world during the investigation. It was hard to know what would fill the void—she was already running three times a week and smoking far more than she should—and Helen wondered what other compulsions might rear up in Angelique's absence. As she'd biked home from Lynn's house, she'd tried to persuade herself not to come. But her head was full of darkness tonight and the news that Sanderson's cover had been blown so quickly had pushed her over the edge.

Nodding to Angelique, she relaxed her body and waited for the first blow. Today had been awful in so many ways and she couldn't rid herself of the unpleasant images swirling round her mind. The look of disgust on Mike Elder's face, his son's cold corpse on the stainless steel slab, and—shot through with these—images of her *own* past. Mike Elder's sneering face seemed to alternate with her father's, while the submissive Moira seemed to walk hand in hand with visions of her own mother, turning the other cheek as her brutish husband beat, tortured and raped his own flesh and blood. Helen had never been a parent—and she knew in her heart that she never would be—but still she felt a fierce, primal anger at those who visited such terrible cruelty on those closest to them. The events of today had taken her straight back to when she was a little girl, remembering the intense fear, impotence and terror that only a child can feel. It filled her with terrible rage, but also terrible sadness. This had been her birthright, just as it had been Jake's.

The crop bit into her back, jolting her from her thoughts. This had always been the way—the endorphins flooding through her as she concentrated on the rhythm and power of her beating. She needed the release now more than ever on this darkest of days. Which was why, as Angelique raised her crop a second time, Helen shut her eyes and uttered a single word.

"Harder."

33

Her boots clicked on the stone cobbles as she walked away down the dark street. It was deserted and deathly quiet tonight. This was one of the reasons why Helen used Angelique—her flat was part of a converted warehouse down by the docks, away from the hustle and bustle of Southampton. It was discreet and off the beaten track, which was how Helen liked it.

Her session had been punishing, but still she couldn't settle. Usually she would have walked away feeling lighter, happier, more optimistic. Tonight, though, she felt a weight on her conscience. Not simply because of what she had endured today, but because there was one task she had still to perform.

She had known it the moment she'd seen Jake's lifeless face, but her conversation with Charlie had brought it home to her. Callous as it was, she had to sever her connection with Jake for good. She told herself that by so doing she was just freeing herself to pursue his killer, but it still made her feel disloyal and unworthy, as if she was somehow embarrassed of her relationship with him.

Unzipping her jacket pocket, she pulled the battered Samsung phone from inside. She had bought it from a market stall in Portsmouth. It had clearly been stolen, but Helen didn't quibble, handing over the cash before heading off in search of another stall that sold knockoff SIM cards. Putting them together, she had an unregistered phone from which she could send messages that would never be traced back to her. She had her own phone, of course, for everyday stuff, but this phone was used purely to arrange her appointments. First with Jake Elder, later with another dominator, Max Paine, and then finally with Angelique. A discreet way to organize a side of her life that Helen wanted to remain hidden.

Helen knew this number would come up at some point in the investigation as the team examined Jake's past communications. She had messaged Jake regularly in the old days, setting up their meetings, confirming times and occasionally canceling their sessions when duty called. Recently their communications had been much more sporadic, but he had messaged her a few months back. It was innocuous enough—a request to resume their professional relationship—and Helen had been kindness personified in knocking him back. Still, it would be on the list of numbers to check out. Her team obviously couldn't place her at the club and there would be precious little to flag her number as one of particular interest, given how irregularly she'd used it. But it was just possible that they might try to trace its location and that could lead to some uncomfortable questions, as she often had the phone on her at work.

This was why this part of her life had to end tonight. Once more, she had cleaved close to someone only for him to meet a horrifying end. On nights like these, Helen genuinely wondered if she was cursed. Everyone she had feelings for, everyone she formed any sort of relationship with, ended up suffering for it. Her sister, Marianne, and her nephew, Robert, had suffered, as had her former lover Mark Fuller and now Jake. Was *she* the connecting factor here? Was it somehow her fault that these people should endure the horrors they did?

Helen suddenly realized she had come to a halt, lost in her own thoughts. Cursing herself for her self-indulgence, she scoured the surface of the road. She soon found what she was looking for and, marching across to the gutter, pulled both the battery and the SIM card from the body of the phone. She checked that the street was clear once more, then dropped all three parts down the drain.

And that was it. Brutal, short and definitive. The last rites on her relationship with Jake Elder.

34

Whose bright idea was it to put mirrors in the lifts?

Charlie was already late for work—she'd forgotten it was Jessica's show-and-tell this morning—and her mood was not improved by the sight of herself in the floor-to-ceiling mirrors. Her clothes were okay, if a little tight—it was her face that depressed her. The lighting wasn't great in the lift, but even so, she looked washed-out, with deep, dark rings under the eyes. She wasn't the greatest advert for being a working mum.

The doors pinged open, and turning her back on the accusing mirrors, Charlie strode down the corridor to the incident room. She paused by the door to smooth her hair down, then pushed through it with an energy she didn't feel. Her late-night stakeout had yielded nothing—Jackson had stayed put all night—and she was paying the price for it this morning. The only consolation—if you could call it that—was that Sanderson had lucked out too.

Charlie headed straight to her desk. As she approached it, however, she slowed her pace, surprised by the sight of two Media Liaison officers talking to Helen in her office. They only turned up when something important had happened, and looking around the office, Charlie noticed that there was something different in everyone's expression today. They looked optimistic and energized.

Waving Edwards over, she cut to the chase.

"What's going on?"

"Got the DNA samples back this morning."

"And?"

"We got a match. Paul Jackson. He's the manager at—"

"Santander in Shirley. I know. I spoke to him yesterday."

"There you go, then."

Edwards turned away, but Charlie stopped him.

"Someone should have called me."

"I did, but it rang out. Then I thought I'd tell you when you came in—we were expecting you in a bit earlier."

"I got held up," Charlie responded tersely. "Anyway, what are we waiting for? We should be down there—"

"It's under control," Edwards replied crisply.

Charlie was already scanning the office. She had a nasty feeling where this was going and wasn't surprised in the least when Edwards concluded:

"DS Sanderson has just gone to pick him up."

35

He knew it was coming, but still it was much more brutal than he'd expected.

He was in the middle of a divisional meeting—the heads of all the local branches gathered together for tea and biscuits. These sessions always ran overtime, the various managers positioning themselves for promotion, while sharing tales from the coalface, but he still enjoyed them. In this environment, he was king. He liked the deference, the banter and, if he was honest, the power.

The meeting room was glass-walled, so everybody saw them coming. His PA—the redoubtable Mrs. Allen—was trying hard to look professional, but in reality she just looked shit scared, saying nothing as she opened the meeting room door and ushered the tall, serious-looking woman inside. He didn't recognize her—she wasn't the one who'd come yesterday—but he could tell by the way she

carried herself that she was a police officer. A fact she now confirmed by presenting her warrant card to him.

"DS Sanderson. I wonder if I could have a word, Mr. Jackson,"
she said, her voice quiet, but clear.

"Of course. My office is just—"

"I think it would be best if you accompany me to the station."

The walk of shame through the office was quick, but felt
interminable—the eyes of every staff member glued to him. Colleagues shuffled out of the way in silence and moments later he
found himself striding down the brightly lit corridor toward the
exit.

Before long, he was in the back of a sedan, moving fast down
the road. As he pulled away from the bank that had been a happy
home for many years now, he caught sight of his managerial colleagues staring out of the meeting room window at him.

This was it, then. The end of his old life. And the beginning of
something new.

36

"What do we say to the press?"

There was more than a hint of excitement in Gardam's voice, but Helen knew he was experienced enough not to get carried away.

"There's massive media interest in this case already and I don't want to whip them up any more," he continued. "I take it you've seen the early edition of the *Evening News*?"

Helen confirmed that she had, trying to put Emilia Garanita's lurid four-page spread from her mind. It was written as if in sympathy with the dead, but in reality was a hatchet job on Jake and everyone "like" him. She could tell that Emilia was hoping that this story would be a long runner and felt a small sense of satisfaction that she might be about to cut her enjoyment short.

"I think we play it straight," Helen carried on. "We say that an individual is helping us with our inquiries and leave it at that."

"They'll know he's in custody. DS Sanderson has made sure of that. What details are we prepared to release?"

"Gender, age if you want, but leave it at that," she replied, making a mental note to talk to Sanderson. "We don't want a witch hunt."

"I think we're probably going to get one, come what may, but I'm sure you're right. I'll give them enough and no more. If you want to come along to say a few words to start us off—"

"I think I'm better used in the interview suite, sir."

"As you wish. I understand he's already downstairs, so don't let me keep you. I'll field the hacks and leave you to do what you do best. The sooner we nip this one in the bud, the better."

Helen thanked him and headed for the lift bank. Paul Jackson was an unlikely suspect in some ways, but he had history with Jake, a taste for the exotic, as well as access to people's credit card details. Killers came in all shapes and sizes and Paul Jackson had a lot of explaining to do. Would he be able to tell her why her good friend had been so brutally killed? As she descended to the custody area, Helen felt a surge of excitement, a sense that they were finally getting somewhere. And unless her eyes had deceived her, Gardam was feeling it too.

37

Charlie waited until Paul Jackson had been handed over to the desk sergeant before making her move. Having brought him in and cautioned him, Sanderson had ten minutes to gather herself while he made his obligatory phone call. Ten minutes would be plenty for what Charlie had to say.

"I didn't think you'd stoop this low."

Sanderson turned, surprised by Charlie's sudden approach. Something—was it embarrassment?—stole across Sanderson's face before she recovered her composure.

"Come on, Charlie, you know the drill. We had a lead, I was the senior officer on duty—"

"Jackson was *my* lead. I spent half the night watching his house . . ."

"So I hear," Sanderson replied knowingly.

"Don't you dare take the piss out of me," Charlie spat back, anger suddenly flaring within her. "I questioned him, wrote the follow-up report. *I* got his bloody DNA, for God's sake—"

"No one's denying that. It was good work. But you know what the boss has been like on this. She wants everything done yesterday—"

"Great. So now you're blaming her—"

"Of course not."

"We're equal rank—you can't steal leads from me. Just because your undercover gig was a bust—"

"You weren't here, Charlie," Sanderson interrupted. "What was I supposed to do?"

"You were supposed to *call* me. That's what any normal person would have done. But you're so busy trying to impress Mummy that you'd—"

"You're out of line."

"Deny it, then. Look me in the face and deny that you deliberately stole my collar to make yourself look good in front of—"

"Go to hell."

"You'd like that, wouldn't you? Be just like the old days—"

"What's going on?"

Charlie was almost nose to nose with Sanderson, but pulled away sharply on hearing Helen's voice.

"We have a suspect in custody," Helen continued, approaching fast. "We have dozens of leads to chase up. So why are my two senior officers going at it like a pair of fishwives?"

Neither Charlie nor Sanderson answered. They didn't dare, given the look on Helen's face.

"You've both been around long enough to know that any problems need to be settled in private, not paraded for the rest of the station."

Charlie stole a glance at the desk sergeant, who'd clearly been enjoying the show.

"DS Brooks, you will accompany me to the interview suite. DS Sanderson, you will return to the incident room and lead the team."

Sanderson opened her mouth to protest.

"And don't even think about answering back," Helen said, silencing her before she'd begun.

Without another word, Helen turned, walking away fast toward the swing doors. Charlie sped after her. She didn't bother looking back at Sanderson—she could tell what she'd be feeling now. Not that this was any consolation—they were both in trouble now and had a lot of ground to make up.

Whatever way you looked at it, Charlie's bad day had just got a whole lot worse.

38

"You are making a monumental mistake and when this is all over, I will be expecting a formal apology."

Helen Grace had already been surprised twice by Paul Jackson in the ten minutes they'd known each other. His agreement to field questions before his lawyer arrived was unusual, as was his decision to adopt such an aggressive tone. He was either extremely confident of his innocence or an accomplished liar.

"As I've said, you're here because your DNA was found on the victim's body," Helen responded calmly. "In saliva on his cheek and ear. It's highly unlikely that our laboratory got that *wrong*. They double- and triple-check their findings—"

"You hear about mistakes all the time in these places," Jackson interrupted. "Petri dishes that haven't been cleaned properly, evidence that has been cross-contaminated—your lot are constantly arresting the wrong people because of cock-ups at laboratories."

"I agree that there have been mistakes, but the fact remains that it is your DNA. The only way cross-contamination could have occurred is if they had a sample of your DNA stored there from a separate incident. Is that the case? Have you ever had to provide a DNA sample for the police before?"

"No."

"Then the only 'mistake' that could have occurred was if your saliva was accidentally transferred to Mr. Elder's face. Can you explain how this might have happened?"

"I've no idea. Perhaps our paths overlapped on the way to work. Perhaps we use the same gym—"

"Mr. Elder works from home, keeps very different hours from you and to the best of our knowledge didn't have a gym membership."

"I can't explain it, then."

"You've never met him?"

"Never. I've said this three times to three different officers now. Perhaps if you tried listening to me, we could sort this mess out."

Helen was about to respond when the door opened and Jackson's lawyer hurried in. Helen knew Jonathan Spitz to be an astute and experienced lawyer and he wasted no time in reprimanding her for proceeding without him. Helen ignored his protests and carried on:

"Mr. Jackson has confirmed that he didn't know Mr. Elder and can't account for the DNA samples we found on the victim's face."

Spitz looked relieved that no serious damage had been done.

"I'd now like to ask your client about his phone history. I'm showing Mr. Jackson a black iPhone. Can you confirm that this is yours?"

Jackson nodded.

"For the tape, please, Mr. Jackson."

"Yes."

"When we spoke yesterday," Charlie interjected, "you said that you'd never contacted Mr. Elder via e-mail, message, phone—"

"Correct."

"Yet dozens of Snapchat messages were sent from this device to Mr. Elder. I have the dates of some of them here"—Charlie pulled a sheet of paper from her file—"August the tenth, August the fourteenth, September the first, September the sixth, September the fourteenth. The list goes on."

"I didn't send them. The phone must have been cloned or something—"

"It's curious, though, that the gap in messages in the second half of August coincides with the dates that you and your wife were on holiday in Santorini. The data roaming charges on your account give us a pretty good picture of your movements, and of course, we're double-checking this with Sally as we speak."

For the first time since they'd started, Helen saw Jackson react. Clearly he was not keen on his wife being dragged into this.

"Furthermore, we've had a chance to look at some of the other messages and texts you sent from this phone. And it's interesting that the same grammatical tics that we see in your texts also crop up in the Snapchat messages that Mr. Elder received. You always seem to leave a gap between a word and a question mark, for example, and you're pretty scrupulous about using commas. Not everyone is as fastidious in their messaging these days."

It was said with a smile, but provoked a blank response from Jackson.

"This is all circumstantial," Spitz butted in. "Do you have any actual evidence against my client?"

"Apart from the DNA evidence, you mean?" Helen rejoined. "I should point out that no other DNA was found on the victim, hence our interest in talking to your client."

Helen let that settle before continuing.

"I'd like now to move on to your movements on the night of the fourteenth. You told my colleague that you left work at seven p.m. and went for a drink at the Saracen's Head."

Jackson said nothing. He appeared to be waiting for Helen's next move before committing himself.

"That's strange, because your phone was transmitting in the Banister Park area of the city—very near to the Torture Rooms—at around eight p.m. that night and again at just after twelve thirty a.m. the following morning. I'm assuming that in the interim you were in the basement club and thus out of reception?"

"I don't know anything about the Torture Rooms or Banister Park. Somebody's obviously messed up—"

"Yet another mistake—you do seem to be unlucky . . ."

"I went to the Saracen's Head. I watched the game, had a few drinks—"

"Why the Saracen's Head, out of interest? You work in Lansdowne Hill. You live in Freemantle. Going to a pub near the hospital seems an excessive diversion."

"For God's sake, I like the beer there, so—"

"What beer do they serve?"

"Shepherd Neame, I think . . . Adnams, a couple of local brews."

"Actually they haven't served Shepherd Neame in over two years," Charlie interjected. "I went there yesterday afternoon, spoke to the bar staff. Nobody remembers seeing you there on Tuesday night. In fact, I couldn't find a single person to back up your version of events."

Spitz looked at his client, hoping for more defiance, but none was forthcoming. Helen took over, adopting a more emollient tone.

"I know you're in a fix here, Paul. You're thinking of Sally, of the twins, of what this will do to them. But lying won't help. We have firm evidence you knew Jake and were active on the S and M scene. Your phone places you near the scene of the crime, yours is the only DNA on the body and I have no doubt that one of those present at the Torture Rooms *will* positively ID you as having been there that night. So let's start again, shall we?"

Helen looked Jackson straight in the eye.

"Tell me what really happened on Tuesday night."

39

She didn't see her coming until it was too late.

Sally Jackson had been in the midst of a particularly difficult conversation when the call came. Paul's PA had seized the nettle, ringing Sally to tell her that her husband had been arrested and taken to Southampton Central. She'd been irritated when the phone rang—she worked at a local family center and was busy explaining to an irate dad why his meetings with his estranged children had to be supervised. These discussions required finesse and patience, not interruptions, so she was tempted not to answer. But when the phone kept ringing, her curiosity was aroused.

She didn't know what to say at first, other than to check that it wasn't a joke and that she was *sure*. But the tone of Sandra Allen's voice—tight, somber, with a hint of embarrassment—convinced Sally that she was. What do you do in these situations? Sally had extricated herself from her work, claiming a migraine, and hurried to her car. But once inside she just sat there, trying to process what was happening. Why hadn't Paul contacted her? Terrified, she'd considered calling a lawyer friend, then, discarding that option, decided to go to her sister's. In the end, she'd done neither, driving home instead. It was like she was on autopilot, heading to the place she felt safest.

"Mrs. Jackson?"

She had just stepped out of the car when the woman approached. She was curious to look at—beautiful from one angle, but scarred on the other—and the situation was made stranger still by the look of concern on her face. How did she know so soon? Who was she?

"I'm Emilia Garanita from the *Evening News*. I understand you've had a terrible shock."

She was so blindsided by the woman's sudden approach—had she been lying in wait for her?—that initially Sally was struck dumb.

"There's no way you can be alone at a time like this, so why don't I sit with you until someone else comes?"

Sally was surprised to see that the woman had taken her arm and was now guiding her toward her own front door.

"Your hands are shaking, poor thing. Give me your keys and I'll do the honors. Then we can have a nice cup of tea."

She stood there smiling, her hand outstretched for the keys. She seemed so confident of what she was doing that Sally now found herself rummaging for her keys. As she pulled them out, however, she spotted her key ring. On it was a small picture of her, Paul and the twins, taken about six months ago at the top of Scafell Pike. They were all smiling—tired but exhilarated by their triumph in reaching the summit.

"I'm sorry—who did you say you were again?" she said, keeping the keys gripped tight in her hand.

"I'm from the *Southampton Evening News*," the woman replied, her smile tightening a touch. "I know you must be wondering what to do for the best and I'd like to help. Within the hour, you're going to have reporters, TV journalists and God knows who else camped on your doorstep. I can deal with them. Let me do that for you," she said, casting an eye across the street as a van pulled up nearby, "or, believe you me, it's going to be a free-for-all. And nobody—least of all you—wants that."

"I don't even know you."

"Here's my ID," she replied, thrusting a laminated press card into Sally's hand. "You can call the office if you like. It's now or never, Sally."

Sally now spotted a reporter she recognized from the local news heading up the road toward her.

"I'm sorry. I don't want to talk to anyone," Sally said, finally finding her voice.

"You're going to have to talk to someone—"

"Please get off my property," said Sally, cutting her short. She opened the door and bustled inside.

She turned to find the woman had a toe on the doorstep—where do these people get their cheek?—and slammed the door shut quickly. She hurried out of the hall, taking refuge in the kitchen, but before she'd even sat down, the doorbell rang. This time she heard a male voice, imploring her to answer. She said nothing in response. There was no way she could talk to anyone. She had the boys to think about, and besides, what could she tell them? She didn't have any information about why Paul had been arrested, what was happening or when he'd be back.

The only thing she did know was that their happy, ordered life was about to implode.

40

He grasped the metal bar and pulled down hard. The weights at the other end of the rope shot up and he held them in that position, his broad shoulder muscles taking the strain. He counted down the seconds in his head—thirty, twenty, ten—before easing the weights back down to base. They touched down without making a noise, bringing a smile to his face. It was stupid to revel in the finesse he brought to the job, but not everyone could do it, so why not?

Rising from the bench, Max Paine surveyed the scene around him. This was by far the most expensive gym in Southampton—complete with floor-to-ceiling views of the Solent—but you got what you paid for. It had the latest equipment, was quiet and full of professional gym bunnies. A particularly well-toned pair of girls wandered past now as he toweled himself down and he took the opportunity to scrutinize their tight backsides. They pretended to be deep in conversation, but they knew he was checking them out and loved it. Max made a mental note to say a few words to them before he left.

He was still following their progress toward the treadmills when his attention was caught by one of the large plasma screens on the wall. There were TVs everywhere in this place, showing sports, lifestyle programs, soaps and of course the ubiquitous game shows that clogged up daytime viewing. He generally ignored them—he was here to exercise—but this time what he saw stopped him in his tracks.

The news was playing, showing a press conference with Hampshire Police. Max didn't recognize the guy leading it and his headphones were switched off, so he couldn't hear what he was saying—but his eye was drawn to the headline bar at the bottom of the screen: TORTURE ROOMS MURDER. Dropping his towel on the bench, he hurried over to the screen, tapping his console to tune in to the relevant channel.

". . . in custody. We won't be releasing a name, but we can confirm that he is a male in his forties who lives locally."

Max Paine listened intently. He had been to the Torture Rooms on numerous occasions and had been scouring local media for updates since he'd heard the news of Jake Elder's death.

"That's all I'm prepared to say for now. As you know, Detective Inspector Grace is leading the investigation, and I'm very confident that we'll make swift progress in this case. There is no need for members of the public to be alarmed, as we are currently treating this as a one-off incident."

Max stood still. Had he been hearing things? No, the guy had definitely said DI Grace. Suddenly he laughed out loud, provoking startled looks from the gym bunnies nearby. This was too good to be true. No, this was *priceless*.

All thoughts of his workout were now long gone. As he strode toward the exit, his mind turned on the possibilities this surprising development threw up. This was an opportunity to make some serious money. What he had to say would pay for his expensive gym membership and a lot more besides.

41

"So this was your third visit to the Torture Rooms?"

"Yes," Jackson replied, without choosing to elaborate further.

Helen nodded, but didn't push it. He had clearly never spoken about this to anyone before.

"What time would you say you got there?"

"Around eight p.m."

"Did you go with someone else or—"

"I was alone."

The way he said it made Helen think he had been "alone" for some time.

"This is not something I've shared," he continued. "It's not something I want shared. It's been a process for me."

"You'd told Jake Elder, though."

Jackson looked up sharply at Helen, then lowered his gaze once more.

"How did you first encounter him?"

"I went to a Munch. They're—"

"We know what they are. Go on."

"Well, I'd looked at some things online. I suppose I've always been attracted to men. But I've never told anyone, never done anything about it until recently. Maybe it's because the kids are older, because I've got more time on my hands. Don't get me wrong—I love my wife—but there's a part of me that's just . . ."

Helen nodded, but said nothing. There was more coming.

"I liked the S and M stuff. Can't say why. I've got a stressful job, a busy life . . . but maybe that's just excuses."

"And Mr. Elder . . . ?"

"Someone at the Munch mentioned him, so I got in touch. We had a session at his flat, and well . . . that was pretty much it for me."

Helen nodded. It was so odd to hear him articulating feelings *she* had felt, but she kept a poker face. She wanted more than this discursive preamble.

"I went as often as I could. Spent I don't know how much money. After a while, it became unsustainable, so I thought I'd venture on to the scene to see if I could find some more . . . companionship."

"That must have been risky," Charlie interjected.

"Of course it was, given my position . . . but there's a kind of unwritten rule about these places. If you see someone you know—someone you recognize from normal life—well, you never mention it."

"What happens on tour stays on tour."

"Something like that."

"And what about Tuesday night?" Helen said, inserting herself into the conversation once more. "When and how did you meet Jake Elder?"

"I saw him on the dance floor. He looked bored. He looked . . . sad."

"Why?"

"I've no idea."

"What happened next?"

"I beckoned to him," Jackson replied cautiously. "I beckoned to him and he came over. I suggested . . . I suggested he might like to go somewhere with me."

"Did you touch him?"

"A little. Just to get him in the mood . . ."

"Why was your saliva on his cheek and ear?"

Jackson sighed, fidgeting.

"Why, Paul?"

"Because I sucked his ear."

"Okay."

"I whispered a suggestion of what we might do and then . . . then I sucked his earlobe. I don't know why I did it . . ."

"Then what?" Helen persisted. She could sense Jackson retreating inward. These confessions were taking their toll.

"He turned me down."

"Why would he do that?"

"You'd have to ask him that." Jackson laughed bitterly, earning a reproachful look from his lawyer. "He said it was because he didn't want to blur the lines between the personal and professional, but who knows?"

Helen eyed Jackson carefully. It was a convenient excuse and Jake wasn't around to contradict him. Was his bitterness just an act?

"Did you go into the rooms at the back of the club?"

"No."

"So we definitely won't find any traces of you—hairs, skin, prints—in those rooms?"

"I never got near them."

"Why not?"

"I don't know—you tell me. Maybe it just wasn't my night."

"A handsome guy like you?"

"There's no accounting for taste," Jackson spat back sourly.

"Are you sure Jake didn't accept your invitation and take you backstairs?"

"Look, I've told you what happened. If you don't believe me . . ."

"Do you like the rough stuff?"

"Don't answer that," his lawyer interjected.

"For God's sake, Paul, our guys are poring over the search history on your phone. We're picking up your computers—from home and work. We are going to find out what you've been looking at, so do *not* hold out on me now."

"Yes, I like the hard stuff."

"Paul . . . ," his lawyer warned gently, but his client appeared not to hear him.

"Have you ever watched Edge Play? Online or in the flesh?"

"Yes."

"Have you ever participated in Edge Play?"

"Occasionally."

"Have you used wet sheets?"

"Yes, I have, but that doesn't mean—"

"Doesn't mean what?"

"That I did anything to Jake."

"Why would it mean that? I haven't mentioned wet sheets in

connection with his death. Neither has the press, so how would you know that?"

"I wouldn't . . . I was just saying that . . ."

"Did you kill him, Paul?"

"No . . ."

"Did you take him to one of the back rooms that night, tie him up—"

"No, a hundred times no . . ."

"Punish him as he deserved to be punished?"

"I would never do that."

"Why?"

"Because it's not my thing."

"You're contradicting yourself now, Paul. We've all just heard you say—"

"I like the rough stuff, but—"

"But what?"

"But I'm always the bottom, okay, never the top," he finally said, glaring at Helen.

"Sorry, I'm a bit—," his lawyer began.

"Bottom means the submissive. The top is the dominator," Helen interjected, keen to keep the focus on Jackson.

"I . . . I don't *like* to dominate." Jackson's voice faltered. "I want to be humiliated, abused, degraded. That's why . . . that's why I could never do something like this."

Jackson raised his gaze to meet Helen's and she was surprised to see that tears were threatening.

"Please believe me. I didn't kill Jake Elder."

42

"Is he lying?"

Helen and Jonathan Gardam were huddled in the smokers' yard, away from the prying ears of colleagues, lawyers and Gardam's PA.

"Hard to say for sure. He sounds genuine, but there's a lot that links him to Elder, to the scene. Also, Lynn Picket banks with Santander—it would have been the easiest thing in the world for him to lift her card details off the system and use them for his own devices."

"Would he really shit on his own doorstep like that?"

"How could you link him to it? Nearly a hundred people work in that bank. Thousands more have access to their system."

"So what's our next move?"

"I'm going to go back to Meredith, see if we can link Jackson to the crime scene. They've got mountains of stuff—cigarettes, beer bottles, hair, spit, semen—if we can put him in the room, then we can prove he's lying."

"And if we can't? What does your instinct tell you?"

"I don't really believe in the copper's gut," Helen replied, dropping her cigarette to the floor. Nicotine was doing nothing for her today, but that still didn't stop her wanting another.

"You must have a view, though," Gardam persisted.

"I'd be tempted to believe him, in the absence of evidence to the contrary."

"Why?"

"He was in the right place at the right time but . . . he just doesn't seem the type to me. This murder was unusual, elaborate and provocative. It's a statement killing—whoever did this *wants* our attention. Maybe he's a good actor, but my feeling is that Jackson doesn't want the world to know that he likes men, likes S and M . . ."

Gardam nodded, even as his eye was caught by the discarded cigarette on the floor. A smudge of Helen's lipstick was still visible on the tip.

"He's married, got twin boys," Helen continued. "He's leading a double life and my instinct is that he wants to keep it that way."

The irony of this comment wasn't lost on Helen—this case just kept rebounding against her—and she toyed with her lighter to avoid looking directly at Gardam.

"Do you want to hold him?" Gardam said, interrupting Helen's chain of thought.

"I'm not inclined to. He's not a flight risk—he's too anchored in Southampton—and I don't want to put too much pressure on him, in case we're wrong. He seems pretty fragile to me."

"Well, I'll back whatever you decide."

"Thank you."

Gardam offered Helen another cigarette, which she took without hesitation.

"I know they're not good for you," he said, lighting Helen's cigarette before fixing one for himself, "but I can't do without them. I have to smoke them here, as Jane thinks I've given up."

Helen nodded, but didn't play along. She'd never been comfortable with the way male colleagues deceived their wives, then enjoyed publicizing the fact.

There was a brief silence, and then Gardam asked:

"Are you okay, Helen?"

"Sure. Why do you ask?"

"You look very pale, that's all. Is anything the matter?"

"I don't think so," Helen lied. "I'm always like this during a big investigation. I'm not a good sleeper at the best of times, so . . ."

"I'm the same," Gardam replied. "Thank God for cigarettes, eh?"

"Indeed."

They smoked for a moment in silence. Then Helen said:

"I'd better get back."

Gardam nodded and Helen walked off, squeezing the last vestiges of nicotine from her dying cigarette as she did so. Gardam watched her cross the yard, his eyes never straying from her, until eventually she disappeared from view and he was left alone.

43

She looked in the mirror and saw darkness staring back.

It wasn't the scratches on her arms or the faint shadow of bruising on her face. It was what she saw in her eyes that shocked her. Something dying, an emptiness taking hold. She had no idea how long she'd been sitting here, drinking herself in, but somehow she couldn't find it in herself to move. The last couple of days had taken so much out of her.

Draining the last drops of her vodka, she reached for her mascara and resumed her preparations. For most of her life she had been friendless, but if there was a staple in her life—apart from self-abuse, drugs and the dolls, of course—it was this. Her war paint had been part of her for as long as she could remember and she never felt whole without it. There was something soothing, exciting and empowering about the ritual of self-improvement, and she loved the feeling of the brushes against her skin. She had always been into this kind of thing—her mother had once said she was very intuitive about "texture." It was one of the few kind things she had ever said to her.

Putting the brushes down, she pulled the tub of hair gel toward her. Scooping up a large handful, she smeared it over her hair and scalp. She often wore her hair up—in a riotous, peacocking display—but not today. Running her hands over her crown, she worked hard to flatten her hair. She liked the severe, asexual look it gave her—she was determined that there would not be a hair out of place.

Satisfied, she rose and walked over to the wardrobe. This was the most painful part and best done quickly. Pulling the whalebone corset from the wardrobe, she stepped into it and raised it up and over her chest. Grasping the strings, she pulled as hard as she could. The corset gripped her rib cage, punching the air from her lungs. She gasped but didn't relent, pulling still harder. She loved the feeling of breathlessness, of constriction, of pain. After thirty seconds, she finally relented, loosening the strings a notch and tying them in a neat bow. Surveying herself in the mirror, she was pleased by what she saw. She looked sleek, smooth, in control.

Time was pressing now, so she slid into her jumpsuit, reaching over her shoulder to zip herself up. Then, marching into the bathroom, she applied the final touches. Colored contact lenses, changing her irises from light blue to a deep chocolate brown. Her hair looked dark and slick, her face uncharacteristically pale, and the eyes that stared back at her were those of a stranger. She didn't recognize herself. She hoped others wouldn't either.

Her preparations were complete now, so there was no point hesitating. Switching off the light, she walked quickly toward the front door. It was time to do battle again.

44

"I'm going to release Paul Jackson."

Helen had dragged the entire team into the briefing room. They looked shocked at the news—Charlie in particular—but Helen wasn't in the mood for a discussion. Jackson might still have a role to play in the case, but in her mind at least, he wasn't the elusive, sadistic killer they were hunting. Crushing though it was to have to admit it, they were back to square one.

"It's only on bail and he'll be under surveillance, but I want us to widen our search and consider other possibilities. We should assume for now that Jake Elder's murder was *not* an opportunist act. The careful choice of venue, the credit card fraud, plus the tactics employed by the perpetrator to conceal the purchase of the items used, suggest a high level of planning."

"Does that mean the perpetrator had a special grievance against

127

Elder, that he'd been plotting his murder for some time?" DC Reid offered.

"Have we found anything in Elder's communications or recent history to support that? Has he angered anybody recently?" Helen responded.

"Nothing on the drugs or money front," Lucas replied.

"Nor in his private or professional life," Edwards said, overlapping. "His life seems pretty . . . empty, to be honest."

Helen felt a sharp stab of guilt but, swallowing it, pressed on.

"In which case we have to consider the possibility that whoever did this has no personal animus against Elder."

"Perhaps it's what he represents?" DC Lucas said.

"Could be a hate crime," Sanderson added. "Antigay? Anti-BDSM?"

"Maybe, but if so, I'd have expected someone to have claimed responsibility for the murder," Helen replied. "Or posted some kind of justification for their actions. Let's keep an eye on that—see if anyone surfaces in the next twenty-four hours."

"Maybe they just get off on the thrill of it," DC Edwards said. "The sense of control, playing God. Maybe whoever did this *enjoyed* watching Elder die—"

"He'd be taking a chance when anyone could have walked in," Helen interrupted quickly, keen not to dwell on this thought.

"Perhaps," Edwards countered, "but according to Blakeman, there's a kind of unwritten rule in that club. If the door's closed, it means 'Do not disturb.'"

"What about exposure?" Sanderson now offered. "By killing him, he's revealing to the world what Elder really was. A dominator, a 'pervert' . . ."

Helen nodded, suppressing her alarm. She had seen this kind

of thing before in the Ella Matthews case, a young prostitute who'd killed her male clients to expose them. Could this latest murder be a copycat killing of her awful crimes?

"But that would suggest that the killer isn't part of the BDSM scene," Charlie objected. "Which doesn't hold water for me. I think our killer knew the club, knew the scene and was very deliberate in his choice of target."

Sanderson said nothing. Nor did her colleagues. As Helen had predicted, everybody knew about their earlier row and they were keen to avoid getting involved.

"In the absence of any specific pointers, we'll have to keep an open mind on the perpetrator's motivation," Helen said, shooting a warning look to both Sanderson and Charlie. "For now, let's deal with what we *know*. Our killer was calm, methodical—"

"Suggesting that he's done this before?" Reid offered.

"Maybe. We should certainly consider the possibility that our killer has a criminal past. Let's look for the obvious—hate crimes, false imprisonment—but I also want us to check out anyone who's been convicted of credit card fraud in the last five years and cross-reference their names against those already on our list. How are we doing with our Snapchatters?"

"Apart from Jackson, we've tracked down seven of the twenty— all of whom have alibis," Charlie replied.

"Not good enough. That's twelve possible suspects who like to conceal their identities and who have a strong personal link to the deceased. Chase them down *quickly*, please."

Charlie nodded but said nothing, so Helen continued:

"Edwards, I'd like you to do some further credit card digging for me. This is our killer's only footprint so far. How did he get Lynn Picket's card details? Check her friends, family, workmen who visited the house—anybody who could have gained access to her bag. Check where she shops, which Internet sites she uses, and ask the tech boys to investigate whether her card details could have been sold as part of a bundle on the Internet or Dark Web. If our killer prefers anonymity, he may favor using a Tor browser."

"I'll get them on to it straightaway."

"I've also asked DS Sanderson to draw up a list of names from last night's Munch. I'm sure word's spread about our presence on the scene," Helen went on, "and it's going to be hard for us to place someone else there, but we can at least follow up on the intel we *do* have."

"I'll circulate the list to everyone," Sanderson added quickly. "Our main person of interest is 'Samantha,' a mid-op transsexual— male to female—who indulges in extreme BDSM and has a history of assault, ABH and so on."

"Finally, I'm going to ask DC McAndrew to keep us all up-to-date with any forensic developments," Helen concluded. "In the absence of any other direct DNA sources on the victim's body, we'll need to interrogate the other traces found in the room and its environs. If there's a match to someone with a criminal past—however trivial—we need to know about it."

There was a silence in the room as everyone looked to Helen once more.

"Well, don't just stand there," she barked at them. "There's a killer out there and he's laughing at us."

And with that, she turned, heading for the sanctuary of her office.

45

Helen pushed the door to and tossed her jacket onto the sofa. She felt drained and dispirited, her high hopes of the morning dashed. She needed time and space to gather her thoughts—gather herself—but she had only just made it back to her desk when she heard Charlie's angry voice:

"You could have spoken to me first . . ."

Helen turned to see Charlie shutting the door behind her. Helen stared at her, then at the door, irritated by this act of insubordination. She was not in the mood to be crossed today.

"I wasn't under the impression I had to run my decisions past you," Helen replied, just about holding her anger in check.

"Jackson is a good suspect."

"I agree, but you were in that interview room. Do you think he's guilty?"

"It's too early to say. We have to go at him again."

"He's being released as we speak."

"Why, for God's sake? We've interviewed him *once*. We can hold him for at least another forty-eight hours—"

"Because if he is an innocent man, I don't intend to ruin his life completely. He has already been the subject of some pretty vile speculation in the press—"

"I appreciate that—"

"Do you? There are people out there who, for valid reasons, want to keep the different parts of their life separate, who've committed no offense—"

"But Elder rejected him. Jackson told us as much. He wanted sex with him and he was rejected. He has a strong motive—"

"So strong that two weeks prior to this murder, he ordered a collection of bondage items with which to commit the crime. This was *not* a crime of passion and you shouldn't dress it up as one."

"You don't know that for sure," Charlie threw back at her, her anger flaring now. "He could have bought those items discreetly, intending to use them recreationally, but on that particular night he was angry and rejected—"

"Put him in the room, then," Helen spat back. "Put him at the crime scene and then we can have this conversation."

The two women had now squared off against each other. Helen's eyes flitted to her office window. She could tell the rest of the team were listening to their argument and she was keen to bring it to a conclusion.

"I think we're making a mistake," Charlie said defiantly.

"Noted," Helen replied. "But ask yourself why you're so hot on Jackson as a suspect. Could it be because you want to prove something to Sanderson?"

"He was my collar and she brought him in."

"And now he's 'yours' again, you want to see it through, one in the eye for your fellow DS."

"That's not true. Yes, Sanderson was out of line—"

"*I* told her to bring him in—because you weren't here."

This time Charlie said nothing in response, stung by the implication.

"You were late and I will not let anyone's lack of professionalism hamper this investigation."

"That's completely unfair," Charlie said, stunned by this personal attack. "I work harder than anyone else—"

"It's a statement of fact. You weren't here when you should have been."

Charlie stared at Helen, speechless.

"But I'll tell you what. As you're so convinced Jackson is guilty, *you* can take the surveillance detail."

"Oh, come on, that's a DC's job at best—"

"It's yours now," Helen asserted.

Charlie opened her mouth to protest, but Helen continued:

"Bring me evidence of his guilt. Show me I'm wrong and I'll eat my words."

She crossed the room and pointedly opened the door of her office.

"But know one thing, Charlie. This case is not about *you*. You may think it is, but it's not. It's about an innocent man—"

Helen's voice faltered as Jake's lifeless corpse once more sprang to mind.

"—an innocent man who deserves justice."

"Why are you being like this?" Charlie said, emotion suddenly ambushing *her*.

"Because it's my job. You'd do well to remember yours."

Helen stared at Charlie, challenging her to respond. But this time she didn't. Instead, she turned and walked straight out of Helen's office and toward the exit without saying a word to anyone. Helen retreated quickly to her desk, keen to busy herself with her case files. She could feel her face burning, as if she were the one in the wrong. She *needed* to regain her composure.

Silence reigned in the incident room beyond, but Helen knew that that was just show. They were all trying very hard to look busy and engaged, but as Helen distractedly turned the pages of the case file in front of her, she knew instinctively that all eyes were on her. Everybody was watching her, but nobody was saying anything.

46

Max Paine flicked through the pages of the newspaper until he found what he was looking for. The *Evening News* was dominated by sensational reports of the Torture Rooms murder, but it was the center spread he was after. There at the top-right-hand corner of the page was the journalist's mug shot and direct line.

Emilia Garanita was no looker, given the extensive scarring on one of her cheeks, but she was a famous face in Southampton— with a number of high-profile exposés already to her name. She was happy to walk where angels feared to tread, going anywhere and talking to anyone who might provide her with a scoop. Paine hoped to use that to his advantage now.

He would meet with Garanita and tell her in confidence the information he was prepared to sell. He would then ask her to make him an offer. Under the pretext of thinking about it, he would then contact Grace and see what *she* was prepared to pay. To the winner, the spoils. He wasn't on some moral crusade, after all. He just wanted money.

He punched Garanita's phone number into his mobile and turned away from the café counter—he didn't want to be overheard. But the call didn't connect, going straight to voice mail instead. He decided to be short and sweet.

"My name is Max Paine. I have information about the Torture Rooms murder that you'll want to hear. Call me on 07977 654878. I'll be waiting."

He rang off, pleased to have made the first move, but irritated not to have been able to speak to Garanita in person. Still, there was plenty of time for that. No point getting strung out this early in the game.

He finished his coffee, flicking carelessly through the rest of the paper, before heading on his way. It was getting late and he had work to do. He thought about taking the *News* with him, but he had Garanita's number on his phone now, so, tossing it casually onto the table, he left. The waitress swooped, scooping up his empty coffee cup, pausing momentarily to take in the front page of the abandoned paper. Something approaching sympathy now creased her features as Jake Elder's smiling, happy face beamed out at her from beneath the screaming headline:

SOUTHAMPTON SEX MURDER

47

They stood staring at each other, neither daring to speak.

The enormous relief Paul Jackson had felt on being told he was to be released turned swiftly to anxiety when he realized what lay ahead. He didn't trust himself to call Sally—he wasn't even sure if she'd answer—so he'd texted her. His message was brief, saying simply that he was on his way home and would see her shortly. It was the kind of anodyne message he had sent a hundred times before. Now, however, it had a very different meaning.

He had hoped to avoid the press by sneaking out of the back exit of Southampton Central, but they were waiting for him there, as they were when he eventually pulled into his road. There was no question of heading in via the back door—the garden wall was too high to be scaled without a ladder—so, getting out of the car, he made a dash for the front gate. Immediately, he cannoned off one journalist, knocking over a photographer in the process. Nobody actually laid a hand on him, but they all contrived to impede his progress. They wanted to provoke him, to get him to lash out, but he kept his head down until he reached the sanctuary of his front door.

His hand had been shaking when he'd put the key in the lock, and the house seemed eerily empty when he finally succeeded in getting inside. The twins had been picked up by another school mum and were still blissfully unaware of what was happening. Sally, however, was waiting for him in the kitchen, seated at the table with her hands folded.

He was about to kiss her, then thought better of it. He pulled out a chair—the trailing leg made a sharp, squealing noise on the polished wooden floor—and sat down. He saw Sally flinch at the noise, and looking at her, he now realized that she was on the edge of tears. The sight made him feel sick. This was his fault. All this . . . hurt . . . was his fault.

"I haven't been able to go out," Sally said suddenly. "They've been ringing the doorbell, banging on the door. I pulled the phone out of the wall, but they got my mobile number from somewhere . . ."

"I'm so sorry, Sally. I never wanted any of this . . ."

"Please tell me it's a mistake," she replied quickly, her voice wobbling. "I heard the headlines. I know what this is . . ."

"Of course it's a mistake, my darling. I'm not a violent man. I would never hurt somebody like that."

"And the rest of it?"

Paul was suddenly unable to look at her.

"That place. Where this man died . . ."

She didn't elaborate further, but the unspoken question was clear.

"Yes. I went there."

"How many times?"

Paul said nothing in response.

"How many times have you been there? And please don't lie to me, Paul."

"Six, maybe seven times."

"What did you do there?"

For a moment, Paul was tempted to lie, to soften the blow. He could start by saying he went to drink, dance . . . But in the end, he simply said:

"I went there to meet men."

Sally nodded slightly, then rose from the table. Paul rose too, moving toward her, but she held up a hand to fend him off. Turning, she walked from the room without looking back, running up the stairs to her bedroom. Paul heard the bedroom door slam shut and, moments later, the sound of her crying.

He walked over to the window, pulling the curtains round to block out the press photographers who were straining to see in from their vantage points on the wall opposite. It was a pointless gesture—it was too late to protect his family. He had never hated himself so much as he did in that moment. He hadn't heard his wife cry in years and now in one awful day he had destroyed her happiness, her peace of mind and her faith in him.

His very public arrest would cause her embarrassment both at home and at work. The revelation that he was bisexual would hurt her deeply too. But perhaps they could have worked through those things—for the boys' sake—were it not for the fact that he had betrayed her. He had lied to her night after night, as he slept with casual pickups. It was this that would damn him ultimately and he knew that Sally would never forgive him. Nor, if he was honest, would he.

48

From her viewpoint across the road, Charlie watched the horrible soap opera unfold. Charlie remained to be convinced that Paul Jackson was innocent, but she still felt for him and his family. Like her, they must have got up this morning with no inkling of what was about to befall them. They might even have been looking forward to the day. But in the time it takes the sun to rise and set again, secrets had been revealed, accusations made and a family's happiness shattered.

Thanks to her job, Charlie came into contact with many unsavory characters, but few were as unpleasant and pitiless as the journalists now camped outside the Jackson house. In time, they would drift away, as new developments emerged, but the next forty-eight hours would be hell. The family could take legal steps to protect themselves from intrusion, but these things took time and in the interim press hounds, radio and TV journalists, bloggers and more would be beating a path to their door.

They would claim that they were only doing their job—"It's a free country" was the common refrain—but Charlie knew they enjoyed it. It was bullying pure and simple, the pack descending on whomsoever they deemed fair game. They would climb walls, scale lampposts, shout through letter boxes, bribe, threaten, cajole—all in the hope of getting a few words with the accused or a photo of his weeping wife. Many people out there thought the same of coppers—that they were only on God's earth to cause grief and upset—but in Charlie's mind, at least, the two professions were very different indeed.

The biting wind whistled round Charlie, and cursing her luck, she retreated to her car. Helen had sent her here as a punishment, knowing full well it would be a wasted journey. It was easy enough to blend in with the journalists and gawpers, but with such a crowd outside what were the chances that Jackson would actually do anything incriminating? If he was smart, he would stay exactly where he was, until the interest in him waned.

Charlie had the disquieting feeling that Helen had turned against her. They had exchanged some harsh words earlier—words that had shaken Charlie to the core—and even though she knew she deserved to be sent to purdah for rowing with Sanderson, she never expected to be publicly dressed down like that. Helen's behavior was out of character—impulsive and erratic—and it unnerved her. Especially when she still felt she had so much to prove.

Charlie hoped her exile would be brief. She missed her family, hated the tedium of a stakeout and desperately wanted to be back in the heart of things. But this case was doing strange things to people—to Helen, Sanderson, even Charlie herself—and she wondered if she had permanently blotted her copybook with her boss. Truth be told, she had never felt so uncertain of her position as she did tonight.

49

"I like the look of this one."

Sanderson was hunched over her desk, running Helen through a printout from the PNC database. The atmosphere was tense following the latter's clash with Charlie, and Sanderson was working overtime to appear efficient, professional and productive. Like her rival, she still had a lot of ground to make up.

"There's a few on the list, but she seems the most likely, given Dennis's description. Real name Michael Parker, now a mid-op transsexual, living as a woman. She's used a number of different identities over the years . . ."

"Sharon Greenwood," Helen replied, reading the details, "Beverley Booker and most recently *Samantha* Parker."

"Exactly. And look at her form. Affray, drugs, theft, obtaining money by deception, false imprisonment . . ."

"What have we got on that last charge?" Helen said.

"Questioned, but never charged, about an incident with a Julian Bown, a married man she took back to her flat. Parker said their acts were consensual. Bown said they weren't, wanted to press for GBH, but dropped it at the last minute."

"And obtaining money by deception?"

Sanderson leafed through her file to find the relevant page.

"Credit card fraud," she said, looking up at Helen. The excitement that always comes with a new lead was rising inside her, but she hid it well. Best not to get ahead of herself when her boss's mood was still so hard to read.

"Dennis said Samantha never missed an Annual Ball, so it's likely we can place her there . . . ," she continued.

"Let's check her out," Helen said decisively. "Does this Dennis know where to find her?"

"I believe so."

"Then I'd better pay him a little visit. In the meantime, let's contact gender reassignment clinics, starting in Southampton and rolling out from there. If Samantha's a mid-operative transsexual, then she shouldn't be too hard to track down. Also, can you locate Julian Bown? If he still lives locally, we need to talk to him."

"Sure thing, boss."

"Stay in touch. This is good work, Sanderson."

"Thank you."

"But that doesn't excuse what happened this morning." Helen lowered her voice. "I'm sure you know that, so I won't labor the point—except to say that I expect every member of my team to work *together* regardless of their rank, temperament or personal history. Is that clear?"

"One hundred percent."

"I'm very glad to hear it."

Sanderson watched on as Helen scooped up her jacket and marched from the office, handing out a few last tasks as she did so. As reprimands go, it had been brief and to the point—Sanderson knew she had escaped lightly. But there was still work to do. The decision to release Paul Jackson may have angered Charlie, but it also reflected badly on her. Helen clearly didn't believe he was guilty and Sanderson's call in arresting Jackson so publicly now looked very misguided.

Charlie had been right about her motivation. Sanderson *did* feel threatened by Charlie, and the chance to grab some glory and emphasize her rival's tardiness was too good an opportunity to miss. She had hoped it would play well for her, but in fact it had achieved the very opposite. But all was not lost and a new lead, and a possible breakthrough in the case, could change everything. She would do whatever was in her power to remedy the situation, because through all the backstabbing, insecurity and confusion one thing remained true—she craved the good opinion of DI Grace.

50

Emilia Garanita hit the hands-free button and punched in the number. She was the last person in the office and this was her final duty on what had been a tiring, but satisfactory, day. She always replied to phone and e-mail messages before the day was out—it was one of the things she prided herself on as a journalist, one of the things that singled her out from her peers. Once she was done, she would head home, open a bottle of wine and read tonight's edition.

It was an indulgence, but she never got tired of seeing her words in print. It was just a provincial paper in some people's eyes—but to Emilia, it had always been more than that. It was a city paper—her city—and it still excited her to see her byline and photo at the top of the page.

Today's spread was particularly good. Everyone knew that people in stressful, high-pressure jobs often had unusual ways of relieving the pressure, but, still, a respectable bank manager was an absolute gift. This story had all the best ingredients—murder, sex, betrayal—and was guaranteed to run and run. Not just because the killer was still at large, but also because the main suspect, Paul Jackson, was clearly leading a double life. He was happily married with two kids, and judging by the look on his wife's face, the revelation about his involvement in the Torture Rooms murder must have come as a complete shock to her, not to mention to their friends and neighbors.

It was the kind of story that would have people all over Southampton speculating about what *their* neighbors were up to after hours, so the *Evening News* had gone to town on it—Emilia once more enjoying a four-page spread all to herself. They'd mocked up an image of the crime scene, constructed a possible narrative of events and gone large on the views of a psychologist about the attraction of hard-core BDSM. That last element had been part of their wide-ranging profile of Paul Jackson. They'd initially run shy of using his name, but once he was released on bail, the gloves were off. Maybe he was guilty; maybe he wasn't. In some ways it didn't really matter—it was still great news, packed with secrets, lies and depravity.

The phone was still ringing, so Emilia clicked off and tried again. But she was growing tired now, so after another fifteen rings she hung up, heading for the exit. Whatever Max Paine wanted would have to keep for another day.

51

"Always nice to see a fresh face," Max said as he straddled the chair and sat down to survey her. "I've not seen you before, have I?"

"I'm just passing through."

"You seem very well kitted out for someone who's in transit."

"Oh, don't let this fool you. I'm very *green* really."

Max Paine smiled. He loved the tease of this job and always responded to clients who were prepared to make their time together more than just a soulless exchange. They were the ones who became regulars, the ones with whom the job was always fun and never a chore.

"Well, let me take you in hand," he suggested, walking over to her.

She was tall and thin with slicked black hair and striking eye makeup. It was a classic Berlin look and suited her down to the ground. Running his finger up her arm, he paused to knead the flesh beneath her shoulder blades. She exhaled happily, so he carried on running his hands down her back, sliding them round to the front. Continuing his progress, he ran them over her chest before bringing them to rest on her crotch. The soft, pliable bulge that now began to harden to his touch revealed that this was going to be even more interesting than he'd imagined.

"Aren't you the girl that's got everything?" he said, rounding her to face her full-on.

"You better believe it," was the impish reply.

Smiling, Max walked away, toward the locked cupboards at the back.

"We have two hours ahead of us, so why don't you choose your weapon?"

He opened the double doors of the wardrobe to reveal his arsenal of crops, whips, paddles, bats, maces and more. There was nothing he couldn't provide for his clients, nothing he hadn't tried.

"You're very sweet, but I wonder if we might use a couple of things *I've* brought along with me. I've never used them and I might need a little help."

Without waiting for an answer, she now walked across to the drawstring bag she'd dropped by the door on arrival. Max watched, intrigued, as she drew a series of restraints and a large Zentai suit from within. The tight-fitting suit looked brand-new, the spandex glistening in the beams of the ceiling spotlights.

"I know we've only just met, but I'd like us to push things a little tonight. I want Edge Play. Can you stretch to that?"

Normally Max wouldn't rush to do this on a first meeting, but she seemed to know what she was taking on, so, nodding, he moved forward to pick up the Zentai suit. But, as he did so, she laid a gloved hand on his arm.

"The thing is, Max," she continued in a whisper, "I want *you* to be *my* bitch tonight. Are you willing to be my bitch?"

Max paused, turning to her. She was attractive and commanding and didn't seem like a psychopath, but you could never be sure.

"That's a bit rich for a first date," he said. "Maybe when we know each other a little better."

"Pity, but have it your own way," she replied, putting the suit down. "These are troubled times. Everyone's running scared at the moment, which is why I was willing to pay so much. But, as you say, another time—"

"How much?"

Paine hated himself for asking, but he couldn't resist. He hadn't paid his rent in more than three months and lived in daily fear of eviction.

"Five hundred pounds if you're a bad boy. A thousand if you're a very bad boy."

His client removed a wedge of twenty-pound notes and placed them on the table.

"What do you say, Max? Can I tempt you?"

Max looked her up and down—there wasn't much to her—then, shrugging his shoulders, he relented. Walking toward her, he smiled warmly and said:

"I'm all yours."

52

"You can't barge in here like this."

"I didn't barge in anywhere, Dennis. I rang the doorbell and your mum let me in."

The mention of his mother provoked a visible flinch. Dennis was pushing fifty, overweight and underemployed and clearly had mixed feelings about living at the family home. Eliza Fitzgerald was a slim, punctilious septuagenarian, who could now be heard preparing tea in the kitchen. Helen imagined she would do it the proper way—warming the pot, using leaf tea—and wondered if her domestic regimen was as meticulous and old-fashioned. Did she still ask her adult son to tidy his room?

"Haven't you people done enough already?"

"'You people'?"

"We don't do anything illegal—we don't do anything *wrong*. You've no right to send spies to our gatherings—"

"Well, if people don't talk to us, what can we do?"

Dennis eyeballed her, but said nothing.

"Everyone in the BDSM community *says* they are shocked by Jake Elder's murder," Helen told him. "Yet nobody has come forward to help us. Which makes me wonder how deep their concern is."

"Fuck you."

"Careful, now, Dennis. Mother might hear . . ."

Dennis shot her another venomous look, but said nothing. The sound of clinking crockery drifted in from the kitchen.

"I think you're rather more interested in protecting yourself. You can dress it up as suspicion of the police, but I think it's more about keeping your little secret safe. Don't get me wrong—I understand that and I have no desire to make your life difficult, so—"

"How did you find me?" he interrupted.

"The Brother*Hood* Web site. IP address of the site runner is registered to this address. Electoral register has an Eliza and Dennis Fitzgerald living here. It took one of our data officers less than five minutes to locate you. Hardly a secret society."

"And are you harassing the others too?"

"No, just you, Dennis. Because you have something I want."

Helen took the photo of Michael Parker from her bag and handed it to him.

"Do you recognize this person?"

Dennis took a cursory look at it, then handed it back.

"Look at it, Dennis. Or I swear I'll arrest you for obstructing police business."

As Helen raised her voice, the clinking of crockery in the

kitchen stopped. Helen could see small beads of sweat appearing on Dennis's forehead.

"We know he's got form, Dennis. Was this the person who hurt you? Is this 'Samantha'?"

Dennis said nothing, but Helen noted that his hand was shaking slightly as he held the photo.

"If you're worried for your safety—"

"It's not that—"

"—or concerned about giving up a fellow member of your community, then I'm happy to make this an anonymous tip-off. But a young man has died here and we need to talk to anyone who might be connected."

Dennis's mother was on the move now, so he spoke quickly.

"I don't know where she lives. But, yes, it's her."

"You never went to her flat, a place of work?"

"She got in touch over the Internet. We only ever met in neutral spaces. Clubs, hotel rooms—"

"Come on, Dennis," Helen cajoled, "give me *something* here."

"But I do know that she sometimes performs at the End of the Road."

Helen breathed out, relieved. The End of the Road was a gay bar in central Southampton that specialized in drag acts and cabaret.

"She's a performer?"

"Sometimes she works behind the bar—other times she performs. Calls herself 'Pandora' when she's onstage. To be honest, I've avoided her since . . . you know . . . but she probably still works there."

"And do you think she could be responsible for Jake Elder's death? Does she have it in her?"

Dennis thought for a moment, then gave her back the photo. "Yes, I do."

Nodding, Helen took the photo from him. Right on cue, his mother appeared in the doorway. Thanking Dennis for his help and reassuring the curious Eliza that there was nothing to worry about, Helen took her leave.

As she walked briskly to her bike, her eyes remained glued to the photo still in her hand.

Was this the face of their killer?

53

"There, that didn't hurt, now, did it?"

Her voice was soft, but had an edge. Max could tell she was excited by what they'd done. And what was still to come.

He had stripped for her—much to her evident pleasure—then slipped on the Zentai suit that she'd brought with her. It was a snug fit—she was clearly far more experienced than she let on—and it covered him from head to toe. Max hadn't done much Zentai before—the oriental stuff wasn't really his bag—but he liked the way he looked. He was like a kind of depraved Spider-Man, every inch of him covered in black spandex.

It was an odd thing to be inside. You could still hear, but the sound was muffled; you could still see, but everything was a little darker. You felt different, not like yourself, the strangeness of the situation underlined for Max by the fact that he was the one taking the beating, rather than handing it out. This was not the norm, and given recent events, he had been tempted to refuse. But she seemed in control of herself, and the blows she was giving him were mild. Besides, he wasn't inclined to believe the fevered tabloid speculation about there being a killer at large in their community. He wouldn't be at all surprised if Jake Elder's death turned out to be an accident with the press turning it into something it wasn't.

Max suddenly realized that she had stopped. He was still bent over the wooden horse, and straightening up, he saw that she had retreated to her little bag of tricks once more.

"Hog ties," she said, holding up the leather and chain contraption triumphantly. "I think we've both had enough of the nursery slopes, don't you?"

Max crossed the room to where she was now pointing.

"No more talking from now on. Just do as I say," she ordered.

Max nodded, enjoying the game.

"Get down on your knees. Good, now arms behind your back."

Max did as he was told. He felt her secure his ankles in the leather restraints. Then, pulling his arms sharply down and back until his fingers were almost touching the upturned soles of his feet, she secured those too. All four restraints—two wrists, two ankles—were joined by a series of short metal chains, making it virtually impossible for him to move.

He was on his knees now and utterly at her mercy. His mouth was dry and he could feel his heart beating fast. She'd said she was into Edge Play—he suspected he was about to find out exactly what her version of that was. He heard her move toward him and seconds later she lowered herself to his level. Her cheek brushed against his and he couldn't conceal his growing excitement when she finally whispered:

"Let the games begin."

54

Paul Jackson stepped into the garage and closed the connecting door firmly behind him. He had tried to talk to Sally three times now. The first couple of times she'd just shut the bedroom door on him, but on the third she'd finally found her voice—telling him to pack his bags and go.

He hadn't been expecting that. He had thought she would let him stay as they tried to work out what to do next. He'd wrongly assumed that that was partly why the boys were being looked after elsewhere—to give them time to talk.

But she didn't want him in the house. In fact she barely seemed able or willing to look at him. The last twenty-four hours had been beyond awful, but this was the straw that finally broke the camel's back and he'd sobbed as he'd begged for her forgiveness. He *loved* her—in spite of everything he'd done, he loved her now more than ever.

But she was deaf to his pleas, refusing to engage with him. And though the thought of facing the assembled journalists filled him with dread, he had eventually complied, pulling the small suitcase from the shelf in the wardrobe and throwing a few odds and ends into it. He never went away, never traveled for his work, and it all seemed like a ghastly pantomime as he tossed his socks, shirts and toiletries into the suitcase, heading off on a journey that he had no desire to make.

Zapping the car open, he raised the boot and dropped the suitcase inside. It fell with a dull thud, the sound echoing off the brickwork that surrounded him. They'd had the garage done only a few months ago. It was supposed to be his space. What a pointless waste of money it seemed now.

He climbed into the driver's seat and picked up the remote control for the garage doors. Was this it, then? His departure from the family home? Inside was nothing but desolation and despair. And outside? A mass of prurient journalists, idlers and neighbors keen to enjoy his disgrace, not to mention two innocent boys who would never look at their dad in the same way again. It was hideous to contemplate.

Which was why he put down the remote control without pressing it, reaching instead for the car keys. Then, winding down all four windows, he sat back in his seat and, closing his eyes, started up the engine.

55

She hurried along the street, taking care to avoid the fast-food wrappers, the empty pint glasses and the occasional pool of vomit. It was Thursday night in Southampton and the drinkers were out in force.

The End of the Road was in the heart of Sussex Place and Helen pushed her way through the postpub crowds to get to it. There was a long queue snaking from the entrance, but Helen bypassed this, heading straight for the bouncer and presenting him her warrant card.

Inside, the party was in full swing. The cavernous bar was a sea of peacock feathers, sequins and elaborate eye makeup—punters and staff alike dressing to impress. Sleekly dressed in her biking leathers, Helen fit in pretty well, receiving several complimentary catcalls as she jostled to the bar. But she ignored them—something told her that speed was of the essence tonight.

She had to bellow to be heard at the bar. The bartender looked unimpressed by her inquiries but sloped off anyway. Cursing under her breath, Helen turned away to examine the scene. Her eye was immediately drawn to a poster for "Pandora," frayed round the edges, but still in pride of place on the far wall. Helen drank in the face—even with the deep gold eye shadow and generously applied rouge, there was a coldness to the face that was unnerving.

"Can I help you?"

Helen turned to find a short, bald man looking at her across the bar. Craig Ogden owned the End of the Road and was clearly thrown by the presence of a police officer in his bar on a busy Thursday night.

"I need to speak to Samantha. You may also know her as Pandor—"

"Both."

"She works here?"

"She does the late shift. Can I ask what this is about?"

"When are you expecting her?" Helen replied, ignoring the question.

"Well, she was due in at ten. But she called in sick."

"When?"

"Just as we were opening," he replied, his frustration clear.

"Where can I find her? Do you have an address?"

"We did, but she moved a few weeks back. Hasn't told us where she is now. She might be living in a skip for all I know. She's not the type to encourage questions and God alone knows where she ends up at night . . ."

"A phone number, then?"

"I can see if we have anything on file, but to be honest, I

inherited her from the last manager and the record keeping at this place has never bee—"

"But she phoned you earlier," Helen insisted. "You must have her—"

"Number withheld. Fuck knows why . . ."

"What about friends, then?" Helen said, increasingly exasperated now. "Or colleagues? Is there anyone here who might know where I can find her?"

"Ask around, by all means," Ogden replied, shrugging. "For my part, I kept well clear of her. Sometimes you can just see it in the eyes, right?"

Ogden was in full flow now, but Helen was scarcely listening, turning to look at the hundreds of revelers who were packed into the club. It would be like looking for a needle in a haystack.

Helen ended the conversation and pushed through the crowds, keen to escape the din. She wanted to get back to Southampton Central, touch base with Sanderson and see if the team had made any progress. Helen had been in an optimistic frame of mind after her chat with Dennis, pleased to have a lead on the elusive Samantha at last. But now she was leaving the End of the Road empty-handed and frustrated, plagued by the feeling that Samantha was vanishing from their radar for a reason. She had vowed to get justice for Jake, but she was still no closer to catching his killer.

A promising lead had just gone up in smoke.

56

The sweat was oozing down his forehead, creeping into his eyes. It was incredibly hot in the Zentai suit and his discomfort was increasing by the second. What had started out as a tantalizing, transgressive game was now becoming unpleasant and unnerving.

He shook his head to dislodge the sweat, but succeeded only in making himself feel dizzy. His heart was racing and the clinging material of the suit was making it hard to breathe. For a moment, he thought he might faint, something he'd never done before. That could be disastrous in a BDSM situation, so, gathering himself, he said:

"Liberty."

This was their safe word, but his voice was cracked and his resulting call weak. He wasn't surprised she hadn't heard it, so he said it again, louder this time.

"Liberty."

Still nothing. He knew she was still here—he could hear her moving. So why wasn't she responding? It wasn't done to tease someone in this situation. If you heard the word, you stopped everything.

"Liberty," he screamed, fear suddenly getting the better of him.

He heard her moving toward him now and tears sprang to his eyes. He was still furious with her, but if she let him go now, then . . . He heard something tearing now. What was that? Was she cutting him out of this suit? Cutting his bonds? Then suddenly he felt something strike his face. He jumped, shocked by the impact, and too late realized what was happening. The tearing sound had been her ripping off some duct tape—tape that she had just stuck over his mouth.

"Let me go."

He bellowed the words, but the tape held, muting his cry.

"I'd love to, sweetheart, but we've only just begun."

The last word was said with such emphasis that for a second Max thought he was going to vomit. Fear now mastered him completely—he suddenly realized that he had made a terrible mistake in playing her games and that because of this misjudgment he was about to die.

57

Charlie stifled a yawn and looked at the clock. It was nearly midnight—she had another two hours before she was relieved. If Helen wanted to punish Charlie, she was doing a good job. Steve had complained about being dragooned into emergency childcare yet again and Charlie was irritated too—with Sanderson, with Helen, but mostly with herself. When had she become so brittle? She used to be the fun, cheeky officer whom everyone got on with. Now she was exhausted, short-tempered and *paranoid*. She didn't regret starting a family for one second, but there were a lot of hidden costs that nobody told you about and she was feeling those now.

Outside, the press pack's enthusiasm was starting to wane. It was cold and a thin drizzle floated down the street, saturating all those still out and about. Most of the journalists had retreated to their vehicles, experience teaching them that you can catch your death on a night like this. Those who remained outside were swathed in thick North Face jackets, praying that the weather would clear. They would have gone home some time ago but for the light that stole underneath the garage door. Somebody had turned it on a while back, and as the family car was stored in there, everyone present was expecting Jackson to make a break for it.

Charlie assumed it was Paul Jackson, as she'd seen his wife head upstairs a few hours ago. The gaggle of photographers that haunted the property was hoping to grab a through-the-window shot of him fleeing his home. There was something about the angle and context of those shots that always made the subject look guilty. Editors loved them, which was why people were prepared to brave the elements to get them.

Charlie flicked through the radio stations again. If Paul Jackson was smart, he'd turn the light off and head to bed. The best way to deal with journalists was to starve them of what they craved. By hanging about, he was just raising their hopes. Finding little to divert her, Charlie switched off the radio and stole another look at the clock. Ten past midnight.

Had Paul Jackson been banished to the garage? Surely not. There were plenty of bedrooms in the house, so even if his wife didn't want anything to do with him . . . Charlie looked over at the garage again. Paul Jackson's sons were elsewhere and his wife had stormed off upstairs, meaning he was in the garage alone. And had been for thirty minutes or more.

Charlie now found herself opening the door and stepping out into the rain. It settled on her face, gentle and cold, but she didn't bother pulling her hood up as she marched toward the garage. If she was wrong, then she wouldn't mind getting a little wet. But if she was right . . .

She walked straight up to the metal garage door and put her ear to it. A motorbike roared past in the road and a couple of news hacks now shouted at her, ribbing her for doing their job for them. She waved at them to shut up, but it made no difference. Furious, Charlie dropped to all fours, her knees soaking up the moisture from the ground. She placed her ear at the bottom of the metal door, where the narrowest chink allowed a little light to escape. She was listening for the sound of the engine, but it wasn't the noise that struck her first. It was the smell.

Now Charlie was on her feet, yanking at the garage handle. But it was locked from the inside and refused to budge. She redoubled her efforts, but still nothing.

"Get over here now," she roared at the startled photographers.

The look on her face made them comply.

"Get that open now."

As they grappled with the door, Charlie raced up the steps. She rang the doorbell once, twice, three times, then opened the letter box and yelled through it. There was no time for hesitation, no time for caution. This was a matter of life and death.

58

He was straining with every sinew, but getting nowhere. The fabric of the suit was smooth and the wooden floor so perfectly polished that the more he moved, the more he spun in pointless circles. He couldn't get any purchase, and his attacker watched now as he exerted himself in vain. It was strangely moving to behold. *This* was what somebody looked like in his death throes.

It had all gone to plan. The only moment of danger had come when Paine had screamed to be liberated. That had been a surprise—a testament to his instinct for danger or perhaps his innate lack of trust in his new "client." It was a mistake, but a small one. Duct tape had been quickly applied to the mouth and the danger had passed.

The foreplay had been completed, the preparatory work done— now it was time for the coup de grâce. Had the thrashing figure on the ground made the connection to Jake Elder's death or was he as clueless as the rest? By the looks of things, he was still in denial, desperately trying to belly-slide toward the door. What was he going to do when he got there? Open it with his feet? It was a crazy last throw of the dice, but there was a possibility that his banging might alert a neighbor. So, crossing the room quickly, the figure lowered the rope from the ceiling pulley and slipped it through the hog ties, tying them together in a secure grapevine knot under Paine's wrists.

Alerted by the sound of the pulley, Paine bucked even more wildly, but, in the end, what could he do? His attacker yanked the rope tight and Paine lurched up into the air. He was only a few inches off the ground, but this sudden development clearly alarmed him—he swung back and forth on the rope, as he made one last, desperate push to escape. It was hard to hang on, but his assailant moved steadily backward, pulling sharply with each step, until Paine was safely suspended in midair. Securing the rope firmly to a wall hook, the figure then stood back to admire its handiwork— Paine, covered from head to toe in spandex, spinning in the air like an obscene mobile.

This had been more arduous than expected, but the hard graft was done. Moving quickly, the figure now walked in and out of the bedroom, lifting a tablet and a smartphone from the bedside table and popping both of them in a zip bag.

Satisfied, the figure headed for the doorway, flipping down the white plastic flap on the thermostat by the entrance. Casting a last look at Paine, his attacker punched the central heating up to the max, then quietly slipped out of the door.

59

The doors burst open and the medical team hurried through in the direction of the intensive care unit. Paul Jackson lay on the hospital trolley next to them, an oxygen mask secured over his mouth and nose. His ashen wife ran alongside, occasionally laying a hand on his, but he didn't react. He had been unconscious when they found him.

Charlie followed a few feet behind, keen to see what was happening, but anxious not to get in anybody's way. Paul Jackson was dying and every second counted. She had eventually roused Sally Jackson, who seemed stupefied at first, barely believing what the desperate police officer was saying. When she had finally unchained the front door, Charlie had raced straight past, navigating her way by instinct toward the internal door that connected to the garage. Jackson had locked it from the inside, so Charlie had had to kick it in.

As soon as she had done so, great clouds of noxious fumes swept over her. Visibility had been poor, but the smell even worse. Clamping her scarf over her mouth, Charlie had pushed through the lethal haze, feeling her way toward the car. Fortunately, Jackson hadn't locked the doors—if he had, it would have been all over for him. As it was, she had managed to maneuver the comatose figure onto the floor, just as the journalists on the other side finally levered the garage door open.

Putting her hands underneath his armpits, Charlie had dragged him out of the garage, laying him in the recovery position in the fresh air outside. Moments later, the ambulance had arrived and Charlie's leading role in events was over. Leaving Sally to join her husband in the ambulance, Charlie had hurried over to her car, receiving a few respectful nods from journalists as she went—their mutual hostility suspended for a few hours at least.

The paramedics had done their best, but Jackson remained unconscious as the medical team now pushed through the double doors and into the intensive care unit. Sally Jackson hesitated, aware that this was as far as she was allowed to go, turning to Charlie as if looking for guidance. Charlie knew from experience that family members in this situation always wanted to do something to help, but the truth was that there was very little they could do. It was in the hands of the doctors and surgeons at South Hants Hospital now. Putting her arm around her, Charlie shepherded her toward a vacant chair. Greater tests lay ahead and she would need to preserve her strength.

As she did so, Charlie reflected on her earlier irritations. She realized now how unworthy those thoughts were, how petty her complaints. Life had its frustrations, but in reality she was blessed. She possessed one thing that Sally Jackson might never experience again—a happy, healthy, loving family. And for that, she was eternally grateful.

60

Helen laid down her flowers and kissed the headstone in front of her. It was gone two a.m. and the driving rain raked the lonely cemetery, but still Helen lingered, pressing her forehead against the cool stone. She had been on her feet for nearly forty-eight hours, but was too wired and upset to return home. She would rather be doing something—anything—than pace her flat, and, besides, this was a duty she never shirked. Marianne was family, so every Thursday night after hours Helen came here, to tend her graveside and leave flowers for the sister she had loved and lost.

Offering a few final words of love, Helen turned and walked down the path. She had hoped a simple act of kindness, of remembrance, might dispel the darkness growing within her—but her conscience weighed heavily on her tonight. She had only just got back to base when Charlie rang. She'd been racing to the hospital, panicking and upset, and her news had hit everyone hard. Paul Jackson had been a decent suspect, but now he was fighting for his life.

Had they driven an innocent man to suicide? The press had to take some of the blame, but so did her officers. It would play hard on Sanderson's conscience whatever the outcome, but it was ultimately *her* fault—the team was Helen's responsibility, and in failing to identify the growing hostility between her DSs, she had committed an unforgivable oversight. If he died, they would all have to answer for it.

Helen had reached the gates now and paused to look down over Southampton. It was a dark, brooding night, relentless bands of rain sweeping over the city, and the lights twinkled mischievously below, as if reveling in the dark deeds that go undetected at night. Helen instinctively felt that their latest thinking was right—that someone within the BDSM community was responsible for Jake's murder. Samantha was potentially a good fit, but if so, why had she suddenly snapped? What had Jake done to provoke such savage treatment? And where was she now? As ever, there were more questions than answers.

The rain continued to sweep the hillside, but Helen didn't move. She remained stock-still, a lone figure lost in her thoughts, surrounded on all sides by death.

61

"It's so nice to meet you. I just wish it could have been in happier circumstances."

Emilia gave David Simons her best happy-but-sad smile. Jake Elder's former boyfriend had arrived on the first train from London and Emilia had been waiting for him. It was highly unlikely that another journalist would have got wind of his arrival in Southampton, but she'd decided not to take any chances, whisking him from the station back to base. They were now tucked away in her small office, breakfasting on strong coffee and the best doughnuts Southampton had to offer. In Emilia's experience, sugar was the best medicine for grief.

Simons was jet-lagged following his flight from Los Angeles, which only exacerbated his disorientation and distress. Emilia could tell that tears weren't far away and she was keen to keep him on track, gently coaxing his story from him.

"So you and Jake were together for . . ."

"Six, seven months."

"And you saw each other regularly during that period?"

"Pretty much every day."

"And how would you characterize your relationship?"

"Good. Very good at first. He was so generous and kind—"

"And then?"

Simons looked up at her, a flash of irritation crossing his face. Emilia sensed he was irked to have been dragged away from happy memories to the painful reality, but she didn't let her concern show.

"Most of the time it was great, but fairly early on, it became clear that there were . . . limits to our relationship."

Emilia leaned forward.

"Meaning?"

"That I wanted more than he did."

Emilia nodded, but said nothing.

"Contrary to the rumors, not all gay men are promiscuous," he continued. "I've only ever had long-term relationships—don't see the point in the other—"

"And you were hoping that Jake might be a keeper?"

"Isn't that what everyone's looking for?"

Emilia smiled, keeping her counsel. Was that what she was after? She'd had relationships, of course, but they had been brief—her work schedule and family responsibilities always conspiring to kill off any potential romance. And now, after so long, she wondered if she was actually capable of commitment.

"So what was the problem?" she replied eventually, interested in his answer for more than just professional reasons.

"His heart wasn't in it."

"Because?"

"Are you always this fucking blunt?"

Now his anger was clear. Emilia had misjudged how brittle he was and hurried to recover lost ground.

"I'm sorry if I sound rude. It's early mornings—I'm no good at them and I've a tendency to put my foot in my mouth. All I'm *trying* to do is get an idea of what you've been through. But please don't answer if you don't want to. I'm very happy to put you in touch with the police if you'd prefer, so you can get the answers you want from them."

This had the desired effect. The police had clearly been in contact with Simons, but Emilia sensed that he'd been evasive about the precise date of his arrival in the UK. He seemed keen to avoid contact with them for as long as possible. In the meantime, Emilia was a useful source of information for him—it would pay him to keep her onside, despite his evident distress.

"I'm sorry. I'm just very tired . . ."

"Of course you are," Emilia responded gently, offering him another doughnut. "And there's no need to talk about anything you don—"

"He was in love with someone else, okay? He loved me in his own way, but there was a part of him I couldn't reach."

"I see. And do you have any idea who this other person was—"

"I glimpsed them talking once, but it was nobody I recognized."

"Can you describe him for me?"

"Actually it was a she. Tall, shoulder-length hair, pretty."

Intrigued, Emilia scribbled the description down before asking: "So what happened?"

"I confronted him about it. He denied that he had feelings for her, but he was lying, so I pushed it. He told me more and . . . well, I was bloody upset, so I called it a day. I've been in this situation before. And I didn't want the end of our relationship to be death by a thousand cuts."

"You went your separate ways?"

"I took some work in the States. Tried to put as much distance between Jake and myself as possible. I'm not sure it worked, though."

Emilia kept her eyes glued to his as she scribbled "female lover?" on her pad. The tears that had threatened were coming now and she had the strong sense that this poor guy, who had loved Jake so much during his short life, now loved him even more in death.

62

He hammered on the door with his stick, but there was no response from inside. What was it with these people? Did they think that paying rent was optional?

Cursing, Gary Lushington looked down at the little book in his hand. There it was in black and white—rent arrears going back over three months. Paine had been a good tenant at first—if you ignored what he got up to for a living—but he'd been evasive and moody of late, which made Gary nervous. That type of behavior usually meant only one thing—him ending up out of pocket. And that wasn't something he was prepared to allow.

Muttering, he leaned against the door and, pulling the key chain from his pocket, began to search for his duplicate set. As he did so, he became aware of a very strange sensation. His back felt warm against the door—no, more than that, it felt *hot*. Gary pulled away quickly, turning to face the doorway.

And now he became aware that this corridor *was* markedly hotter than the couple he'd already visited on his rounds. He'd assumed his clamminess was the result of all those stairs—they were harder for him now that he had to use a stick to get about—but then he realized that the heat he felt was emanating from within the flat. What the bloody hell was Paine thinking? It was a nice autumnal morning, for God's sake—there was no need to have the heating on full blast.

Suddenly Gary was seized by a nasty thought. Perhaps Paine had gone away, leaving the heating on. He might even have done a bunk, leaving his landlord with a hefty heating bill as a final fuck-you.

Slipping the key into the lock, Gary turned it hard and pushed the door open. Calling Paine's name angrily, he stepped forward, but almost immediately found himself stumbling backward again. Crashing into the wall opposite, he remained rooted to the spot, momentarily stunned into silence. The temperature within the flat was *overwhelming* and a wave of choking heat now flooded out, crawling over the shocked landlord and escaping down the corridor beyond. But it wasn't this that rendered Gary Lushington speechless, nor even the sight of a figure hanging from the ceiling. No, what really stopped him in his tracks this morning was the smell.

63

All eyes were on her. The team had gathered in the briefing room for the morning update, looking to Helen for guidance and inspiration. But she felt empty this morning—despite a few hours' sleep she was still running on fumes—and had nothing new to give them. She had never been this deep into an investigation with so little to go on, and the morning papers—with their graphic accounts of Paul Jackson's suicide bid—had done little to improve her mood. Everyone at Southampton Central, from her DCs right up to the chief super himself, had been rattled by this unexpected development.

"The good news is that Paul Jackson is stable," Helen said, as she continued her briefing. "He's still in ICU, but he's conscious and the early signs are that there won't be any permanent damage to his brain or lungs. He's in a bad way, but the doctors are reassured that there's no immediate danger to his life, which is in no small part thanks to the decisive intervention of DS Brooks."

Charlie acknowledged the compliment with a brief nod, but kept her eyes fixed to the floor. Was this to avoid meeting Helen's gaze or Sanderson's? Helen hoped it was the latter—evidence perhaps that her DSs had decided against antagonizing each other further.

"I know you were all shocked by last night's events," Helen said, addressing the team once more. "But right now we have to keep our focus on the case. How are we doing on the Snapchatters?"

"We've ruled out seventeen of the twenty now," Edwards informed them. "Nothing that links any of them to the club. Once we've run down the last three, we'll widen our field—look at Elder's e-mails, texts—"

"We've also just heard that David Simons is in the country," DC Lucas interrupted gently. "The Border Agency confirmed he landed at Heathrow last night. We'll get him in as soon as we can, but he's not in any hurry to contact us."

"Keep on it. In the meantime, let's focus our attentions on possible suspects within the BDSM community, specifically 'Samantha,' formerly known as Michael Parker. The End of the Road has provided a mobile phone number, but it's not currently in use. I want us to investigate when and where that phone last made calls. Also, we have three former addresses for her, all of which she's spent time at within the last two years. We need to be knocking on doors, seeing if any neighbors or friends know where she might be now. Also, let's talk again to people who were at the club, the taxi drivers who were working that night—let's see if we can place her at the Torture Rooms. Any relevant info—good or bad—I want to hear about it straightaway."

Helen was about to move on to allocating individual tasks,

when she saw the custody sergeant approaching. Nodding to Sanderson to take over, Helen drew him aside. The look on his face suggested he had something important to tell her.

"Uniform were called to an unusual death this morning," he said quietly. "We don't have all the facts, but it appears the victim was suspended from the ceiling in some sort of all-in-one bodysuit."

Helen's heart sank, even as he said it. Gathering herself, she replied:

"Any marks on him, any signs of violence?"

"Not that I'm aware of. The boys are saying the place is in mint condition and that the whole thing looks kind of staged."

Helen nodded, but her heart was beating fast.

"Do you have the address?"

The custody sergeant handed Helen a piece of paper, then withdrew. Helen was glad he'd done so, because as she looked at the address in her hand, she got a nasty shock. She had visited the address on only two occasions, but she knew exactly whom it belonged to. A man she loathed and hoped she'd never see again.

Max Paine.

64

What was wrong with her? She should be feeling relieved, elated, excited, but she felt none of these things. Her body ached, her brain throbbed—she was a mess.

Samantha lay on the bathroom floor, resting her forehead on the cold tiles. Returning to the flat last night, she had downed an entire bottle of vodka. Perhaps it was the adrenaline of the evening, or perhaps the vodka was just low-grade—either way, she'd brought it all back up again an hour later. She normally never vomited, but last night she couldn't stop, gagging on the bitter bile that was all she had left at the end.

If she'd had the energy, she'd gladly have killed herself. Her life was an endless merry-go-round of high hopes and crushing disappointments—each one harder to stomach than the last. She knew she was a work in progress, but still . . . Why were the highs so high and the lows so low? Perhaps all those shrinks had been right after all. Perhaps she *was* a bad person.

Putting an unsteady hand on the sink, Samantha hauled herself upright. Turning on the tap, she cupped her hands together to collect the cold water and drank greedily from them. Then she threw the soothing water onto her face—she was burning up—and ran her wet fingers through her hair. A deep, sulfurous burp ensued and suddenly she was vomiting again, the water she'd just consumed disappearing down the plughole with obscene haste. It was as if the water couldn't stomach her, rather than the other way around.

Samantha dropped back down to the floor, exhausted and defeated. There was no point fighting it now and she finally gave way to despair. It was cruel, but there was no point denying it. She had tried to embrace this world, but it always rejected her, raising the level of punishment each time. She was gone—dead behind the eyes now—and felt hollow, empty and utterly alone.

65

The SOCOs had already lowered the body to the ground and removed his clothing for further analysis. The victim now lay on the floor, naked save for a sterile sheet. It wasn't much dignity, but it was the best that they could do in the circumstances.

Crouching down, Helen used the tip of her pen to lift a corner of the sheet. She knew what to expect, but still it was horrific to behold. In life, Paine had been a handsome man, but now his face was waxy and mottled—numerous burst blood vessels giving his expression an unpleasant patchwork quality. He looked like he had exploded from within.

Helen shuddered silently. She had disliked—no, she had despised—Max Paine. He was a violent misogynist who took pleasure in bullying and degrading women. She had used his services a couple of times and had had cause to regret her decision, escaping a dangerous situation only by fighting her way out of his clutches. But still she wouldn't have wished *this* on him. This didn't seem like a similar situation—this wasn't a question of Paine overstepping the mark. This was a well-organized and premeditated attack on his life. This was an execution.

What connected Jake Elder and Max Paine? They were two very different characters who'd chosen the same profession. Helen knew both of them—one intimately, one in passing. Was that important? If so, it was hard to see why. Max Paine was hardly a friend of hers and as far as she was aware, the rest of the world wouldn't miss him either. So what was the point of his death? Were he and Jake chosen specifically or had they just hooked up with the wrong client? It seemed increasingly likely that their attacker *was* from the BDSM community, but the motive was still unclear.

Dropping the sheet, Helen stood up. She would not mourn Paine, but his death was still distressing and alarming. If the two victims were connected, then Helen was the obvious link. But if they weren't, the outlook was even worse. Helen and her team had put so much work in trying to link their killer directly to Jake Elder, but maybe they had been barking up the wrong tree? Perhaps it was the act of murder, not the identity of the victim, that was driving the killer here.

If so, then there was no telling when he might stop. Killing was like a drug—the appetite becoming sharper and more urgent with each successive act. If their killer was getting off on his total control over his victims—and his seeming ability to strike without attracting attention—then what would possibly induce him to stop? Helen had a nasty feeling that he was just hitting his stride.

Having exchanged a few words with Meredith, Helen headed through the front door. Introspection and fear would get her nowhere. Their perpetrator had just raised the stakes significantly and she *had* to respond. It was time to summon what resolve she could if she was to stop him from killing again.

66

"If anyone asks, you say it's a police incident and move them on. No exceptions."

The constable guarding the entrance to the flat nodded solemnly. The PCs seldom said anything when Helen spoke to them. Was that out of respect? Or fear? Helen couldn't tell.

"You're not to move from here until you're relieved. Somebody gained unauthorized access to the crime scene on Wednesday morning. If it happens again, I'll be asking you for an explanation. This is off-limits."

"What a pity. I skipped breakfast to get over here before the others."

Helen knew that voice. Turning, she saw Emilia Garanita walking toward her.

"I was just talking about you," Helen replied.

"All good, I hope?"

Helen didn't dignify that with a response, instead turning and walking fast away from the flats toward her bike.

"I will find out, you know."

"Find out what?" Emilia replied, as she hurried to keep up.

"Who your mole is. And when I do, I'll have their badge and you up on a charge of bribing a public official."

Emilia tut-tutted gently.

"Why do you always see the worst in people? I'm just a jobbing journalist, playing by the rules—"

"You're a ghoul who trades in people's misery," Helen retorted.

"Come off it, Helen. I only report the facts. I can't help what people read into that."

Helen stopped in her tracks and turned to face Emilia.

"I saw the hatchet job you did on Paul Jackson. What was the headline? 'The double life of the boardroom spanker'?"

"I don't write the headlines—"

"Bullshit. It had your fingerprints all over it. You have no regard for the consequences of your irresponsible journalism."

"Back up a little. I have a duty to the public—"

"You have a duty to be a human being."

For a moment, Emilia looked stung, as if Helen's accusations had finally landed. Then she seemed to relax again, a thin smile crawling over her face.

"Is there a reason why you're getting so wound up about this particular case?"

Helen stared at Emilia scornfully, but said nothing.

"You haven't been at any of the press conferences, so I haven't been able to ask you about your personal reaction to Jake's death."

"I've got nothing to say about that."

"But you were acquaintances. Friends even . . ."

Helen stared at Emilia but said nothing. She'd known this moment was coming—Emilia was not the type to forget a tasty bit of gossip or past arguments—but now that it was here, Helen still felt rattled. There was no point denying her connection with Jake, but this was not an avenue she wanted to go down. There was no telling where it might lead—blackmail? exposure?—and this time she had no weapon with which to squash the wily journalist.

"We were friends, but I hadn't seen him for a couple of years and I'm treating this case as I would any other."

"Please don't lie to me, Helen," Emilia replied. "You were very close to him—you must be in turmoil. I'm surprised they let you lead on this."

"You're way off the mark," Helen lied.

"Am I? I spared you last time because you persuaded me that that was the right thing to do. But I'm seriously starting to question the wisdom of my decis—"

"You *spared* me?" Helen replied, incredulous. "You spared yourself. If you'd printed that stuff, I would have had you up on a charge of illegal surveillance. Don't kid yourself that you're a decent person, Emilia, because you're not."

"Fighting talk," Emilia replied tersely, irked by this character assassination. "Let's see where it gets you, shall we?"

Happy that she'd had the last word, Emilia turned and walked back in the direction of the flats. She had won the first battle. The question now was whether she would win the war.

67

Helen barely registered the other road users as she biked back to Southampton Central. She was riding slowly for once—she needed to buy herself time to think. This case was becoming ever more complicated, with no immediate or obvious solution in sight. What had started as a terrible personal tragedy had grown into something darker and Helen now faced a fight on two fronts—bringing in a devious and elusive serial killer, while fending off the very real threat of exposure.

Strange to say, the latter terrified Helen as much as the former. Privacy and discretion had always been her watchwords—it was the only way she knew—but now she was backed into an impossible corner. It would not be easy to spike Emilia's guns, nor tell what she might do with the information she now held close. Emilia would know that any attempt at extortion would be rebuffed—Helen would rather sacrifice her career than be turned—so what other option did she have but to publish? A detailed and lengthy exposé, highlighting the terrible conflict of interest that Helen had swallowed in the interests of gaining justice? Helen could well imagine how that story would play with the top brass.

Helen knew that there was only one possible solution, but still she recoiled from it. She had never wanted anyone to know her properly, never wanted anyone to get close to her. Her life was like it was for a reason. But the cat was out of the bag now and the only remedy was to confess, before Emilia beat her to the punch. The thought made her feel sick—how could she even find the words to begin?—and there was no question of her opening herself up for general entertainment. No, if she did this, it would have to be targeted, controlled and brief. And it would have to be now—there was no telling what Emilia would do and Helen refused to be driven off this case by public outrage.

Leaving her bike in the Southampton Central car park, Helen stopped to look up at the windows above. There was no point putting it off.

It was time to talk to Gardam.

68

Charlie stared at the unshaven lump opposite her, trying to hide her distaste as he crammed a dripping fried-egg sandwich into his mouth. Chewing noisily, the middle-aged cabbie eventually looked up, catching her gaze.

"You having something?" he asked.

"I've already eaten," Charlie replied, lying. She was trying to lose a bit of weight and the fare at the transport café didn't fit the bill.

"Suit yourself," the cabbie replied, taking a noisy slurp of his coffee, before popping a chipolata in his mouth. Charlie was paying for his breakfast this morning and he was clearly going to get the most out of her generosity.

"You spoke to one of my colleagues yesterday?"

The cabbie nodded.

"You told her you were working on Tuesday night?"

"I work every night, love. Don't have a choice."

Charlie smiled sympathetically.

"And you had an unusual pickup between the hours of midnight and one a.m."

The cabbie shrugged. "You get all sorts doing a night shift. But this one was a bit odd."

"Odd how?"

"Well, it was a bloke for a start. I thought she . . . he was a bird at first. Long legs, long hair, nice clothes and that. But the voice was too low and he had an Adam's apple, so . . ."

"So what specifically was odd?"

"You mean apart from that?" the cabbie replied, laughing.

"Come on, there are lots of gay pubs and cabaret bars in that area. You must see stuff like that all the time."

"It was more the state of him," he conceded.

"Go on."

"I could hardly understand where he wanted to go at first. He was white as a sheet and he'd been crying. He was trying to suck it in, but his makeup was a horrible mess." He laughed again. "I wasn't going to let him in, but he gave me a twenty up front, so . . ."

"Where did you take him?"

"To an address in St. Denys—Newton Street. Only cost a tenner, but he didn't care. Got straight out of the cab when we got there and didn't look back. You ask me, he was about to puke. I don't know what they take in these places but—"

"Can you describe him to me?"

The cabbie paused, then said:

"Tall, like I said. Thin, very thin. He was dressed in a kind of catsuit, so you could see there wasn't an ounce of fat on him. Hairless too—no stubble or anything."

"Can you describe his face to me?"

"Dark eyes, no eyebrows except what was drawn on—"

"Anything on the sides of his face?"

"Yeah, now you mention it, he had a little scar on the right side of his face. Makeup couldn't hide that."

Charlie nodded, then pulled a photo from the file on her lap.

"Was this the person you picked up on Tuesday night?" she asked, offering the cabbie the photo. He took it between his greasy fingers, then after a moment's consideration handed it back.

"Yeah, that's him."

Charlie took the photo and, having confirmed the address of the drop-off, thanked the cabbie and hurried on her way. Finally they had something to work with.

Her cabbie had just placed Samantha near the scene of the first murder.

69

"Thank you for seeing me straightaway," Helen said, her confident tone failing to conceal her anxiety.

"My door is always open," Gardam assured her calmly. "How bad is it?"

"Bad. He's definitely our second victim."

"How can you be sure?"

"The MO is slightly different, but the victim was made to suffer as much as is humanly possible and it was a highly 'professional' execution. This was a statement killing, just like Elder's."

Gardam took this in—he looked as sick as Helen felt. Then he said:

"So the flat is owned by this Max Paine? How sure are we that he's our victim?"

"One hundred percent."

"Right," Gardam replied. "I thought we were still trying to contact his next of kin—"

"We are, but I know him. That's what I wanted to talk to you about."

"I see. Have you come across him in a case before, or . . . ?"

The "or" was left hanging and Helen knew she had to fill the gap. If she didn't say it now, she would lose the confidence to do so.

"This is very difficult for me to say . . . but it would be unprofessional of me not to do so," Helen said, just about getting the words out.

Gardam said nothing. He was watching her intently, which only made it worse.

"I know Max Paine—in fact I know both victims, because I've used their services."

Gardam's face didn't move at all, but Helen could tell he was shocked by what she'd just told him.

"I used Paine's services twice, about a year ago. Before that, I used to visit Jake Elder on and off, but I haven't seen him in over two years."

This wasn't the whole truth. Helen had decided to omit the beating she'd given Paine—this was difficult enough without admitting to a criminal act.

"Right. I see," Gardam finally responded, not quite finding the words.

"I don't really want to go into the details," Helen continued. "But I thought you ought to know."

"And you didn't think this was worth telling me after Elder's death?"

"No, I didn't," Helen replied firmly. "I hadn't seen him in ages and couldn't add anything useful to the investigation by doing so.

But now that a second man known to me . . . Well, I wanted to be up front with you and offer to remove myself from the case—if that's what you'd like."

Helen had debated long and hard whether to offer this up, but she knew she was duty-bound to. It was the only thing she could do, given the circumstances.

There was a long silence. As Gardam processed his response, Helen examined his face for signs of an instinctive reaction. What was he thinking? Had she irreparably damaged herself in his eyes?

"Thank you for sharing this, Helen," Gardam finally replied. "This can't have been an easy thing to bring up."

"It wasn't, believe me."

"Can I ask if anybody else knows of your connection to the victims?"

Helen paused, then, closing her eyes, bit the bullet.

"Emilia Garanita knows about my connection to Jake Elder."

"Bloody hell."

"But she obtained this knowledge illegally and if she's smart, she'll keep quiet. She knows nothing of my connection to Paine."

Helen could have said more but didn't. In reality it was highly unlikely she'd be able to stop Emilia with the threat of prosecution—the original offense having been so long ago—but she had to play any card she could with Gardam in order to try to stay on the case.

Gardam pondered his response. Impatient, Helen now blurted out:

"Look, if this is awkward, I can take sick leave. I don't want to, but if you feel it would be for the best, then it's something we should consid—"

"Well, let's review what we've got," Gardam interrupted. "You knew both victims and have a personal connection to the case. Were you in a relationship with either of them?"

"No. Of course not. I liked Jake as a human being, but that's it. Paine meant nothing to me."

"Right."

What was that in his tone? Was it pity?

"And do you think you'll be able to discharge your duties in this investigation as normal?" Gardam continued.

"Definitely."

"You're not *too* invested in it?"

"I don't think so. I'd tell you if I was."

"And how sure are we that Garanita will keep shtum?"

"Fairly, though there's no guarantee, of course," Helen lied quickly.

Gardam looked at her, his mind turning. Helen was suddenly aware she was holding her breath and exhaled gently, trying to calm herself.

"Well, it's not an easy decision. But . . . I'm minded to keep things as they are for now," Gardam said decisively. "These deaths are alarming and I need my best people on it."

Helen nodded, more relieved than she could say. She was embarrassed to feel tears pricking her eyes.

"And don't worry, Helen," Gardam reassured her. "This will remain between us."

Helen thanked him and went on her way, keeping her eyes to the floor. Outside in the corridor, she leaned against the wall and brushed the offending tears away. Odd though it was, she almost felt happy. It had been a tough conversation to have to have, but she was pleased she'd grasped the nettle. It had cost her something to take Gardam into her confidence—to reveal her weakness to him—but she now felt free to drive the investigation forward. Marching toward the incident room, Helen pulled her mobile out and dialed Meredith's number. There could be no more delays, no more setbacks now. Jake Elder and Max Paine deserved justice and Helen was determined to see that they got it.

70

Charlie drained the dregs of her coffee and tossed the paper cup in the bin. Would it be bad to have another one straightaway? She was tired, but more than that, she was cold, despite the autumnal sunshine. She had been pacing Newton Street for over an hour now and had little to show for it, except a mild headache and blocks of ice for feet.

Her cabbie was certain that he'd dropped his ride off near the top of the road. There were several blocks of flats there, but a little basic detective work in the shops and cafés had established that Samantha had been seen coming out of Ellesmere Heights on occasion. It was a fairly sorry-looking setup and no one was answering the buzzers, despite Charlie having pressed them all several times. There had been nothing to do but watch and wait, so she'd parked herself on a bench outside the launderette with a coffee and a free sheet, arming herself with a puffed-out but empty laundry bag by way of cover. She seemed to spend most of her life on surveillance these days and she hungered for something a bit more challenging. The numerous lattes she was consuming were doing nothing for her waistline.

As the minutes, then hours, ticked by, Charlie's decision to keep this lead to herself began to trouble her. It was quite probable she was wasting her time, and besides, Helen had reiterated the importance of everyone sharing information from now on. But still . . . every lead Charlie had pursued so far had proved fruitless. Paul Jackson was a disaster and they were still trying to locate David Simons, though in truth no one genuinely thought he was a suspect. Which just left Michael Parker, aka Samantha. Charlie knew why she was keeping this lead to herself, and she knew it didn't reflect well on her, but still she sat here, ignoring the occasional buzz of her phone, intent on seeing it through.

How much longer could she stay? She would have to account for her time eventually and the longer she left it, the harder it would be to explain away. She was already in Helen's bad books, so why risk their friendship further by escalating her war with Sanderson? When all she might end up with for her pains was a stinking cold?

She rose to head back to the coffee shop and almost walked straight into Samantha. It took a moment for her to compute who it was—Charlie was busy apologizing for getting in her way when her gaze was drawn to the bloodshot eyes and the faint scarring on her right cheek. Samantha hurried on, and Charlie, realizing her mistake, flung her newspaper into her laundry bag and walked swiftly in the same direction.

Normally she would have waited longer, but Samantha seemed so determined to make it home that she was fearful of losing her.

Samantha hurried up to Ellesmere Heights and pushed roughly inside, her gait unsteady and stumbling. The heavy door swung back on its hinges, then began its inexorable progress back to a closed position. Charlie jettisoned her fake laundry bag and ran. If she didn't apprehend Samantha now, she would have to hand over her lead and take the consequences—and she was damned if she was going to do that. The gap was only inches wide, but Charlie shoved her foot into it, wincing slightly as the door pinched hard. But her intervention had been subtle and silent—she could hear Samantha stumbling up the stairs above, seemingly oblivious to her intrusion, so, easing the door open again, Charlie slipped inside.

71

"I have a name for you."

Helen was now standing in front of the team. A new case file in hand, she was determined not to waste any time.

"His landlord has identified the victim as Maxwell Carter, more commonly known by his professional name of Max Paine. He was a dominator who worked from his flat, so obviously one of our first lines of inquiry is whether he was meeting a client last night. There were no papers or diaries at the scene, so, DC Reid, could you liaise with uniform on the house-to-house inquiries—see if we have any witnesses to activity at the flats last night. We'll also need to interrogate his digital footprint—did he run Web sites, was he on Twitter, Tinder? There were no devices in his flat, but we did find chargers for an iPhone 5 and a tablet, so check if he backed up at all and if so where to. Fast-track any warrants—we need to know who he was communicating with in the last few days of his life. McAndrew, can you take the lead on this?"

"On it," McAndrew replied, rising and hurrying off.

"Max Paine is a local boy," Helen continued, "with one marriage behind him and a son, Thomas, aged six. He divorced three years ago—his wife, Dinah, now lives in Portswood with their little boy. I will talk to them once we're done here. For now, let's focus on the facts. As with the Jake Elder murder, the killer has been very cautious, very precise. We won't have Jim Grieves's findings for a few hours, but so far Meredith has found no DNA evidence of our perpetrator within the flat."

The way Helen said the word "within" made a few of the team look up. Clearly she was building up to something.

"However, she has just confirmed to me that her team have found a partial footprint in the corridor leading away from the flat. The lino on the floor had been cleaned recently and we've got the faint outline of a size six boot. It was raining last night—the ground outside the flats was soft and dirty, so—"

"Does that suggest his visitor was a woman?" DC Edwards asked.

"Or a man with small feet. We've got an impression of the tread, which is ridged and in waved grip lines. DC Lucas, can you keep on forensics until we have a match?"

"Will do."

Helen handed out the rest of the duties to the team—witness statements, Munch follow-ups, financial investigation, family histories—before calling time on the meeting. It felt good to be leading again, but even now something nagged away at her. She had asked for the whole team to attend the briefing—to push forward together on the new leads—but one officer was notably absent. Which left her wondering:

Where the hell was Charlie?

72

Charlie hammered on the door, but still there was no response. She had followed Samantha up to the fourth floor, calling out her name. But she appeared not to hear and in any event Charlie was too slow to stop her entering flat 15, slamming the door behind. By the time she made it there, the music had already started up. Deafening techno shook the walls of the building and no amount of knocking could raise its inhabitant. What was she doing there?

Charlie walked across to the landing window and looked down on the street below. Having spent a good five minutes wearing the skin off her knuckles, she'd given up knocking and descended to the entrance once more. Just inside the main door, next to the fire regulations, was a number for the caretaker. He was clearly more used to dealing with leaking roofs and blocked toilets, but once

Charlie impressed upon him the urgency of the situation, he had been happy to comply. So why was he taking so long to get here?

This was a calculated risk and Charlie knew it. Technically she should have waited for a warrant, but as long as her entry was not illegal, she would probably be fine. Samantha was only a tenant and the caretaker had the authority to open her door. Furthermore, she had failed to stop when requested to do so by a police officer . . . Charlie knew she was scrabbling a bit, but she would need to have her story off pat, should the need arise. Helen would see through it, but might let her off if the arrest proved decisive, and something told Charlie she needed to get into that flat as fast as possible. Samantha could be doing anything in there. Destroying evidence, preparing to flee, perhaps even making an attempt on her life? What was the reason for the deafening music? What was she trying to hide?

The squeal of brakes snapped Charlie out of her thoughts. Moments later, she heard the front door open. Shaking hands with the agitated caretaker, she ushered him upstairs until they were once more outside flat 15. The caretaker seemed to hesitate—as if tacitly asking Charlie if she was sure she wanted to do this—but Charlie wasn't in a mood to be put off.

"Open it, please."

He turned the key in the lock and the door slid open.

"Do you want me to stay?" he asked half hopefully.

"You can wait outside. I'll call you if I need you."

Grumbling, he complied. As he traipsed down the steps, Charlie didn't hesitate. Pulling her mobile from her pocket, she called base to request backup, then stepped confidently into the gloomy flat.

73

"This is him at Thomas's birthday party."

Helen was sitting with Dinah Carter in her dingy living room, turning the pages of the family photo album. To Helen's surprise, Paine seemed to have had a strong relationship with his son—but this had been cut short. Thomas's dad was now on a metal slab across town, in the tender care of Jim Grieves.

"When did you last see Max?"

"Maxwell," Dinah corrected her. "He was always Maxwell to us."

"Of course," Helen replied, noting the hostility to Max's professional name. "When did you last see him, Dinah?"

"Two weeks ago. He came round to take Thomas to football practice."

There were no tears yet, just blank shock. Dinah was still

trying to grapple with what she'd been told. The grief would come later.

"How did he seem?"

"Fine."

"And did you speak to him at all after this?"

"We exchanged texts. Making arrangements and so on, but that was it."

"When was the last time you received a text from him?"

Dinah was already scrolling through her phone.

"Sunday night."

Helen read the message, which was everyday, anodyne, then said:

"And you've been separated for how long?"

"Separated for seven years, divorced for three."

"And can you tell me why your marriage broke up?"

"Different lifestyles."

"Can I ask what you mean by that?"

"Really? You have to ask?" she replied tersely.

"His choice of work."

Dinah nodded.

"He wasn't working as a dominator when you met him?"

"No, he wasn't. He was a laborer, for God's sake. I'm not saying he was an angel. Neither of us were. I was open to stuff—we had a good sex life—but then he started watching a lot of porn, more and more BDSM stuff. He wanted me to go along to meets and stuff and I went to a couple out of loyalty, but I've never been comfortable . . . doing that sort of stuff in public. And once I was pregnant, that was it. I called time on it and asked him to do likewise."

"But he didn't?"

"He said he tried, but he didn't really. He was hooked. Said it was part of who he was. I don't think it was at all. In fact it changed him, I always said."

"In what way?"

"He was always very generous, very kind, and he loved being a dad. But he started staying out all hours, lying about where he'd been. I loved him, but I didn't love that side of him and in the end it all became too much."

"Was it you who ended the relationship?"

"Yes. He got a flat and not long after that changed his name and . . ."

Helen nodded. It was clear that Dinah hated her ex-husband's alter ego, feeling perhaps that the name change was a rejection of her, of his past.

"Did you ever see his flat?"

"No, I wouldn't go round there and I wouldn't let Thomas either."

"Did you ever come into contact with any of his clients? Anyone he worked with?"

"No," Dinah replied impatiently. "I wanted nothing to do with it. Because that wasn't him. Our Maxwell bought me flowers every Friday, took Thomas to the Saints, saved up to take us away on holiday. Whatever else came after, that was the *real* Maxwell. The man we both loved."

Helen nodded, her gaze falling on the photo album that lay open in front of her. Looking at the photos of a smiling Maxwell, laughing and joking with his son, Helen reflected on how often people surprise you. She had been guilty of writing Paine off as a violent misogynist, but he was clearly capable of love, tenderness and devotion. Maybe it was impossible to know somebody else in this life. Perhaps it was only in death that one's true self was revealed.

74

"Samantha?"

The music was deafening, drowning out Charlie's voice. Outside the flat, it had been unpleasant and jarring; within the flat it was horrendous—the insistent, high-pitched computer beat and thumping bass arrowing straight through her. Charlie's first instinct on entering had been to turn back—her head throbbed and she felt unsteady on her feet, the vibrations crawling up through her bones, but she was here for a reason and was determined to see it through.

"Samantha?"

Her cry was once again lost in the audio barrage swirling round her. This was the third or fourth time she'd called her name now without response, so, summoning her courage, she pressed on. It was dark in the flat and the carpet was old and ruffled up in places, making it fertile ground for trips and slips. Charlie found a light switch on the wall to her right, but the low-energy lightbulb emitted only a weak, yellowing light that barely helped.

Plowing on, Charlie came to a doorway. Cautiously, she poked her head inside to find a deserted kitchen. The fridge door hung open and a pile of dirty pots clogged the sink. It didn't look as if the room had been used for some time. Directly opposite was another door, this time leading to a tiny, faded bathroom. Again it was deserted and the small room smelled so overpoweringly of vomit that Charlie beat a hasty retreat.

Once more, Charlie hesitated. The source of the noise seemed to be farther down the corridor, which arced round to the left ahead, disappearing from view. This was the bowels of the flat—hidden from public view—and Charlie was suddenly nervous of what she might find there.

Pulling her baton from its holster, she moved forward. There was not enough room in this place to extend it properly—you'd never get a proper swing—so she kept it short. Experience had taught her that this often worked best when it came to hand-to-hand combat in confined spaces.

She made her way carefully down the corridor. The farther you got from the front door, the darker it became, and she had to feel her way round the corner. The floorboards creaked loudly beneath her feet, threatening to give way, so Charlie upped her pace, eventually coming to a door that hung ajar. A sliver of light crept from within, illuminating a faded poster of a topless model that hung on the exterior of the door. Any beauty or glamour the image might have once possessed was lost now under the welter of depraved graffiti that covered it.

Taking a breath, Charlie grasped the handle and pushed the door open. This time the wave of sound knocked her back on her heels. It felt like she'd been struck, but gritting her teeth, she stepped forward. The sight that met her eyes took her breath away.

The small room was in a terrible state of repair—bare boards, peeling plaster and exposed wiring hanging from the walls. There was no bed, little in the way of furniture—instead the room was piled from floor to ceiling with dolls. Barely an inch of space was visible beneath the avalanche of painted faces, frills and stuffed limbs. Charlie stood still—she felt as if dozens of lifeless eyes were now fixed on her, chiding her for her intrusion.

Now the dolls were moving. Charlie took a step back, raising her baton in defense, flicking it out to its full length. The mound of dolls parted suddenly and from beneath them a figure emerged. It was Samantha, but not as Charlie had seen her before. She was naked now, her pale form decorated only by the livid bruises on her ribs and the smeared mascara that had dried in streams on her face. Her expression was lifeless, her eyes cold, and when she opened her mouth, Charlie could see that her teeth were yellow and brown. She looked the intruder up and down, then said:

"I've been expecting you."

75

We think we're anonymous, but we never are. However we might try to protect ourselves, however smart we think we've been, it is impossible not to leave a footprint of some kind. Max Paine's killer had left his or her mark in the corridor outside the flat and perhaps he or she had left a digital mark too.

The latter was increasingly the case in police work, and DC McAndrew was no stranger to content warrants and cyberspace. Rolling her neck with a loud click, she returned her attention to the screens in front of her, making a mental note to go to her Pilates class later. Too much data sifting played havoc with your posture, and she could feel her back beginning to protest at her lack of activity.

Click, click, click. McAndrew and the team were working on the supposition that Paine's attacker had deliberately cleared the flat of electronic devices—anything that could send or receive messages.

Such a tactic might work in the short term, but it was nothing more than a temporary fix. Paine hadn't been very assiduous about backing up, but the apps, downloads and messages from his tablet and smartphone were synced to the cloud. McAndrew sifted through them now, searching for the important clue that seemed to have eluded them so far.

She flicked quickly through the dating apps, before finding what she was really after. His e-diary. Scrolling straight to yesterday's date, she took in his diary entries—a doctor's appointment at eleven a.m., coffee with a friend at twelve p.m., a Tesco's delivery at three p.m. After that came his work commitments—Paine was a nocturnal worker. A "Mike" at six thirty p.m., "Jeff" at eight p.m. and then the final appointment of the night at nine p.m. None of the names gave them much to go on—no surnames and the first names probably false—but the last meeting of the day was even more oblique. Just a time and next to it a single initial:

"S."

76

"If you want me, you're going to have to come and get me."

Samantha remained stock-still, despite Charlie's repeated demands for her to move. She lingered within the sanctuary of her strange doll cocoon and as neither of her hands was visible, Charlie had no intention of approaching her. Charlie had been stabbed, assaulted, even strangled in the line of duty and had no desire to risk another such attack.

"That's not going to happen and backup's on its way," Charlie barked, crossing the room quickly to switch off the deafening music.

"Isn't that what they always say, just before something bad happens?"

"Threatening a police officer is a criminal offense," Charlie growled back, irritated and angry.

"I think I can wear it, sweetheart."

Charlie stared at her. She was treating this like a game. Was she just enjoying the moment or was there something else going on here?

"Well, that's all you're wearing, Samantha, so why don't you find yourself a robe? You've no idea what the sight of a naked woman will do to some of my uniformed colleagues."

"Especially one like me," Parker responded, suddenly getting to her feet. The dolls fell away to reveal her full nakedness. She was utterly hairless and stick thin. With her toned body and full eye makeup, she could pass very convincingly for a woman, except for the bulky male genitalia between her legs. Charlie raised her eyes to hers and kept them there.

"Could you grab something for me, honey?" Samantha nodded toward a large wardrobe in the corner of the room. "There's a jump-suit two hangers from the left that should fit the bill."

She ran her tongue over the last two words, amused by her little joke. The faint sound of sirens could be heard in the distance now, but this seemed to have no effect on Samantha. Her eyes were fixed on Charlie.

Charlie edged toward the cupboard, not once breaking eye contact. Samantha seemed calm, relaxed even—it was hard to see where the danger might come from. Was it possible there was some-body actually in the cupboard? The thought was crazy, but taking two quick steps toward it, Charlie threw the wardrobe doors open.

Nothing but a ragged collection of dresses and suits. Keeping one eye on Samantha, she reached for the second hanger from the left. A crimson jumpsuit hung on it and Charlie lifted it out. As she did so, the hook of the hanger snagged on the top of the hanging pole and Charlie had to turn briefly to free it. As she did so, she saw her go. Samantha sprang from her position in the middle of the room and sprinted through the open doorway. She had waited patiently, playing for time, but now she was making her bid for freedom.

Charlie dropped the hanger and ran after her. Samantha made it through the door and tore off down the dark corridor, hurdling the detritus in her path. Charlie was only seconds behind her, busting a gut to keep up.

Samantha raced to the bend in the corridor and took it hard, bouncing off the wall but keeping her balance. Charlie lunged at her, but in the darkness failed to see a discarded vodka bottle on the floor. Her left foot went from under her, the bottle skidding away, and she hit the ground hard. Her momentum carried her forward and then she was scrabbling to her feet, ignoring the throbbing pain in her shoulder as she burst round the corner.

Now it was a straight race. The long, creaking corridor ran all the way to the front door—to freedom. Samantha had a head start and looked odds-on to get there first, but Charlie knew she had to stop her. Redoubling her efforts, she surged forward. Samantha was only twenty feet from freedom now.

Charlie had shut the front door behind her on entering and she was glad of it now. As Samantha approached the door, she was forced to slow down. And as she yanked the door open, Charlie saw her chance. Launching herself through the air, she cannoned into Samantha, slamming her naked body against the back of the door, before the pair of them fell to the floor in a heap. Dazed, Samantha tried to struggle to her feet, but the wind had been knocked out of her and within seconds, Charlie had her knee in the small of her back. Pulling her arms roughly behind her, she slapped on the cuffs and yanked Samantha to her feet.

They stared at each other for a moment, breathless and bruised, before Charlie eventually said:

"I think we've had enough fun and games for now. Let's make you decent, shall we?"

Samantha stared at her, shivering even as the sweat ran down her cheek, then suddenly spat hard in Charlie's face.

77

"What in God's name were you thinking?"

Helen had sped to Ellesmere Heights as soon as she had got Sanderson's call. Charlie had disobeyed a direct order by apprehending the suspect alone, so in spite of the presence of Sanderson, Lucas and numerous SOCOs, Helen didn't hesitate in taking her to task.

"You could have been killed or injured . . . You call, then you wait for backup—you *always* wait for backup."

"Like you do, you mean," Charlie retaliated, wiping the last remnants of Parker's saliva from her face.

"Excuse me?" Helen countered, stunned by Charlie's aggressive tone.

"You've broken protocol on numerous occasions. And have you *ever* been pulled up on it?"

Charlie would not normally have answered back, but she had just brought in the prime suspect and was not in the mood to be lectured.

"Only in life-or-death situations and besides, it's different for me. You have a family—"

"So it's one rule for you, one rule for everybody else."

"Why the hell are you doing this, Charlie?" Helen replied, beyond exasperated. "You've got nothing to prove to me, nothing to prove to yourself. There's no need to keep putting yourself in danger like this."

"I didn't know what she was doing in there," Charlie countered. "I could have waited another five minutes, but what if she'd done something to herself? You can see what state she's in—drunk, emotional, unpredictable—"

"Come off it, Charlie. You've always been impulsive, but that's not what this is. This is about you getting one over on Sanderson. This was *her* lead."

"So why didn't she bring him in?" Charlie retorted, casting a quick glance at her rival, who loitered by the flat entrance nearby.

"I told every member of the team to report back to me straightaway with any developments, but you deliberately kept this to yourself. You missed an important briefing, went off on your own. To prove what? That you're willing to risk your life for your career? You've got to get a handle on this—it's affecting your judgment, your ability to do the job—"

"Well, that's rich coming from you."

Helen looked ready to explode, but Charlie continued:

"Ever since we found Jake Elder, you've been acting oddly."

"Don't think our friendship gives you the right to talk to me like that. I am your superior officer," Helen snapped back, anger flaring in her.

"Then try acting like one," Charlie interrupted. "You were in pieces after we found Elder and you've been aggressive, overemotional and unpredictable ever since. Take a look in the mirror, Helen. It's not me that's acting weirdly. It's you."

Charlie turned and walked away toward her car. Helen's first instinct was to go after her, but even as she took a step in her direction, she became aware of the large audience watching on. There was no question of continuing the argument now. Helen had already let herself down by rowing with another officer—the same crime she'd pulled Charlie and Sanderson up on only a day ago—and she risked losing all authority if she made their confrontation look personal.

But in truth it *was* personal. Charlie had always been Helen's closest friend and ally at Southampton Central, but now it looked very much like her old comrade had cut her off for good.

78

Are some wounds too deep to heal? Is damaged love ever beyond repair?

Sally Jackson sat by her husband's bedside, clinging doggedly to his hand. She'd kept a vigil here since he'd been released from ICU, hoping that her support and encouragement might speed his recovery. Hoping that the Paul she knew would come back to her.

He was out of danger now, but he still found it hard to talk and was asleep for much of the time. Sally didn't mind—she'd hated being excluded from the intensive care unit, powerless to influence events and ignorant of what was happening within. Here at least she could try to help. In Paul's waking hours, she kept up a constant chatter, talking to him about mundane family matters as well as looking forward to things they might do with the boys once he was better.

Sally had no idea if it was true or just wishful thinking. It was hard to imagine they could ever go back to the way things were given the trauma of the last forty-eight hours. He had been in such a dark place, so despairing, that he had tried to leave them. Perhaps in her position some people might have felt rejected, but she didn't. She just felt guilt. Paul had asked for her help, for her understanding, and she had been too weak to give it to him. Paul had betrayed her—of course he had—but she had repaid him in kind and it made her feel dreadful.

Her conversation had petered out a while ago now. Much as she tried to remain upbeat, it was hard not to be consumed by dark thoughts. She'd overheard the nurses gossiping about a second victim and she suspected they were wondering if her husband would be the third. None of it made any sense and it filled her with trepidation for the future. Yes, she was here, doing all the things she should do, but really what hope was there for the future when the fissure in their lives was so great?

Wiping a tear away, Sally chided herself for being so morbid. There was no point looking too far ahead—she had to keep her mind anchored on the here and now. The rest—the future—was another world for them. She would remain here and do what was needed for Paul, for the twins. She would stay because she still cared deeply for her husband. She just didn't know him anymore.

79

"This is your opportunity to tell us what happened. If I were you, I'd take it."

Samantha said nothing in response. She had seen the station doctor and was calmer now, though it was clear that she wasn't comfortable in these surroundings. She fidgeted endlessly, shifting in her seat, tugging at her clothes, obsessing about the broken nails she'd suffered when being escorted to the station. On more than one occasion, she had asked for replacements, as well as foundation, lipstick, mascara, but Helen had refused her requests. They would be good bargaining chips in the hours to come.

"What would you like to know, Helen? May I call you Helen?"

"If you like."

Helen tried to keep the edge from her voice, but didn't wholly succeed. She was still stewing on her argument with Charlie and was not in the mood to be teased or mocked. Charlie had **never** spoken to her that brutally before—such an open act of defiance threatened not only their relationship but also morale within **the** team. It was tempting to blame Charlie's sudden and unexpected promotion for this problem, but actually Charlie was right. Helen *had* been behaving oddly—this case was messing with her **head,** making her act in ways that were both unprofessional and unkind.

"And what should I call you?" she asked, trying to put **these** troubling thoughts from her mind.

"My name is Samantha."

"Samantha Parker?"

"Just Samantha."

Helen noted her aversion to her given surname—a small **but** telling sign. Opening her file, Helen digested the contents, taking **a** moment to compose herself. Her anger and discomfort still burned, but the details of the case, and the rhythm of questioning, **were** comforting and familiar. Helen hoped that slowly she would **regain** her equilibrium in the hushed confessional of the interview suite. She was leading it alone, which was unusual, but in the circumstances what choice did she have? To include either Charlie **or** Sanderson would seem like favoritism. Another rod for her **own** back, Helen thought to herself.

"Samantha it is, then. But you've been known by other **names,** haven't you?"

"We all have many different personalities within us."

"And, of course, there's your professional work as a drag **act,** which requires an alter ego?"

"We're called performance artistes and, yes, a little creativity **is** required."

"Would you say you're well-known on the club scene?"

"Pretty well."

"And in the wider BDSM community?"

"It's a larger world than you'd think and, yes, I play my part."

Helen nodded but said nothing, noting that Samantha was happy to be led toward an obvious trap.

"So you've visited the Torture Rooms, then?"

"On occasion."

"And you've run into Jake Elder during your time. If you need to refresh your memory, here's a phot—"

"I believe I've seen his face around," Samantha said, without looking down at the photo. "At Munches, events and so forth."

"And what about Max Paine? Have you ever met him? Ever used his services?"

"Once or twice. He's got a bit of a reputation, but then again every girl likes to be slapped sometimes, doesn't she?"

Helen ignored the assertion. "Last night he had an appointment. His diary said he was meeting 'S.' Was that you?"

"Don't tell me something's happened to him," Samantha came back calmly.

"Please answer the question. Was that you?"

Samantha sat back in her chair.

"Yes."

"So you kept your appointment?"

Samantha nodded.

"Did he beat you?"

"Not particularly."

"So how did you get your bruises?"

For the first time, Samantha hesitated, her cockiness temporarily deserting her.

"I forget."

"Not good enough."

"I honestly can't remember. I was in a bit of a state last night."

"Why?"

"None of your fucking business."

It was aimed directly at Helen. She sidestepped it and continued:

"Where were you between the hours of ten thirty p.m. and six thirty a.m. last night?"

"At my flat."

"Can anyone verify that?"

"No."

"How about Tuesday night? Cast your mind back three days—where were you then?"

"Out."

Helen said nothing. The silence sat heavy in the room.

"I was at the ball, okay? It's a very popular event."

"To be clear, you were at the Annual Ball at the Torture Rooms nightclub."

"The Torture Rooms *nightclub*—Jesus Christ, you sound like my grandmother."

"Yes or no?"

"Yes."

Helen scribbled a note to herself to call Meredith. If Samantha's presence at the club that night could be confirmed, it would make a massive difference to their case. Otherwise they would always be open to the defense of false confession—a thorny problem in high-profile cases.

"Did you encounter Jake Elder on Tuesday night?"

"I saw him mooching about like a bear with a sore head. Poor boy looked like he needed cheering up."

"Did you talk to him? Interact with him?"

"Did I . . . interact with him?" Samantha replied, wrapping her mouth round the words. "Not that I recall, but then, the night is a bit of a blur. As your colleague has probably told you, I have an issue with alcohol. I'd pay for the good stuff, but as it is . . ."

"So nothing out of the ordinary happened that night?"

"No. Same old, same old . . ."

"Have you ever used wet sheets?" Helen asked, changing tack sharply.

"Of course."

"Other forms of restraints? Leather straps, hog ties—"

"Who hasn't?"

"A witness—a cabbie—picked you up that night after the Annual Ball. Said you were in a terrible state. Angry, distressed, unpredictable. If it was such a mundane evening, why were you so affected by it?"

Samantha said nothing, but Helen could see her eyes narrowing.

"What happened that night, Samantha?"

There was a long pause, as Samantha toyed with a broken nail. Then she leaned forward, rewarding Helen with an ample view of her cleavage as she did so, before whispering:

"That's for me to know. And you to find out."

80

Gardam leaned against the two-way mirror, his eyes glued to the contest in front of him. In his younger days, he had loved the tussle of suspect and interviewer, reveling in the feints and parries, the carefully laid traps and the elegant evasions, but he seldom got the chance to enjoy it now. His was a desk job, important but managerial, far from the front line, far from the fun. So he had to amuse himself vicariously, watching others do the job he once loved.

The experience was always sweeter when the interview took place under high pressure. The discovery of a second body and the ensuing media excitement had left no one in Southampton Central in any doubt about the need for a quick resolution to the case. Two men had been sadistically murdered, but worse still, their initial suspect now languished in hospital, following a botched suicide attempt. Southampton was being made to look like a den of vice and its police force far from competent—Gardam had already had the police commissioner, the local MP *and* the mayor on the phone, bending his ear about it.

His get-out-of-jail card in these situations was always Helen. She was an officer of such standing that nobody—least of all the local politicians, who liked to appear strong on law and order—could take serious issue with the way investigations were run. Yes, there were false starts and accidents, and you could never predict how people caught up in cases like these would react, but Helen's track record at getting results in the big investigations was second to none.

Gardam had used her name many times to smooth ruffled feathers, assuring his critics that justice would prevail, and in his heart he *did* believe that this case would be no exception. But another part of him knew that it was already very different. He and Helen had worked together on complicated investigations before, but never as closely as this. Something profound had changed in their relationship.

Was he genuinely falling in love with her? He'd had office crushes before, but he'd never been tempted to act on them. This was something else. She had opened herself up to *him*. He had replayed their recent conversation over and over in his mind. Did she know how he felt about her? Was it even possible she knew that he watched her? He hoped not, because that made her confession even more unprompted. She had bared her soul to him, revealing things she hadn't confided to anyone else. He had the strong sense that she did this not just to unburden herself, but also to test him, to see how he would react. If he'd been obviously shocked or judgmental, she might have backed off, but he had been accepting and encouraging, so she had elaborated, drawing him into her world. He hoped in time she would go further.

But that was for another day. Now there was work to be done. Still, it didn't stop Gardam drinking in his subordinate now, noting the way she spoke, the way she held herself, the manner in which she teased and coaxed her suspect toward her traps. It was magical to watch and Gardam knew that his other duties would be neglected until she was done. While she was here, performing for him, the rest of the world could go hang.

81

"So why do you do it?"

Samantha arched an eyebrow, but said nothing, examining her nails.

"Is it about you? The victims? What is it about them that gets you riled?"

"Why should I hate *them*? They are nobodies."

"So maybe it's about you, Michael."

"Don't call me that."

"It's your name, isn't it? Michael James Parker." Helen pulled a couple more sheets of paper from her file. "Born just outside Portsmouth, second child of Anna and Nicholas Parker, brother to Leoni. Are your parents still alive?"

"No, thank fuck."

"But Leoni is. She's had to post bail for you on a number of occasions, hasn't she?"

"If you say so."

"I see you've got form for credit card fraud. Tell me about that."

"I was working at a café. Management took all the tips and I needed some money to survive—"

"So you lifted customers' credit cards and then what?"

"I feathered my nest."

"Until you got caught."

"Precisely."

"Also charges of affray, assault . . . and false imprisonment."

"That was bullshit."

"Your victim didn't think so."

"It was a game that went wrong."

"Went wrong how?"

"I thought the guy had balls. Turned out he hadn't."

"It's never your fault, is it? Everything we've talked about so far—"

"Why *should* it be my fault?"

Samantha snarled as she said it. Her female carapace was slipping now, her voice low and breathy, revealing a masculine side that was usually hidden from view.

"Tell me, when did you realize that you wanted to be Samantha, rather than Michael?" Helen said, changing tack once more.

"I didn't realize—I knew."

"So it was from birth."

"Of course. I was just born wrong."

"And this desire to be a woman, how did it express itself when you were a kid?"

"How do you think? I had a mother and a sister."

"You borrowed their clothes?"

"Sure. My mother said she never knew, but she did."

"And your father?"

Samantha suddenly threw her head back and laughed.

"He definitely didn't know. Not initially at least . . ."

"And when he did?"

"What do you think?"

"He beat you?"

"Have a look at my past medical records. You'll see a lot of accidents there."

"How long did this go on for?"

"Until he sent me away. He decided my mum and sister were the problem, so he packed me off to boarding school."

Helen watched Samantha closely. The pain of this separation was still evident.

"It was all boys and I hated it. Nowhere to dress, no one to talk to and then puberty, God help me."

"Your voice broke?"

"And the body hair, and walking round with a giant pair of balls between my legs like a fucking ape."

"What did you do?"

"I cut myself, played the fool—I messed up in pretty much every subject I took. Still I was bullied to shit. Turns out the boys there didn't like sissies any more than my dad did."

"So you've always been a victim of violence?"

"Pretty much, though they saved the best till last. I took their abuse for five years, and then one day I thought 'fuck it.' I turned up at the sixth-form disco dressed as Samantha. Immaculate, I was, far better-looking than the rest of the sad sacks there. And you know what? Nobody said a bad word to me. No, they waited until

I was on my way back to the dorm. Doctors said I was lucky not to lose my sight."

Samantha was looking directly at Helen, her eyes boring into hers.

"And the scar . . . on your face?"

"A present from my dad when I was eventually expelled."

Helen nodded. She instinctively disliked Samantha, but her story was not so dissimilar to hers. The wounds inflicted by family are the deepest of all.

"Do you still self-harm?"

Samantha gave Helen a withering look that answered strongly in the affirmative.

"Do you think that's why you're drawn to recreational violence? To BDSM?"

"I'm not a shrink, sweetheart. Are you?"

Helen smiled and shook her head. She didn't like her attitude, but she was talking, which was good.

"Tell me what you like to do when you're having a session. What's your taste?"

"The usual."

"Meaning?"

"Restraint, role-play, punishment, isolation techniques, sensory deprivation—"

"Edge Play?"

"It's been known."

"Give me some examples."

Samantha looked at Helen. She had been warming to her, becoming almost garrulous and sociable, but now Helen saw her hesitate.

"In one of Max Paine's previous entries against your name—or your initial at least—he's written 'Phoenix.' Can you explain that to me?"

Samantha looked dead straight at Helen. Was she looking for an excuse not to answer the question? A way out?

"We're not due to break for another thirty minutes, so please answer the question."

"I'd like a lawyer now."

"Your brief is on her way and should be here soon. In the meantime, what does Paine mean by 'Phoenix'?"

"It's a scenario."

"A scenario you act out?"

"Of course."

"Describe it to me. Samantha, you can look away all you want, but I prom—"

"It's a scenario in which the bottom comes out on top, okay?"

"So the victim—you—are in control."

"Right. Sometimes you act out a little bit first, where the top verbally abuses you, beats you up, but then the tables are turned."

"Meaning that eventually *you* are the one handing out the punishment."

"The Phoenix rising."

As she said it, a smile crept over Samantha's face. Did she feel she was finally getting the upper hand with Helen too?

"Did you act out the Phoenix with Max Paine?"

"Sometimes."

"I don't mean in the past," Helen butted in. "I mean on Thursday night. Is that what you wanted? Is that what he offered you?"

Samantha took a long time to think about her answer, before she finally said:

"Yes."

82

The silence in the room was deafening. Normally the incident room was the epicenter of noise on the seventh floor—mobiles ringing, printers whirring and officers arguing, laughing, speculating. But not today. It was tense and hushed, the spectacle of both Sanderson and Charlie avoiding each other putting everybody else on edge.

Sanderson finished her tea and contemplated heading to the canteen for another. She'd been chivying the computer operatives into carrying out their data checks on Paine's devices for over an hour, but with little success. This was especially galling given Charlie's arrest of Parker. Despite her argument with Helen, Charlie would still get all the plaudits, if they managed to secure a confession from their prime suspect. Sanderson *had* started the day in a conciliatory mood, thinking she should perhaps apologize to Charlie and try to make things right. But Charlie had gone her own way, stitching the rest of them up, and now she had the upper hand. So her apology had been swallowed.

"Okay, let's park the smartphone for now, focus on the tablet instead," she said, her patience finally wearing thin.

Her abruptness earned her a reproachful look from the data analyst, but Sanderson ignored it. She knew she was behaving petulantly, but she couldn't help herself. As her aggrieved subordinate punched the keyboard, Sanderson's eyes strayed across the room. She could see Charlie out of the corner of her eye, leafing through files. It made Sanderson smile. Hard though she was trying to look busy, she knew that all of Charlie's thoughts were bent on the interview downstairs—an interview she was excluded from. This would be a big feather in her cap if things played out as she hoped.

"Here you go," her neighbor said, failing to conceal the hint of triumph in her voice. Sanderson turned to her, irritated with herself for being so distracted.

"What have you got?"

"Someone's using Paine's tablet."

"Where?" Sanderson said, suddenly engaged.

"Not sure yet. They're hooked into a server in the city center. Give me another five minutes and I'll give you a more precise location."

Sanderson was already heading to the door.

"Buzz me in the car. I'm heading down there now."

Sanderson pushed through the door and down the corridor, half walking, half running. She didn't want to overdo it, but she couldn't look this gift horse in the mouth. There *was* a chance that she could still redeem herself. More than that, there was a chance that DS Charlene Brooks had pulled in the wrong guy.

83

"So what do you think?"

Gardam had been waiting for Helen outside the interview suite. She'd been keen to get back to the team, but he'd pressed her for an update. So they now found themselves in the smokers' yard once again.

"I think she's a good suspect. She's admitted engaging in extreme BDSM practices with Paine on the night he died, she knew Elder and I'm pretty sure we'll be able to place her at both scenes. She's definitely damaged enough—she's been a victim of violence all her life and I suspect it's the only language she knows. Plus it's clear that she has an unhealthy interest in subjugating other people."

"She told you all this?"

"She doesn't seem to mind—in fact she seems to enjoy it."

"So why hasn't she confessed? If she's so willing to talk?"

"It could be that she's innocent—though she's never said as much. It may be that she's cornered and wants to enjoy the game for as long as possible. Or it may be that actually admitting what she's done is too hard for her. Don't forget she's a victim too."

"So what's the next play?"

"We keep digging—see if we can link her to BDSM purchases made with stolen credit cards. Anything we can turn up will increase our leverage."

Gardam nodded and drew hard on his cigarette. A brief silence followed as Helen did likewise. They were alone today and the smokers' yard had a curiously intimate feel.

"I really should give these things up," he said, exhaling.

"Me too. But somehow every time I make the decision to quit—"

"Something comes up."

Helen nodded.

"Occupational hazard, I guess," Gardam continued, flicking his ash onto the ground. "How long have you been a smoker . . . ?"

"Since I was a kid," Helen replied. "There wasn't much else to do round our way when we were bunking off school. It was my sister who really got me into it."

"I was the same. I wanted to be like my older brothers. Of course, they both quit years ago and now the bastards do triathlons just to rub my nose in it."

Gardam finished his cigarette and rubbed it out on the wall behind him.

"Maybe we should both quit together?" he said. "Keep an eye on each other."

"Let's not run before we can walk, eh?" Helen replied, extinguishing her cigarette. "We've still got a long way to go on this one."

"I guess you're right," Gardam answered, pocketing his packet of cigarettes.

Helen waited to be dismissed, but Gardam made no move to do so.

"Was there anything else, sir?"

"No. And don't feel you need to call me that. 'Jonathan' is fine, as long as it's not in front of the troops."

"Of course, thank you."

"Good night, Helen."

Helen took her leave and headed back to the seventh floor. Perhaps she had been wrong about Gardam. Against all the odds, they were starting to get along.

84

"It's so nice to have someone to talk to. Someone who *understands*. It must have been hard losing your dad so young, but you turned out okay, didn't you?"

Emilia Garanita nodded and gave Dinah Carter's arm a squeeze. The latter was clearly terrified that her son would be left traumatized by his father's sudden death, and she desperately needed some female reassurance. Emilia was happy to oblige—she was good at making people feel better and what she'd told her so far was *mostly* true. The fact that her dad was not dead, but serving a sentence for drug smuggling, was a minor detail. It *had* been tough for her becoming a surrogate parent to her many siblings at such a young age, but the experience had been beneficial for her in the long run and now she didn't regret it. It was certainly useful in situations such as these.

Dinah Carter had been reluctant to open the door. She'd already had journalists round offering her money, but she'd run scared of them. Emilia sensed that they had been too aggressive, too obviously grasping for a piece of Dinah. Emilia by contrast had tried the softly, softly approach, mainlining on her sympathy for the bereaved ex-wife. And it had worked—Carter hadn't shut the door on her. Emilia suspected it was more than just her empathetic manner that had made Dinah hesitate—the extensive scarring on her face helped too. Emilia wasn't proud of the way she looked, but it certainly had its uses. People could see she had suffered—there was no need to explain—and more often than not, that got her through the door.

They had already spoken at length about Dinah's son, Thomas, but there was a finite amount of copy in this, so Emilia moved the conversation on. The moral majority out there had limited sympathy for a man of Max Paine's alternative lifestyle, however loving a dad he might have been on the weekends. What they—and Emilia—were interested in was who might have killed him.

"Did DI Grace tell you what lines of inquiry they're pursuing, in relation to Maxwell's death?"

Dinah shook her head, fiddling nervously with the buttons on her cardigan.

"Do they have a suspect in mind?" Emilia asked. She was aware that another suspect—Michael Parker—had been arrested in connection with the murders, but she wasn't sure how serious this new line of inquiry was yet.

"Not that they told me. They just wanted to know what kind of man Maxwell was. I told them about how he used to be, the good side of him, but beyond that . . ."

"And do you have any suspicions yourself? Do you know anyone who might have wanted to harm Maxwell?"

For the first time, Dinah hesitated. She looked nervous, even a little tense.

"Has anyone harmed him before?" Emilia sensed a breakthrough. Still Dinah paused, then:

"I don't know if I should be telling you this."

"I won't print anything you don't want me to."

It was an easy lie to tell and Emilia had done so many times before. Did Dinah smell her duplicity? She still seemed uncertain whether to trust her new friend, whether she should unburden herself. Then, making a decision, she said:

"He was attacked once before."

Emilia nodded and looked concerned, giving this piece of info the weight Dinah obviously felt it merited.

"When was this?"

"About nine months ago. He had to cancel a day out with Thomas. I was livid, shouted at him down the phone, so he sent me a photo. Poor sod had been beaten black-and-blue."

"Have you still got this photo?"

"Probably. On my old phone."

"It would be great to have a quick look before I go," Emilia said quickly. "What did the police say about this?"

"I . . . I didn't tell them."

"May I ask why?"

Dinah said nothing, but Emilia could tell there was more.

"Surely you must want to catch Maxwell's killer? For Thomas's sake, if not your own. Why *wouldn't* you tell them?"

"Because it was a police officer that did it."

"How do you know?" Emilia asked.

"Because he told me. He wanted to do something about it, but how can you, when it's one of their own?"

"Did he say why he was attacked?"

"No, just that it was unprovoked. He didn't like talking about it much—he was embarrassed, I think, because it was a woman that did it."

"It was a female officer?" Emilia responded, failing to contain her surprise. "Did he give you a name?"

"No."

"A description?"

"No, but he said she was well-known round here. He knew who she was, but he wouldn't tell me. Wanted to protect me, I guess."

Or protect himself, Emilia thought, but said nothing. She was prepared to play along with Dinah's fantasy of Maxwell as the innocent victim for now. Thanking her for her time, Emilia began to wrap things up. She had come here with relatively low expectations, but was leaving with a major new lead. Could it be true? If it was, it presented some very interesting possibilities.

A narrative was taking shape in Emilia's mind that would trump all the stories she'd penned so far in her brief, colorful career. She would need to be sure of her facts, of course. And there was one person who would be able to help confirm her growing suspicions.

This was Emilia's next stop—one she hoped would finally blow this story wide-open.

85

"Nobody moves unless I say so."

Sanderson signed off and waited for the other members of the team to confirm that they would hold their positions. She had been keen not to repeat Charlie's mistake and had summoned backup as soon as she had pinned down where Paine's device was being used. It was routing via a server that was registered to an estate agent's on Banner Street in Portswood. It was pushing eleven p.m., so the agency was closed, but a light was burning in a third-floor window. The buzzers by the door adjacent to the agency suggested that the second and third floors of the building were flats. Perhaps they had an agreement to share the router or perhaps whoever was upstairs had gained access to it by some other means. Either way, the team were about to find out.

Sanderson had tried and failed to contact the estate agency via its out-of-hours number, leaving her with no choice but to apply for a warrant. This had taken a couple of hours to source, but now she had the authority she needed to act. She rang the buzzer for the third-floor flat. No response. She rang it again, but still nothing. Losing patience, she gestured to the nearby PC to barrel charge the door. The weak lock yielded easily, the door swinging wide-open, and Sanderson was inside and bounding up the stairs.

She moved past the second-floor flat, which appeared to be unoccupied and quiet. Another burst of speed and she crested the top landing. Marching straight to the flat door, she hammered on it.

"Police. Open up."

She beat the door again, then moved aside quickly, allowing her uniformed colleague a proper run-up. Giving her the nod, she pulled her radio from her pocket.

"On the count of three. One, two . . ."

The door to the flat suddenly opened, prompting the uniformed officer to abort her swing at the last second. Sanderson hurried forward—to be confronted by a sheepish-looking student.

"What gives?" he said, trying and failing to be insouciant.

Sanderson pushed past him. She scanned left and right, darting in and out of the cramped rooms, but she already knew that this was not their killer's lair. It was a down-at-heel student flat—nothing more. You could tell by the smell of weed, the laddish posters, the unwashed pots and pans and, most tellingly of all, the sight of an unshaven young man in his pajamas playing Minion Rush on a battered tablet.

86

Samantha lay on her bed, staring at a spider crawling across the ceiling. It was a while since she'd been in a proper police cell. Normally they just put her in the custody cage with the drunk and the violent. This time they'd moved her to a solo cell. Had they done this to give her more time to reflect? To try to isolate her? Either way, it showed that they had plans for her.

She watched the spider scuttle its way to the corner of the room, settling itself back into its web to lie in wait for its prey. Was this Helen Grace's tactic too, lying in wait in the darkness, hoping that Samantha would offer herself as a sacrifice? If it was, she'd be a long time waiting. Grace had built up a considerable reputation over the years and Samantha had been surprised and disquieted at having to face her. She had thought she might get to talk to Brooks. But instead she had found herself opposite the boss, dancing on a wire.

Grace was determined, resourceful and well prepared. Oddly, she was also adept at putting you at your ease, which made her more dangerous still. You could never be entirely sure what her next move would be, which was unnerving at first, but as she'd grown into the interview, Samantha had begun to enjoy the sudden changes of direction and the attempts to wrong-foot her. It reminded her a little of the ghastly fencing displays she'd had to sit through during her brief period in private education. Lunge, retreat, parry, riposte. Lunge, retreat, parry . . . Grace hadn't landed a telling hit yet, though Samantha could tell she thought she was close. Was she out there right now, drawing all the strands together until she was ready to pull the net tight?

What she wouldn't give to be a fly on the wall, watching Grace sifting the evidence with her team and debating her next move. She had seemed so confident, so businesslike when they started the interview, as if it was only a matter of time before she got her "man." But, by the end, her frustration was coming through loud and clear as she pressed Samantha for a confession. She had enjoyed refusing to play ball—that bitch was clearly full of herself and needed taking down a peg or two.

Grace was used to getting her way, to being on the winning side. But not this time. Perhaps she would be patient, waiting for her prey to come to her. Or perhaps her next move would be a full-frontal assault. Either way, one thing was clear to Samantha. DI Grace was clutching at straws.

87

"It would have been a lot easier if you'd contacted us earlier, Mr. Simons."

David Simons said nothing in response—he looked about as pleased to be in the interview suite as Charlie did. She'd been on the cusp of calling it a day when he had finally presented himself at the custody desk. Sanderson had just returned to the station and was locked in a private briefing with Helen, leaving Charlie no choice but to field the interview, as the only senior officer available.

"I might say the same thing to you," Simons replied. "I'm the only person on this planet who gave a shit about Jake Elder and yet I've no clue what's happening. Are you going to charge this guy Parker or not?"

"I'm afraid I can't comment on an ongoing operation—"

"Yada yada yad—"

"But I can assure you we are making good progress," Charlie interrupted, resisting the temptation to punch Simons in the face.

The truth was of course a little different. Samantha was in custody but had not been charged, which made Charlie very nervous indeed. There was a lot riding on this for her, especially after her bitter argument with Helen.

"In the meantime, I'd like to go over a few details with you. Starting with where and how you first met Jake Elder?"

Begrudgingly, David Simons began to talk, giving brief details of his relationship with the first victim. Charlie listened, nodding and taking notes when necessary, but in truth her mind remained elsewhere. She didn't expect any revelations from Simons and her thoughts were full of the day's traumatic events. Her shoulder still ached from her fight with Samantha, but she would have happily worn that if she had helped bring this troubling case to a conclusion. As it was, she had all but destroyed her relationship with Helen, and Samantha remained a suspect, but no more.

Had the price been worth paying? She was determined not to come second best to Sanderson—but had it really been necessary to confront her mentor and friend so harshly? She and Helen had always got on and though it was true that Helen was in a very troubled place at the moment, she owed Charlie more than bitterness and aggression. She had been right to call Helen out on her behavior, but a lot of what Helen had said about *her* had also been on the money. Charlie did need to get a grip on herself. The fact that she wasn't planning on telling her partner, Steve, about her fight with Samantha told Charlie all she needed to know about the wisdom of entering that flat alone.

Would an apology cut it? Was it even advisable? Charlie had brought Samantha in and while there was still a good chance that she would be charged, it was probably best to say nothing. Once she had put Sanderson in her place, then she could try to repair her relationship with Helen. For now, there was nothing for it but to hunker down and see things through to the bitter end.

88

The kettle shrieked as it reached the boiling point, jolting Helen from her thoughts. She had been briefed by Sanderson before leaving the station, her DS confirming that Paine's tablet was a dead end. The device had been found by two students in a park bin miles from his flat, its memory erased and the exterior wiped clean.

Frustrated and drained, Helen had spent some time in her office leafing through Meredith's latest reports, which worryingly did *not* include a positive DNA source for Parker at the Torture Rooms, before she decided to call it a day. It was late and she craved the sanctuary of her flat.

Once safely home, she'd tried to read, but when that failed to distract her, she'd opted for herbal tea and a hot bath instead. But, as ever, she couldn't stop her mind from turning. She didn't really remember filling the kettle, which was testament enough to her inability to drive Samantha from her thoughts. She was such a good fit for these crimes, but if she was guilty, why was she so cocky? She seemed to be enjoying the dance, as if she alone knew the punch line that was about to be delivered. Helen had the unnerving feeling that they were missing something significant.

Helen poured the boiling water into the cup and watched the color leach out of the tea bag. She had been looking forward to a soothing drink, but now she couldn't face it. What was the point of going through this ritual? She could have a cup of tea, lie in a warm bath, but she would still be thinking the same thoughts, teasing away at the same knotty problems. She'd smoked too many cigarettes and she didn't have the energy for a run—it was a bitter irony that she no longer had Jake to turn to, to rid her of her dark energy.

Throwing her tea into the sink, Helen turned to face the window. It was late now and the pubs would be emptying soon—perhaps some late-night voyeurism would help Helen unwind. The lights were off in her kitchen, shrouding her in darkness, but the moon was full and bright and as Helen looked out of her window, she saw him. It was only for an instant, but there was no mistaking it. A man was standing in the derelict building opposite, watching her.

Helen's instinctive reaction was to pull away, but she managed to control herself, turning and walking slowly toward the back of the flat, as if nothing had happened. Then, as soon as she was out of view, she dashed to the front door and wrenched it open. She had no idea who was watching her, but he wasn't going to escape her tonight.

89

Helen burst out of the fire exit and into the communal gardens at the back of her flats. Whipping her key fob from her pocket, she buzzed herself out and sprinted round the corner. She now doubled back to her road but instead of turning left into it, she carried on past, coming to a halt by the lolling chain-link fence that surrounded the derelict building—its only form of defense against the squatters and junkies who occasionally used it.

Finding a low point in the fence, Helen slipped over and padded toward the back of the flats. The building cast a tall shadow and Helen had to choose her path carefully—the ground was littered with broken glass and discarded needles. As she worked her way toward the empty shell, her mind was turning on what she'd seen. Was this the same figure she'd glimpsed a few months back? She'd thought nothing of it at the time, assuming it was just another drug user seeking temporary sanctuary. Now she chided herself for her complacency.

She had reached the back entrance and, bending down, picked up an empty beer bottle. It wasn't much, but it would have to do—in her haste she had left her baton and holster in the flat. Stepping into the building, she reached out a hand to steady herself. There was no light in the cavernous space—just moonlight creeping through the holes in the roof. It was an oddly magical sight, the moonbeams descending from above, but perilous too. Helen could barely see where she was going and knew that a wrong step might send her plunging into the basement below. More than that, she sensed that the person she was hunting was still inside somewhere. He might strike at any minute—if that was his intention—and Helen would be virtually defenseless.

She hesitated. Through the gloom she could make out a staircase in the far corner. Creeping forward, testing each floorboard as she went, she kept her head upright and alert, searching for danger. She remembered her words to Charlie earlier, but it was too late to call for the cavalry now. By the time they arrived, Helen felt sure her quarry would be gone.

Reaching the staircase, Helen looked up, suddenly feeling very small in the deserted building. There were fifteen floors above her, but she felt certain the figure she'd seen had been on the penultimate floor. She had fourteen floors to climb. What was her best strategy—slow and steady or swift and decisive? The stairs were made of concrete and seemed the one element of the building that hadn't rotted away, so, summoning her courage, Helen raced up the stairs.

Fourth floor, fifth floor, sixth floor. Helen drove herself on, keeping her pace steady. She was bouncing lightly from step to step, moving as silently as she could, but it was hard to move this fast without creating a little noise. Would this prove costly? Was she walking into an ambush? Fear once more seeped into her consciousness. She was not by nature fearful, but something about this place was messing with her head. She didn't want to end her days here.

She had reached the thirteenth floor now. Gripping the beer bottle firmly, she dropped her pace, taking the stairs two at a time in giant, silent strides. If he was going to come for her, it would be now. But she wasn't going to walk into his trap tamely.

There was nowhere for him to hide now, so Helen burst into the room, her arm raised to protect herself. The floorboards protested and a cloud of dust flew up, but no attack came, so Helen moved on to the next room, expecting to be thrown backward with a savage blow at any minute.

Still nothing. Then suddenly there was a noise. At the other side of the building—what was it? A crash? Someone putting his weight in the wrong place? Helen bounded forward. She was sprinting as if her life depended upon it, eating up the yards to the far wall, and suddenly she burst out into a large open space. A penthouse apartment that was never built, it was now a vast receptacle for dead birds and drugs detritus. Other than that, it was empty—save for the door to the fire escape that lolled open.

Helen raced over to it. Pushing out into the fresh air, she came to an abrupt halt. The fire escape on which she now stood was old and rusty and could potentially give way at any moment—suddenly her impulsive bravery seemed foolhardy in the extreme.

Taking a step back, she looked through the grille to the steps below. The metal staircase zigzagged down the building and Helen scrutinized it for signs of movement. But all was still, apart from a few startled pigeons and the fire escape door moving back and forth in the wind.

Suddenly a thought occurred to Helen, and mounting the fire escape, she climbed to the top floor. This was the only remaining place her voyeur could be hiding. But it was as deserted as the rest of the shell.

Crouching down, Helen breathed out, trying to slow her heartbeat. Despite her endeavors she had been left empty-handed. There was *no one* here. She had been so sure—had seen the figure so clearly. She couldn't have imagined it all.

Could she?

90

"I don't think we have a choice. We have to charge her."

Charlie's tone was flinty and unyielding. Despite the failure of Samantha to confess, she seemed determined to nail her for the brutal double murder.

"If we don't, we've got at best another twenty-four hours and I don't think that's enough. She's too confident of herself—we need more time to wear her down."

"You really want to dive in again, after what happened last time?" Sanderson replied, as coolly as she could. "We have got to be sure."

"She was the last person to visit Paine on the night he died."

"That we know of."

"And she's never once protested her innocence, despite numerous opportunities to do so."

"Nor has she confessed. So what have we actually got?"

Helen watched her two deputies debate the evidence. It was still early and she was exhausted and irritable after her nighttime excursions. She hadn't slept a wink last night, replaying what she'd seen over and over to see if she could have been mistaken. Her defenses were up and every tiny noise had seemed so ominous that in the end she'd given up trying altogether and headed into the office. She knew that today would be crucial for the investigation, so when Sanderson and Charlie arrived, she called them both into her office.

She had thought about apologizing to *both* of them for her recent behavior, but the events of last night still hung heavy on her mind and with the clock ticking on Samantha's custody, there was no time to waste. So they'd pressed on with the case, just about managing to ignore the tensions bubbling beneath the surface. Helen would have to force the pair of them to work together if necessary, as they were both good officers whose recent misdemeanors were mostly a product of her own fractured focus.

"What have we got on the credit cards?" Helen asked suddenly, interrupting the debate.

"The Zentai suit and hog ties that killed Paine were bought with a different credit card to the one used to buy Elder's wet sheets," Sanderson replied.

"Have we cross-referenced the stores and Web sites that the two different cloned cards were used in? To see who might have stolen the details?"

"Yes, but it's already a massively long list. The supermarkets, Boots, W. H. Smith, Amazon, PayPal, iTunes . . ."

"Can we link either of the cloned cards to Samantha? We know that as Michael Parker she had form for this kind of thing."

"Nothing on her home computer, phones or devices. And we didn't find any cards at her flat."

"Does she work anywhere other than the bar?"

"Not that we know of."

"What about the deliveries of the bondage items themselves?" Helen said, turning to Charlie.

"As with Elder, the BDSM stuff was delivered by courier to a vacant address. A domestic property awaiting new tenants."

"Get on to the estate agents that rent them out. See if there's any connection between the different properties and a particular agency."

"Sure thing."

"What about the boot print?" Helen continued. "Meredith said the print she found at Paine's was a size six. Parker is a size seven, but that doesn't necessarily rule her out."

"There was loads of stuff in the flat geared toward sizing down, corsets, heels—," Charlie responded.

"Trying to make herself as petite as possible."

"Exactly. But no sign of any boot or shoe that fits."

Helen nodded, but her frustration was clear.

"We've got the tread pattern," Sanderson interjected. "It's quite unusual, so we'll chase down which outlets sell it."

"Good. We're not letting Samantha believe she's anything other than our number one suspect and we exhaust *every* avenue, up to the last minute, to link her to these murders. Understood?"

Sanderson and Charlie nodded and left. Helen picked up the phone to dial Meredith Walker, but as she did so, DC Reid knocked on the door. Replacing the cradle, Helen beckoned him in. Reid approached, clutching a DVD. He handed it to Helen without a word, clearly worried about being the bearer of bad news.

Helen slipped the DVD into her laptop and the screen filled with a CCTV feed.

"What is this?"

"CCTV taken from a street near the Eastern Docks. One of the night watchmen down there saw someone matching Parker's description, so we checked it out."

Reid reached over and fast-forwarded the footage, before eventually pressing play. Helen leaned in, looking closely at the date and time stamp.

"This is the night Max Paine was killed?"

"Correct."

The camera gave a decent view of the dockside and Helen now saw a woman walk into view. She paused the image. Slicked-down hair, a large, light-colored coat over a skintight suit—it was Samantha, all right. Helen resumed playing the footage and watched as the woman struck up a conversation with a man idling near a stationary van. Parker appeared to take the man's hand and put it between her legs. Moments later, the two figures climbed into the back of the van.

"The van doesn't move for the next three hours. Then Parker exits. She doesn't look in a very good state and gets out of there as quickly as she can."

Helen nodded, but her eye was already straying to the time stamp at the bottom of the screen, and she rewound the footage to the moment Parker got into the van with her bit of rough. The clock read 22:02.

"How accurate is the time on this feed?"

"To the second."

Helen breathed out, then suddenly stepped forward, kicking her office chair with all her might. It careered across the room, slamming into the wall before toppling over. Without bothering to offer an explanation, Helen walked out of the door and away across the incident room, dozens of pairs of eyes following her as she went.

91

"Not up to my usual standard. But pretty damn good in the circumstances, wouldn't you say?"

Samantha offered her nails to Helen, clearly pleased with the few cosmetics items she'd managed to source.

"Very nice," Helen told her, keeping her temper in check. It had taken the best part of twenty minutes to pull Samantha up from the cells, but the interval had done little to calm Helen. Jim Grieves had put Paine's time of death as somewhere between ten thirty p.m. and six thirty a.m. the following morning. Notwithstanding the fact that Paine died slowly, Parker's presence at the docks at ten p.m. meant it was more than likely that someone had visited Paine's flat after her.

"I want to keep myself looking my best. You never know what's around the corner, do you?"

Her tone was teasing and playful.

"Absolutely. But I don't want to string this out any more than we have to. I expect you're anxious to get home."

Samantha shrugged, disappointed with Helen's response. Was she expecting—hoping—for more aggression from Helen?

"You're right. It doesn't do to leave my babies alone for too long."

"Quite."

Samantha's dolls were in fact all in evidence bags at Meredith's lab. Surely Samantha would have guessed that, so was this yet another game? Helen looked down at her file, leafing casually through the pages, saying nothing. She could see in her peripheral vision that Samantha was twitchy and ill at ease, as if this exchange was not going as she'd hoped.

"I'd like to clarify a few details about your night with Max Paine."

"Of course."

"We talked a little about 'the Phoenix' last time."

"Got your juices flowing, did it?"

"I want a little more detail about what you got up to specifically," Helen demanded, ignoring Parker's jibes.

"A lady never tells."

"Was it straight S and M or something more exotic?"

"The latter."

"Details, please."

"Restraint and suffocation. I want total control."

"And how do you achieve that?"

"Force of personality."

"What about the restraints? Do you ever use hog ties, for example?"

"Of course."

"Have you ever used them frontways on? Securing the hands to the ankles so the back is bent forward?"

"Yes, it's more painful that way."

"Did you do that to Paine?" Helen said, looking Parker directly in the eye.

"Yes," she replied, refusing to be intimidated.

"Did you use any other restraints?"

"Tape, leather—I was very thorough. I wanted every inch of that boy to be covered."

"And can I ask what time you left Paine's flat?"

"I honestly can't remember."

"Roughly."

"Around eleven, I suppose."

"And then you went home."

"As I've said before, yes."

Helen sat back in her chair. She had won this battle but lost the war and suddenly felt drained of energy. Her sincere vows to bring Jake's killer to justice seemed a mockery now.

"Why are you lying to me, Samantha?"

"I'm not."

"You didn't leave Paine's flat at eleven—you left much earlier and headed straight down to the docks for some rough trade."

"That's bullshit."

"We've got you on CCTV, so there's no point lying. Is that how you got those bruises? Things get nasty in that van, did they?"

"I was *with* Paine," Samantha insisted.

"Yes, but he was fine when you left him."

"I've told you what happened, how he died—"

"You've recycled the details of Jake Elder's death. Max Paine died in a Zentai suit, with his arms tied *backward* in hog ties. You tried hard, but you were wrong on pretty much every detail."

"You're lying."

"Did something similar happen at the Torture Rooms? Why *were* you leaving in such a state? Did someone reject you, push you away?"

Samantha hesitated too long, giving Helen her answer.

"I thought so."

"This is bullshit."

"You know, this is a first for me. I've never had a suspect who's so keen to be charged with a double murder. You've been wasting my time, haven't you, Samantha?"

"You've got it wrong," Samantha said, now visibly flustered.

"No, you've got it wrong," Helen said, rising. "We're done here."

Helen stabbed off the tape and walked to the door, pausing as she opened it.

"Good luck, Samantha."

Then, without waiting for a reply, she left.

92

It was midmorning and the Pound Shop was heaving. Beleaguered mums juggled maxi-packs of Monster Munch, while old-age pensioners scoured the shelves for bargains, keen to eke out their weekly budget a little further. It was an odd place to be plotting a murder.

The tall, slender figure sailed through the crowds, amused by the sights on display. All these people were so bound up in their own lives, scrabbling in the bargain bins, ladling pick-and-mix into crumpled bags, that they couldn't see what was right in front of them. What would they say if they knew? Would they be horrified? Or excited?

The police were no better. Grace's team had pulled in a messed-up she-male who might interest them for a while. But they were wide of the mark, and though Grace would presumably cotton on soon, she wouldn't be in time to prevent the next death. It was only hours away and already those same feelings were rising. Excitement. Tension. Control. Release.

This one would be a little bit different, though. It wouldn't do to become predictable and now was the time to really give the police something to think about. Whereas the others had been works of art, this would be more down-to-earth, more homespun. This one would make them sit up and take note.

The cashier was ringing through the basket, chatting amiably. In her own mindless way she was becoming an accessory to murder. This was probably the most exciting thing that would ever happen to her and yet she was totally unaware of it, believing that this was just another routine sale of mundane domestic items.

But it was more than that. Much more than that. This was the beginning of the end.

93

"I need everything you've got."

Meredith Walker had been about to tuck into a well-earned sandwich when Helen Grace burst through the doors. Her colleague seemed angry and frustrated, and as Meredith was brought up to speed with developments, it wasn't hard to see why. The pair of them were now shut away in Meredith's office, reams of paper spread out on the desk in front of them.

"Every last detail. The answer *has* to be here somewhere."

"You'd think, wouldn't you?"

"This guy's not a ghost—he's flesh and blood. He can't just visit these scenes and leave no trace."

"I'll admit it's odd, but he has clearly been *very* careful. He wears a bodysuit, perhaps a mask, and never takes his gloves off.

There are no prints on Paine's thermostat, nothing on the door handles or on the Zentai suit, the hog ties—"

"What about more circumstantial stuff? From the corridors, outside Paine's flat, in the bins."

"We're still sweeping, but any defense would have a field day with the possibilities of cross-contamination—"

"I need *something* here."

"I understand that, but we can't magic up the evidence."

"What about the Torture Rooms? What have we got there?"

"Twenty-three different sources of DNA at the crime scene. I think your lot have been over these already."

"What else?"

"We've got a number of DNA sources in close proximity to the corridor which we haven't been able to match."

"What do you mean by 'a number'?"

Meredith lifted a file on her desk to reveal another, from which she now pulled a sheet of paper.

"We have . . . a few beer bottles, a cigarette butt, a used condom, a glove. All of them containing DNA which we can't match to anyone on file."

"He's unlikely to have had sex—the MO doesn't suggest it's that sort of crime—but perhaps one of the others?"

Meredith half nodded, half shrugged—she looked as unconvinced as Helen sounded. Helen rubbed her face with her hands and stared at the sheets of paper on the desk. So much data, such little progress.

"Do you think we'll catch him?" Helen said suddenly.

"It's early days, Helen."

"There's always going to be one that gets away, though, isn't there?"

"He'll make a mistake. They always do. And when he does, you'll be waiting for him. I have every confidence in you."

Helen thanked Meredith, then headed off. She was grateful for her support, but the truth was that this case was so unusual and so puzzling that she was genuinely concerned about the outcome.

For the first time in years, Helen was beginning to doubt herself.

94

"They haven't got a bloody clue."

David Simons's tone was withering.

"They arrest someone, let him go. Arrest someone else, let *her* go . . ."

Emilia nodded and let Simons rant. Like many in the BDSM community, he had had his hopes raised by the arrest of Michael Parker. News of Parker's sudden release was therefore a kick in the teeth that had been met with a wave of anger. Many were confused, others scared, but none had the personal connection that Simons had. Which was why he was blowing a gasket now.

"It's incredibly frustrating," Emilia said, when Simons eventually drew breath. "We all want to get justice for Jake and the investigation seems . . . unfocused at best. Which is why I wanted to talk to you."

Simons suddenly looked up, intrigued and surprised.

"Forgive me for revisiting painful memories, but you said when we talked before that there was someone *else* in Jake's life? A woman he had feelings for?"

Simons stared at her, clearly unhappy to be reminded of this.

"I know this is difficult for you," Emilia continued, "but it's really important. What did Jake tell you about the nature of their relationship?"

"Not a lot—I had to prize it out of him."

"And?"

"And it was complicated. At first, he denied he had feelings for this woman. Then he said he was over her, but I'm not sure that was true either. He used to follow her around at one time, after she'd dropped him—"

"He *stalked* her?"

"I didn't say that. But he had issues . . . letting go."

"So what happened?"

"She walloped him," Simons said, smiling grimly.

"She attacked him?"

"He gave her a fright and got what was coming to him. She whacked him with her motorcycle helmet, I think, and he left her alone after that. He didn't like telling me, of course, but I needed to know everything. For all the good it did me . . ."

Emilia hesitated—scribbling down "motorcycle helmet"—then asked:

"You mentioned that you saw them together once—Jake and this woman. Did you see her face?"

"Only for a moment, but I was intrigued, so . . ."

"Would you recognize her now?"

"Why? Why are you asking me these questions?"

"Look, David, I know this probably seems odd, but I'm trying to put together the fullest picture of Jake's life that I can. For reasons that you'll understand in time, I'm not convinced we can have confidence in the police investigation, and somebody needs to carry on the fight on Jake's behalf."

Simons looked at her and then said:

"Yes, I think I would."

Emilia delved into her bag. Pulling a photo from inside, she laid it on the table.

"Is this her?"

Simons leaned forward. Emilia watched him closely. She was trying to remain calm, but her heart was in her mouth. Finally, Simons looked up at her and said:

"Yes, it is."

95

Angelique lay on the bed, her eyes glued to the television. The news was on, leading with the latest developments in the Jake Elder case, and the early-evening audience was being treated to grabbed images of Michael Parker—"Samantha"—scurrying back to his flat while being harried by local journalists.

Despite her height, Samantha looked so diminished, so pathetic, that it was a wonder the police ever had her in the frame. She was clearly a nasty piece of work, but did they really believe she had the organizational skills to pull off such an intricate double murder? Details of Paine's death had seeped out online, triggering a wave of reaction on social media. Some commentators were sickened, others strangely impressed by the elaborate nature of the crime. But nobody had publicly pointed the finger at Samantha, despite the common practice these days of trial by innuendo. That should have told the police something—sometimes it pays to listen to the word on the street.

As it was, they had accused two innocent people with predictable results. What would Samantha do now? She had always been wound tight—how would she react now to the shit storm that was coming her way? Huddling up inside her stale little flat with nobody to comfort her but her dollies? It wouldn't be at all surprising if she went the same way as Paul Jackson, though something told Angelique that Samantha might be rather more effective at finishing the job.

What were Grace and her team doing now? Now that they were back to square one? Did they still have faith in their leader? Would they trust her to get a result? Not knowing was tantalizing, but there was nothing to be done about it. The next few days would reveal everything and in the meantime there was nothing for Angelique to do but watch and wait.

96

"I want us to look again at the credit cards."

Helen had made Charlie jump when she appeared by her desk. However long you worked with her, you never got used to her stealth.

"We've run them several times," Charlie replied quickly. "Both credit card owners used many of the same stores and Internet sites, so the point of fraud is going to be hard to pin down. Look at the list—Amazon, Ticketmaster, Trainline, Sainsbury's, Gumtree, iTunes, Pets at Home—"

"Let's come at it from another angle, then. If it's Internet fraud, then it's going to be virtually impossible to trace, so let's focus on the retail outlets. We've been assuming that our killer has specifically cloned cards to facilitate these murders. But it's more likely he was involved in petty crime first, only later graduating up to more serious offenses."

"So we want to look for seasoned credit card fraudsters—"

"Exactly. Get on to the local outlets that the fraud victims used regularly. It would be easy enough for an employee to lift their details when ringing through a transaction, so let's see if any employees—past or present—had form for credit card fraud. Don't limit yourself to recent offenses—this kind of crime is a long time in the making."

"But if they're on file, wouldn't we have got a match to a DNA source at one of the crime sites?"

"Not necessarily. It may be they were questioned but never charged. Or it may be that our killer is just too cautious. He didn't even touch Paine, yet managed to kill him. The same may be true of Jake Elder."

Charlie nodded, but it was a depressing thought. Were they chasing shadows?

"I originally thought forensics would be crucial, given the lack of credible witnesses," Helen continued. "But now I don't think we even have that luxury. So we're looking for tiny mistakes, small pieces of the puzzle that put together—"

"Lead us to our man. You should know, though, that even with just the retail outlets highlighted it's a seriously long list—"

"I know it's a needle in a haystack—"

"Look, I'm happy to do it—of course I am."

"Good. Thank you."

Helen turned to go, but Charlie had more to say.

"Look, Helen, I know I said too much yesterday."

"It's not your fault, Charlie. It's mine."

"Whatever, I just wanted to let you know that I'm really sorry and that I'll do whatever is necessary to help you break this case."

"Thank you."

Helen should've gone further, apologizing for *her* erratic behavior, but she didn't really trust herself and something in Charlie's demeanor meant it wasn't necessary. The mark of a true friend.

"Call me if you find anything," Helen said, turning to leave.

"Sure. Where are you going?"

Helen paused in the doorway of the incident room and turned back to Charlie.

"To climb inside the mind of a killer."

97

Control. Sadism. Restraint. Victim. Dominator. Knowledge. Power. Anger. Disgust. Self-hatred. Pain.

Helen scribbled fast, covering the whiteboard with her scrawl. She had commandeered one of the more remote interview suites, covering the table with files and dropping the blinds. She wanted to be alone with the perpetrator, testing her rudimentary profile of him again to see whether she'd missed anything obvious. She read through their behavioral indicators, probable motives, evidence analysis, trying to picture what went through their killer's mind at the point of death.

"Can I join you?"

Surprised, Helen looked up to find Jonathan Gardam standing in the doorway.

"Sorry—I was miles away. Come in."

Gardam pushed the door to and walked toward the board. He stood for a minute, taking in the words written on it.

"How's the profile coming on?"

"Slowly. We haven't got much to go on."

"Tell me."

"Really, it's pretty basic . . ."

"I'd like to help if I can. I was a decent DI once upon a time."

Helen hesitated. She preferred to do her soul-searching alone, but Gardam's tone brooked no argument and perhaps she could make an exception. She wasn't getting very far by herself.

"I think the key element is control. Control of himself, control of his victim, control of us. He's a high-functioning individual with an inflated sense of his own importance, someone who feels the world doesn't understand him. He wants to engage but will only do so on his terms, leaving statement killings for us to interpret."

"So he enjoys the game?"

"Absolutely. I think he likes to tantalize, to tease, to play God."

"Is he likely to live alone, then? To have a home environment that he can control?"

"Possibly, but he may have a partner, even a family. Maybe he controls them like he controls his victims or it may be that they dominate *him*."

Gardam nodded, taking this in.

"Do we think his victims were targeted specifically?"

"If they were, I would expect to see more signs of overt violence against them."

"So does he have something against people in the BDSM world?"

"Possibly."

"Does he have a moral issue with S and M? Was he on the wrong end of a bad experience? Could some incident within the community have triggered this?"

Helen considered this.

"I don't mean to pry," Gardam ventured, "but you must have come across these kinds of people—what sort of world is it?"

"It's not as weird as you'd think," Helen replied quickly. "People go into it for all sorts of reasons, but generally it's professional, discreet and consensual."

"But there must be people who want to push it to the extreme . . ."

"In private encounters, perhaps. Professional sessions have strict safety rules, which are religiously observed."

"So this guy has graduated beyond the entry level? He's experienced?"

"Judging by his knowledge and activities, I'd say he knows this world well. He doesn't seem to want to be punished or exposed or abused—he wants to be the one with the upper hand. It is possible he comes from a place where he has no control, no sense of hope. He could be an abuse victim, someone trapped in an unhealthy relationship, someone saddled with emotional baggage that he can't expiate any other way."

"Do any of those apply to you?"

Helen stopped, surprised by the question.

"Look, tell me to fuck off if you want to, but you're our best asset in trying to understand this guy. I appreciate you don't want to broadcast this side of your life to the team, but between us . . ."

Helen stared at Gardam, then said:

"I do it because it works."

"Because you feel . . . guilt?"

"Guilt, regret, anger."

"And it works for you? It gives you reassurance, comfort . . ."

"For a while."

"But then those feelings come back again?"

Helen shrugged, but didn't deny it.

"Do you think those feelings will *ever* go away?" Gardam persisted.

"I'm not sure. It sounds stupid . . . but sometimes I feel . . . that I'm stained. That I'm marked by what's happened in the past . . ."

"It's a mark no one else can see."

"*I* can see it."

Gardam looked at her for a moment. He seemed to be struggling for the right words. Finally he said:

"Do you really think you're . . . cursed?"

"That's exactly how I feel."

"It doesn't have to be that way, you know . . ."

"Believe me, if I could find a path through this, I would."

"Then let me help you. You've taken the first steps by confiding in me. Don't let this opportunity go to waste. Let me . . . help you."

He took a step forward, holding out his hand to her. The smile on his face was kindly but firm.

"I know you're lonely, Helen. I know you feel lost . . ."

Helen took a step back, but still Gardam advanced.

"And I hate to think of you alone in that flat, with all this going on." He gestured at the board.

"I'll be fine. Look, I think it's best that—"

"You opened yourself up to me for a reason. So don't be scared now."

He put his hand on Helen's cheek.

"This will be good for both of us."

Helen lifted her hand to remove his, but suddenly Gardam pulled her toward him. Now she felt his mouth on hers. She raised her hand to his chest to push him off, but he kept coming, his teeth biting down on her lower lip.

Helen pulled away sharply. But his arms were still around her and as she tried to wriggle out of his grip, she collided with the table.

"Don't run from this, Helen," Gardam chided, running his hand down her back and onto her buttocks.

He moved toward her again, but this time Helen struck first, dragging her nails down the side of his face. Gardam recoiled in shock, giving Helen the opportunity she needed. She drove her knee hard into his groin—once, twice, three times.

Gardam crumpled to the floor.

Helen stepped over him, moving fast across the room. Reaching the doorway, she burst through it, leaving her boss lying on the floor, gagging quietly into the carpet. Helen didn't look back once. Now she just wanted to be away.

98

The eyes of the world were on her now.

Samantha hated mockery, hated attention, hated judgment. But she was getting all three in spades now. She'd pulled the curtains to, turned off her mobile, but still the intercom buzzed, buzzed, buzzed. She knew bugger all about electrics, so in the end she'd ripped it off the wall, hurling it at the door with a stream of invective. Shortly after, the handful of journalists who'd harried and jostled her on her way home had gained entry to the block. She could hardly call the police, and her useless landlord wasn't answering his calls, so they were still at the door, calling, hammering, joking. To them this was all in a day's work.

She had stuck it for a while, ignoring their pleas for an interview, sitting in silence in the living room. But in the end it had got to her and she'd retreated to the back of the house. Cranking up the stereo, she'd treated them to a bit of Dark Metal. They would love it, of course—it would add "color" to their articles—but she didn't care. She just wanted to block out the world for a while.

The police had stolen most of her possessions, her clothes, even her babies. But they had missed a couple. A pair of dolls she'd picked up at a flea market and had called Duke and Duchess on account of their finery. They now resided in the corner of a bedside drawer, temporarily exiled there due to lack of space in the room. Samantha pulled them from their hiding place and laid them on the floor in front of her. They were all she had for company now, yet even they seemed to be looking at her oddly today, their dead, black eyes giving back nothing but suspicion and disappointment. She had seen that look a lot when she had been a kid.

God, how she craved a drink, but there was no way she could head out to get one. She had gambled and lost, reveling in the attention the police gave her as she led them in a merry, pointless dance, only to be tossed aside once they realized she was lying through her teeth. All she'd wanted was a moment in the spotlight, but what a bitter harvest she'd reaped.

She wanted company, but there was none to be had. She wanted sanctuary from the world, but even that seemed to have been taken away from her now. This dingy, rotting flat had been her haven for so long. But that was all over. Now it was just a home without a heart.

99

Sanderson finished her drink and considered the wisdom of having another. It was only a pint of weak lager—not exactly Oliver Reed standards—but still she hesitated. She'd known many a copper ruin a perfectly good career by slipping into bad habits. The Mermaid pub had been the location for several falls from grace over the years, hidden away in a backstreet close to Southampton Central.

She should have been at a Spinning class, but somehow she couldn't face all that shouting and positive energy tonight. The alternative was going back to her badly heated flat and empty fridge, so she'd retreated to the warmth of the pub instead, ignoring the occasional glances of the hopeful males at the bar, to enjoy an overpriced pint of continental beer.

"Can I get you another?"

Sanderson looked up to find Emilia Garanita standing over her.

"I'm meeting someone here shortly, but I've got half an hour to kill. Judging by the looks you're getting, you could use a chaperone."

Sanderson assumed she was lying, but didn't immediately tell her to sling her hook. Garanita had been useful in the past and maybe some company was better than none. She would need to be on her guard, but what the heck?

Minutes later, Emilia returned with two pints.

"I would have thought you'd be burning the midnight oil."

"Taking a break. We've done as much as we can for tonight."

"I daresay."

Sanderson detected the note of sarcasm, but didn't begrudge Emilia her skepticism. Sanderson had set several lines of inquiry in train, but she had little confidence that any of them would pay dividends in the short term. Furthermore, Helen seemed to have gone AWOL, underlining Sanderson's sense that things were drifting. The investigation appeared to be stymied, morale fractured and her own career going nowhere. Her conflict with Charlie risked dividing the team and she still feared that her popular rival would be the natural winner.

"So how *are* things going?" Emilia said brightly.

"Do you mind if we don't talk shop?"

"By all means, but if there's anything you want to tell me, off the record . . ."

"I'm good."

"Well, let me help *you*, then. I know things aren't going your way."

Sanderson looked up from her drink.

"It must be tough now there are *two* DSs, especially as Brooks and Grace are so close. I'm not a betting woman, but when Grace eventually moves on, I'd say Brooks was favorite to take her place, wouldn't you?"

Sanderson stared at Emilia, but said nothing.

"Must be galling being pushed out, which is why I wanted to talk to you."

"Look, things haven't been easy—I'm sure you've heard the gossip—but I don't do quid pro quos, Emilia. If you want to know more about the case, there's a press conference starting in ten minutes at Southampton Central—"

"I'm not interested in that. The kind of questions I've got for you can't be asked at a press conference."

Sanderson looked at Emilia, intrigued now in spite of herself.

"What I'm about to tell you is in confidence. I have important information regarding these murders."

Emilia let her words settle, then continued:

"If we act on this information, the implications for Hampshire Police will be profound, so I need to know I can trust you. Can I trust you, Joanne?"

"Of course."

"Good."

Emilia smiled and leaned in close, dropping her voice to a whisper.

"Because I'm about to make you an offer you won't be able to refuse."

And now Sanderson knew Emilia had been lying about meeting a friend. She had come here for *her*.

100

"You're going to have to handle it on your own."

"I can't go out there without an SIO. I'm a bloody Media Liaison officer."

"Then do your job—liaise with the media," Gardam replied curtly.

"Not having DI Grace is one thing—I'm used to that—but I can't go out there without you. They'll smell a rat and call me on it."

"Then find Brooks or Sanderson."

"Believe me, I've tried. And next time—FYI—I would appreciate a call rather than an e-mail. Bailing at the last minute is not on—"

"But it's happening, so get over it. This is not a fucking debate."

DS Maddy Wicket looked sufficiently put out for Gardam now to soften his tone.

"Look at me. I can't face them like this."

Maddy stared at the scratches on his right cheek.

"What happened?"

"Thought I'd go for a run to make a change from the police gym. Ran straight into a bloody branch and now I look like I've been mugged. Hardly the best advert for local policing."

Maddy wanted to disagree, but even she saw that Gardam was right.

"We could cancel, if you want," Gardam suggested. "Unless you want to knock it back a couple of hours and try to raise Brooks in the meantime?"

Predictably Maddy now latched on to this. She loved nothing more than riding to the rescue and started to run through their options. Gardam nodded, but he was no longer listening. He was back in the interview suite with Helen.

She had come to him. She had worked him hard, appearing frosty and defensive at first, but that had all been part of her game. Slowly she had unpeeled herself and in the last few weeks she had come on to him directly. You don't tell a man that kind of thing without expecting a reaction. It was an explicit invitation and when he acted on it, she'd attacked him.

Was she running scared? Was it because he was married? No, her reaction was far too aggressive to be explained like that. In other circumstances, he would have had her up on an assault charge, but he couldn't do that here. Had she done this kind of thing before? He rather suspected she had. Her previous boss had been a woman, but the one before that had been a man. He had left suddenly, having crossed swords with her—had she tricked him in the same fashion?

She needed saving from herself—she *wanted* to be saved—and

she'd led him to believe that he was the man to do so. He loved her pain, but wanted to purge her of it, to protect her from the darkness out there. He had always thought of her as an injured bird requiring warmth, comfort and love. But now he knew that Helen Grace was nothing more than a heartless prick tease.

101

Helen shut her front door, locking it behind her. Leaning against it, she closed her eyes and tried not to cry. She had left the station and headed straight home, driving too fast, barely registering the other drivers. Her head was pounding and she now pulled her cigarettes from her pocket, but they tumbled from her grasp. Her hands were shaking—she was still in shock.

She kept replaying the last couple of hours in her head. It was over twenty years since anyone had been sexually aggressive toward her, and she would never have expected it to happen at Southampton Central. The station had been her sanctuary for so long, the place where she could be a normal, functioning human being—but Gardam had destroyed all that.

What the fuck was he thinking? She'd told him about herself in confidence and as a friend. She'd been worried about the impact of her past on the case, but that **was it.** She had never encouraged his interest in her. Quite the opposite: she had put his close attention down to him being a good manager, a frontline officer who knew what it was like to lead a major investigation. What signs had he picked up on to make him think that he could behave like that?

It was scarcely believable and she wanted to wish it all away, but she still had his skin under her nails and the scent of his aftershave on her face. She hurried to the bathroom and, pulling off her jacket and blouse, scooped handfuls of hot water over her face, neck and hands. Before long her hair was dripping, her makeup smeared, but she was clean.

Toweling dry her hair, she looked at herself in the mirror. What should she do now? Should she report him? What he'd done was totally unacceptable, but he hadn't harmed her and if he contested her account of what happened, how on earth could she *prove* that she was telling the truth? It would be his word against hers.

She should report him. She *had* to report him. But the thought made her sick to the stomach and besides, she might very well come off worse—Gardam had friends in high places. There'd be no question of carrying on with the investigation, of getting justice for Jake. But could she really go back to work as if nothing had happened and report to Gardam in the usual way? She now knew what he thought of her and it was impossible to stop thinking about it.

Buzz.

The noise had been somewhere on the periphery of her consciousness, but now she heard it clearly.

Buzz.

There it was again. It was coming from somewhere within the flat. Scenting danger, Helen drew her baton and extended it, creeping forward toward the source of the noise.

Buzz.

It was coming from the kitchen. What the hell was it?

Buzz.

Losing patience, Helen now stepped quickly inside. There was no one in the kitchen, but the sight that greeted her still stopped her in her tracks. Her private phone was sitting in the middle of the kitchen table. The mobile that she had dropped down a drain three days ago. It was powered up and now buzzing in receipt of a text message.

Helen inspected the room. Who had put it there? Were they still in the flat? The kitchen window was secured, but what about the living room? The bedroom? Baton raised, Helen charged from the kitchen, checking the windows, the cupboards, under the bed. Her heart was beating fast, but there was no sign of an intruder. She was alone.

Who had seen her drop the phone? Who had returned it to her? *Why* had they brought it back?

Helen walked quickly into the kitchen. Pulling a tea towel from the hooks, she covered her hand and carefully picked the phone up. Through the cotton fabric, she pressed Read. The message sprang up—it was from Angelique and it was short and sweet:

We need to meet.

102

Helen parked her bike three blocks away, then began to walk hurriedly toward Angelique's flat. The sun had set now and Helen stuck close to the wall, avoiding the sodium glow of the streetlights. She had no idea what she was walking into, but she didn't want to announce her arrival.

Had Angelique followed her that night? Seen her drop the phone down the drain? If so, why had she fished it out and how had she gained access to her flat? Helen's cleaner had been in today—it was possible she'd forgotten to lock the door properly, but she was usually very scrupulous about security. Had Angelique got a key somehow?

It made little sense, but the shadow of a memory now rose in her mind. Helen remembered looking through the list of names drawn up by Sanderson, detailing people who'd attended her Munch or who were regular visitors there. There was an Angelique on that list somewhere—Helen was sure of that—but she'd thought little of it at the time. Sanderson hadn't met her, they had nothing specific on her and there was no guarantee it was even the same person. But she had been on the list—she was part of the community. It was very possible she was a size six shoe and from memory she did like to wear boots. Did she know Paine? Had she frequented the Torture Rooms? And if she was responsible for these crimes, what was driving her?

The chief question in Helen's mind was why she had gone to such lengths to summon her. If she wanted to be anonymous or discreet, there would have been easier, less sinister ways to do so. So what was this, then? Some kind of power game? A signal that she was in control?

Helen paused at the top of Angelique's street. It was near the docks and largely made up of converted warehouses and a few specialist shops—most of which never seemed to be open. There didn't appear to be any CCTV on the street, so Helen moved quickly forward, walking down the opposite side of the road to get a better look at Angelique's building.

It was plumb in the middle of the quiet street, backing onto another large set of flats. There appeared to be no back entrance, nor any fire escape either. Her only means of entry was through the front door. This made Helen nervous, but it had one advantage. There were two other sex workers operating from the flats, which meant that the front door was often in use, especially after dark. Helen crossed the road, taking up a position a few yards away from the front door, shielded by a couple of large municipal bins.

Helen breathed out, trying to calm her racing heart. Was she foolish to come here? She had no choice, really—she had to find out why Angelique was playing games with her—but it didn't make her any less apprehensive. This was not her turf, nor was she arriving under circumstances of her own choosing. She was dancing on the end of somebody else's line.

A noise made her look up—a man with an overcoat and a briefcase was hurrying away from the flats. Helen gave him a couple of seconds' start, then emerged from her hiding place—to see the heavy front door swinging to a close. Darting forward, she grabbed at the handle, arresting its progress just in time.

Moving inside, she eased the door shut, then looked up the stairwell. There was no one in sight and all was quiet, so Helen walked quickly but quietly up the stairs. Soon she was on the third floor, outside Angelique's flat. Now she didn't hesitate, pulling a credit card from her jacket pocket. If the deadlock was on, she would get nowhere. But if it wasn't . . .

She eased the card through the gap between the door and the frame and, moving it upward, felt for the latch. The card hit metal, and having gained traction, Helen kneaded it back and forth, maneuvering the metal tongue out of its mooring. She increased the pressure of her body on the door and moments later it opened with a gentle sigh.

Helen stepped inside and listened. A distant beat drifted down from above—someone upstairs had the music ramped up—but there was little sound in this flat. Nor was there any light—the whole place stood in utter darkness. Silently slipping her baton from her pocket, she extended it and took a step forward.

The floorboard creaked under her weight, so Helen took a step back. Changing her route, she now clung to the wall, moving faster and with less clamor. The flat was a small one-bed affair and wouldn't take long to scout. Helen was suddenly keen to have this over with—it occurred to her that perhaps the place was so quiet because there was no one here. Wouldn't that be rich if she was creeping around an empty flat, braced for an attack that was never going to come?

She had reached the kitchen and darted her head in. But it was deserted. She moved forward now into the living room, ducking low to avoid any possible attack. Whatever misgivings, there was no point taking unnecessary chances. But this room too was deserted. She could see through the open door opposite that the bathroom was empty as well, which just left the bedroom.

Helen padded toward the door, which hung ajar. Perhaps the place was unoccupied? Perhaps Angelique was waiting until Helen was inside before following her in? She shot a look over her shoulder, but all was still, so, using the point of her baton, she pushed the door open.

Still nothing. So Helen cautiously took a step forward. The curtains were closed and it was dimly lit, but something made Helen hesitate on the threshold. Something—or someone—was in here. They had the advantage, but Helen suddenly flicked the light on to level the playing field.

And there was Angelique, lying on the bed. She wasn't moving, so, checking the corners of the room, Helen moved forward. As she got closer, it became clear that Helen had come too late. Angelique lay there in her catsuit, her limbs tethered to the four corners of the bed with Japanese bondage cords. Her face was blue and as Helen now leaned over, she saw that the unfortunate dominatrix had a ball gag secured in her mouth. Worse still, her entire head, from chin to crown, was covered in cling film.

Helen had been right all along. She had just walked into a trap.

103

"Now tell me, what happened to your colleague? DC McAndrew, was it? I rather liked her."

Sanderson smiled tightly, as Maurice Finnan presented her with a cup of tea and ushered her toward the living room.

"On operational duties, I'm afraid."

"And now they've sent a sergeant along. I *am* going up in the world."

It was said lightly, but Sanderson sensed the question behind Maurice's joke. Clearly he was sharp as a tack beneath his cultivated eccentricity.

"Nothing too exciting, I'm afraid. Just some follow-up work."

Maurice sipped his tea and said nothing.

"You very helpfully provided us with a list of vehicle registrations that you've seen near Jake Elder's flat."

"I did."

"Would you mind if we went through a few of them with you now . . . ?"

Maurice was only too happy to help, so Sanderson crossed the room and sat down next to him. Maurice pulled his reading glasses from his top pocket and cast an eye over the list of registrations.

"This one, DE59 VFB. A blue Transit. Can you remember the driver at all?"

Maurice thought for a second, then replied:

"No, I'm afraid I can't. Normally I've got a pretty good memory for these things, but . . ."

"What about this one? BD05 TRD—a Corsa."

"Little fellow. Raincoat, with one of the little rucksack things for computers—"

"Laptop bag."

"That's it."

"And VF08 BHU. An Astra estate—"

"Big guy, unshaven, a laborer or something like that."

"Very good, and what about this one—LB52 WTC?"

"Well, that was an unusual one—a motorbike."

"Right. And the driver?"

"A woman. That's what made her stand out. I didn't think they were into that kind of thing."

"Could you describe her for me?"

Sanderson took down the particulars, barely believing what she was hearing. She hadn't wanted to believe Emilia at first, telling her to take a running jump. But as the journalist had laid out the evidence in front of her, troubling questions had been raised in her mind. Garanita had photographic evidence going back several years that suggested Helen had used Jake Elder's services and it appeared she knew Max Paine too. Why had she withheld this from her team? What did she have to hide? Sanderson's head had been spinning by the end of their conversation and she had hurried here, hoping against hope that Maurice would contradict Emilia's story, but he hadn't. Quite the opposite. He had in fact just given her a perfect description of Helen Grace.

104

She'd called in sick, but actually had never felt better—her lie was simply designed to let her work at home in peace. In the past, when she was still learning the ropes, she'd come a cropper by being too open about her stories. Leads had been "borrowed," witnesses snaffled, and suddenly her exclusives had become yesterday's news. There was no way Emilia was making the same mistake again. Not with the story that was going to define her career.

It was clear from her chat with Sanderson that no suspicion had yet alighted on Helen Grace. The loyal DS was disbelieving at first, but over the course of their chat she could see a step change in her perception of her boss, but also in her view of Emilia. The journalist sensed that Sanderson was dissatisfied professionally and she'd played on that—highlighting the opportunities Grace's exposure might throw up, while also appealing to her sense of duty. "One bad apple can make the whole force look bad," she'd said, somehow managing to keep a straight face as she did so.

Sanderson had bitten on it and run off to do her bidding, leaving Emilia free to write her copy. She had already drafted the leader page—a masterpiece of pithy exposé—and had the building blocks in place for pages two and three. What she needed now was some context.

People thought they knew Helen Grace, but she'd had such a rich and difficult life that it was a story that was always worth retelling. It was Emilia's profile piece at the center of the paper that would be the true heart of this story—after all, nobody had better access to or a deeper history with Grace than she did.

In the interest of fairness, Emilia had listed Grace's many triumphs—the unmasking of Ella Matthews, her heroics in rescuing Ruby Sprackling, not to mention her apprehension of a pair of serial arsonists. Set against this was Grace's propensity for violence—the fatal shooting of her own sister most notably—and her dark obsession with sadomasochism.

Like Emilia, Helen Grace was a woman with two faces. Looked at from one side, she was Southampton's finest serving police officer. Looked at from another, she was a deeply troubled woman who seemed to curse everything and everyone she touched. Some, like her loyal comrade Charlie Brooks, survived the ordeal, but others were not so lucky. Mark Fuller had killed himself while in captivity, her nephew, Robert Stonehill, had had to flee after Helen exposed him, and at least three serving police officers—two of them at detective superintendent level—had had to resign after crossing swords with her. Disaster, death and violence seemed to stalk Helen wherever she went.

Her whole life seemed to have been a prelude to the events of the last few days. Jake Elder had been obsessed with her—he had stalked her and been assaulted as a result. Max Paine had also pushed his luck with her and, by the looks of the photo his widow had given Emilia, had been viciously attacked. Emilia had asked around and discovered Paine had a predilection for unwanted advances. Emilia could see the scene clearly—Paine trying it on and receiving a nasty beating for his pains. In their differing ways—one emotionally, one sexually—they had both tried to force themselves upon Helen Grace and paid a heavy price for their boldness.

How had this all come about? Had their paths crossed together by chance or was it by design? Had they threatened to expose Helen, as Emilia had previously, unless she played ball? Or had Helen's anger been simmering for years, just awaiting a spark to ignite it?

Emilia had historic photos of Grace visiting Elder, plus a positive ID and testimony from David Simons confirming that they had a troubled relationship. She also had robust evidence from Dinah Carter and a decent ID—how many well-known female officers with a penchant for sadomasochism were there? Emilia had most of the answers now, but still this final piece of the puzzle eluded her.

Why had Helen Grace finally crossed the line? What had finally pushed her into becoming a murderer?

105

He didn't have to wait long. The front door opened slowly and moments later, she emerged, hurrying off down the street in the direction she'd come from. From his elevated position, she seemed so small, so vulnerable, that for a moment he almost felt sorry for her. But it was only a fleeting emotion—the rage that had sustained him for so long devouring this brief spasm of pity.

What was she thinking now? She had been at the scene for a short time, but had reaped a bitter harvest. By contrast, he had enjoyed himself enormously. This murder had been the most meaningful. And the most satisfying. Angelique had begged for mercy once she realized what was happening—as much as you can beg when you've got a plastic ball clamped into your mouth. But he had barely heard her as he went about his business—it was so much noise in the background. She was just an offering—an offering to lay at the feet of Helen Grace.

Helen had almost reached the end of the road now. Had she left her bike out of sight to avoid drawing attention to herself? If so, she was wasting her time. This was about her—this had always been about her.

Suddenly she slipped from view, disappearing around the corner and away from him. But their meeting was not far away now.

You can run, Helen. But you can't hide.

106

The incident room was deserted. Sanderson had left it until late to return to base, hoping that the rest of the team would have called it a day, given that there were no breaking leads. As she teased the handle of the main door, she was pleased to find it locked—she didn't want to have to explain her presence here. Letting herself in quickly, she secured the door behind her. She couldn't risk being disturbed, given what she was about to do.

Picking her way through the desks, she made her way to Helen's office. Her boss operated an open-door policy and never bothered locking her office. Helen liked to be one of the foot soldiers and was at pains not to erect false barriers between her and the team. This was useful now, as Sanderson walked into her office unimpeded, but it made her betrayal all the worse. Whatever she thought of Helen now, she had always been an inspirational figure in Sanderson's life.

Crossing to the desk, she opened one drawer, then another. But it was as she opened the bottom drawer that she found what she was after. Helen had long straight hair and always kept a hairbrush in her office, in case she suddenly found herself facing top brass or, worse, the press. Slipping on latex gloves, Sanderson picked up the brush and carefully extracted three hairs from the bristles. Dropping the hairs into a small evidence bag, she sealed her haul and, placing the brush back in the drawer, pushed it firmly to.

Twenty minutes later, she was buzzing herself into the Police Scientific Services building. It was a short hop up to the lab on the third floor, where she found Meredith Walker waiting for her.

"This had better be good," Meredith said on seeing her. "I'm missing *First Dates* to be here."

"New lead in the Elder case. DNA source. We need it done—"

"ASAP, I know."

The forensics officer turned to begin her work.

"Oh, and, Meredith . . ."

She turned to look at Sanderson once more, intrigued by her serious tone.

"It's for my eyes only."

107

They ate in silence. Jane was well tuned to his moods and could tell when Jonathan had had a bad day at work. Her default tactic in those situations was not to probe or hassle him; instead she would hand him a glass of cold white wine and get on with the business of cooking their dinner.

She had cooked one of his favorites—linguine alle vongole— but he could barely taste it tonight. He was on autopilot, twirling the pasta slowly round his fork, then lifting it to his mouth, barely conscious of what he was eating. He didn't care a jot for the consequences of his actions today—he felt confident he could ride out any formal complaint Helen might make. It was the betrayal that burned. He had wanted her like he hadn't wanted any woman for years and she had pushed him away. Why had she toyed with him if she wasn't interested?

Gardam finished eating and pushed his bowl away. Looking up, he caught Jane staring at him. She'd obviously been concerned when he returned home with two deep scratches on his cheek, but seemed to accept his story of a jogging accident. Now, though, Gardam wondered if she was having her doubts. The scratches were long, straight and clean. Would you expect that type of injury from a low-hanging branch? The question was whether she would respond to these doubts, asking him outright. He wanted her to ask. He would tell her that he hadn't slept with another woman, but he wanted to. He would tell Jane that he found her predictable, bourgeois and anodyne—both in the bedroom and out. He would tell her that their marriage was comfortable and routine, characterized by his career ambition and her appetite for a nice, middle-class lifestyle, but that when you boiled things down, when you got down to primal needs and desires, she meant little to him. Helen was the woman who occupied his thoughts now. Despite her savage rejection, she remained there still—in his brain, in his gut, but worst of all in his heart.

108

It was nearly midnight and the air was biting cold. Helen walked briskly through the trees, working her way to the deepest part of the wood. She had come this route many times during her runs and knew it like the back of her hand. She was following a path that few knew of, which gave her some comfort, some respite from the paranoia now gripping her. Here at least she would be safe.

Angelique had been left for her to discover. This was a new phase in a game that was clearly directed at her. All three victims were known to Helen—she had used their services and allowed them to see a part of her that no one else did. Was jealousy driving someone to destroy these people? Or something else? And what did the text message sent by Angelique's killer summoning Helen imply? That she was being set up? Or just that she was meant to know? Perhaps the killer had just lost patience with the real target and had decided to bring her into the game.

Time would tell, but if Helen wanted to survive, she would belatedly have to get smart. Pulling her private mobile phone from her jacket, she flipped open the back and removed the SIM card. She looked around for any signs that she was being watched, but seeing nothing, she removed her lighter from her jeans and ignited the flame. It was an oddly beautiful sight—the plastic melting slowly as the metal chip of the SIM card blackened and distorted. Holding it in her gloved hand until it was destroyed, Helen dropped it to the ground, into a small hole she'd dug with the heel of her boot. Kicking earth over the hole, she then moved away quickly, clutching the phone in her hand.

On the edge of the woods, she hesitated. A couple was wandering home across the common, arm in arm. Helen waited until they had disappeared before she ventured onto open ground. She had always felt at home here, but now she felt exposed and vulnerable. Upping her pace, she soon found herself sprinting, keen to get this over with.

Within minutes, she was by the cemetery lake. Checking the coast was clear, Helen pulled the body of her phone from her pocket and threw it as hard as she could, watching it arc through the sky before landing in the water with a splash. The noise echoed briefly, then died away.

Helen had already turned on her heel and was marching toward the southern exit. She had to regroup now, which meant heading back to her flat. She would have to search every inch of it and secure every lock before she would feel safe, but she would do whatever was necessary. It was her home, after all—her only safe space now—and she was damned if she was going to be driven from it.

109

Charlie held her hand to her mouth, sickened by the sight in front of her. It shouldn't have made a difference to her that their third victim was a woman, but it did. Charlie could see the naked terror frozen on her pretty face; she could feel her desperation to breathe, to live, even as the oxygen in her lungs ran out. Her nostrils were dilated, her mouth wide-open—one almost felt she might lurch back into life suddenly with one big breath. But her lifeless eyes, staring monotonously at the low ceiling, gave the lie to that.

She went by the professional name of Angelique, but her real name was Amy Fawcett. The flat was registered in her name and the imprint of her real life could be seen in framed photos hung up in her private space at the back of the flat. She was a musician and performance artist, who paid the bills by her extracurricular work at night. She didn't appear to be a prostitute—there were no condoms in the flat, no history of arrest—in fact this work appeared to be a sideline, which made her death all the more tragic. There was a photo next to her bed of a young Amy gripping a viola awkwardly under her chin. It had brought tears to Charlie's eyes when she first saw it—such was the guileless innocence and optimism of the image—and she'd had to absent herself from the team for a few moments. She needed a break—she realized that now—but quite when and how she would get one was another matter.

They were still in the midst of a major investigation with no clear suspect in mind. Charlie had crunched the credit card details and sent them to Helen, but progress was incremental rather than revelatory and Charlie had the uneasy feeling that things were starting to go south. Normally, Helen would have been all over this, stalking the crime scene, bullying the forensics team and coordinating the uniformed officers on the street. But she was notable by her absence this morning. Charlie hadn't been able to raise her on her landline or mobile. Was she sick? Surely not, Helen was *never* sick.

She had tried Sanderson, thinking it might be wise to defer to her greater experience, but she couldn't get hold of her either and was told by one of the girls at the station that the DS was "unavailable" and "on operational duties." What those were, Charlie couldn't fathom—what could be more important than a triple murder?

It fell to Charlie then to marshal the troops. This should have felt exciting—calling the shots at a murder scene was the natural culmination of her career thus far. But the gnawing uncertainty that something bigger was going on, from which she was excluded, was sapping her energy and optimism. Equally debilitating was the sight in front of her—a beautiful and talented spirit whose life had been brutally cut short.

110

Helen hadn't wanted to leave Angelique like that, but she'd had no choice. She could hardly call it in, so instead she had deliberately left the front door open. She had no doubt that one of Angelique's neighbors would notice and investigate further. It wasn't ideal and might delay her discovery for a few hours, but there was no other way. Helen couldn't risk incriminating herself, and besides, she had work to do.

She had lowered the blind and turned off her phone. The whole of the kitchen table was covered in papers and files—the sum total of her work on these murders so far. She had the strong sense that she had been looking the wrong way the whole time, guided to do so by a killer who was organized, diligent and determined. Helen blamed herself—she had been willfully blind to the growing evidence in front of her, burying her personal connection to the victims because it was inconvenient and unsettling. By retrieving her private phone, by summoning her to the third murder, the killer had let it be known that he would not let her involvement with Jake, Max and the unfortunate Angelique remain hidden.

Helen had a growing sense of who might be responsible, but she refused to let paranoia guide her thinking. She had to follow the evidence, focusing on the choice of victims, the manner of their deaths and the way their killer had gone about organizing these murders. The devil was in the details in these cases and Helen returned once more now to Charlie's credit card searches.

This was their killer's only weak point, the one area where he might show his hand. They now had a third victim to work with and two new instruments of torture—Japanese soft-cord bondage ties and a ball gag—which had presumably been purchased for the occasion.

Helen knew that their perpetrator favored online bondage retailers, so, plugging into the police network via remote access, she started to run the searches. She eschewed the chain sex shops in favor of the more boutique operations. And before long she found what she was looking for—the necessary items paid for by a Geoffrey Plow, an eighty-seven-year-old former teacher, now living in Shirley. He was an unlikely recipient for S&M products, but more telling still was the fact that the delivery address did not match Plow's. The items had instead been delivered to a vacant retail outlet in Woolston.

Helen didn't hesitate now, e-mailing Plow's bank and using her name and reputation in the subsequent phone call to persuade the manager to release the necessary information to her. Moments later, her home printer was spewing out Plow's debit card activity for the last three months.

Helen was excited to see that the list of transactions was fairly short. Whereas the other two credit card victims were keen shoppers, spending frequently at a large number of stores and sites, Plow was parsimonious. He presumably didn't have much in the way of income, given his meager spending, and he didn't seem to shop online, preferring face-to-face transactions. He was also a man who didn't like to go too far afield. Most of his purchases were made locally in Shirley and he was clearly a repeat customer. One location particularly stood out—one he seemed to visit daily. Wilkinson's on Park Street.

Helen knew that Wilkinson's had figured on the other fraud victims' transaction lists and she pulled them from the files now. Her finger ran down one, then the next, and sure enough both had been regular shoppers at the same store.

Which was where Helen was heading now. If she was right, the answer to this deadly game of riddles was waiting for her there.

111

Sanderson paced up and down, fervently wishing she were a smoker or a nail biter. But she was neither—never had been—so there was nothing to do but wait.

The divers had been in the lake for nearly twenty minutes and Sanderson had by now got used to the strange, repetitive rhythm of their work. Dive, resurface, discuss, dive, resurface, discuss . . . Each time they came back up, she was convinced that this would be the breakthrough she needed. And each time she saw that they were empty-handed, another little part of her died.

This was a massive gamble on her part. She had gone over Gardam's head straight to the chief constable. It had been hard enough to get him to agree to surveillance; it was harder still to get him to agree to the expense of a dive. But in the end the chief constable had agreed that there were grounds for concern, and Sanderson's decisiveness initially appeared to have paid dividends. Helen Grace had had a five-person team on her as she made her way across Southampton Common. They had lost her initially as she disappeared in the depths of the woods, but a pair of young officers posing as lovers had picked her up again a little later on, as she emerged back onto open ground.

Sanderson had been beyond relieved at this news—she'd feared Helen was on to them and had deliberately lost her tail—and had radioed another member of the team to watch her from a safe distance. This officer had clearly seen Helen throw something in the lake and from then on, Sanderson hadn't stood still, petitioning the chief constable for a dive, detailing more people to the surveillance effort and drawing DC McAndrew into her confidence to run some further checks.

Standing by the side of the lake, a brisk autumnal wind whipping around her, she wondered whether she had made a mistake. What if the item that Helen had discarded was something else entirely, something personal and unrelated to the case or, worse than that, merely a piece of rubbish? She shuddered at the thought of how she would explain that to her paymasters.

A shout made her look up. One of the divers was signaling that he'd found something and was returning to the shore. Sanderson set off toward him and moments later she was in possession of a mobile phone, neatly encased in an evidence bag. She didn't recognize it, but it could be Helen's—there was a lot they didn't know about her boss, it appeared. Slipping on gloves, she opened the back of the phone, but there was no SIM card inside. Sealing the bag, Sanderson now pulled her phone from her pocket and called McAndrew— even without the SIM card there was lots they could do with the phone's memory, the serial number and so on. Concluding her call, she handed it to a colleague to ferry back to Southampton Central and resumed her position on the edge of the lake, hopeful that there might yet be more discoveries.

They were inching forward, but painfully slowly, and Sanderson wondered how long it would be before Helen smelled a rat. Time was ticking and Sanderson knew her case against Helen would have to be bulletproof before she made her move. If she fudged the execution or, worse still, was just plain wrong, it wouldn't be Helen's neck on the block—it would be hers.

112

"Check again."

Helen virtually barked her order at the startled manager. Peter Banyard, the new manager of the Park Street Wilkinson's, was not used to dealing with police officers, but he knew bad manners when he saw them and bridled at the request.

"I'm more than happy to check again, Inspector, but I can assure you that this is the complete list of all our employees."

Helen ran her eye down them again. Jeff Armstrong, Terry Slater, Joanne Hinton, Anne Duggan, Ian McGregor . . . There was nobody here she recognized, no one who might be relevant.

"Could these names be fake?"

"Of course not," the aggrieved manager responded. "We check their ID, get National Insurance numbers, their bank details—"

"How far does this list go back?" Helen interrupted.

"Eighteen months."

"Okay, I'll need a list going back five years, everything you've got."

"Then I'll need a warrant. I think we've already gone way beyond the call of duty—"

"You'll have one before the end of the day. Thank you for your time."

Helen was already halfway out of the door, heading fast for the store exit. The fraud victims had all shopped here for several years, so it was possible their credit and debit card details had been garnered some time back. And yet . . . she had known Paine for only eighteen months and Angelique considerably less than that. This felt recent and Helen knew that she was missing something significant. Their killer was still out there, thinking, plotting, waiting for his moment to strike.

113

"Amy Fawcett's body is currently at the mortuary—Jim Grieves is working on a more accurate time of death—"

"But . . . ," Sanderson interrupted, wishing McAndrew would get to the point.

"But I've run the Automatic Number Plate Recognition and DI Grace's bike was in the vicinity of Fawcett's flat last night."

"What do you mean, 'in the vicinity'?"

"Three blocks away."

"What time is this?"

"She heads into the docks area around nine p.m. And leaves via the same route shortly before ten."

"Okay, call Grieves on the hour every hour until he gives you a time of death. He won't like it, but he'll have to wear it."

"Sure thing."

They were standing in Helen's office. It was the least suspicious place for a private conference, but even so, it felt profoundly odd to be talking about her while standing in her space.

"Look, Ellie, if you feel uncomfortable doing this," Sanderson said quickly, "you just have to say—"

"It's okay. I'm fine. And you can rely on me to be dis—"

"I know I can. Why do you think I asked you?"

This earned a crooked smile from McAndrew, so Sanderson continued:

"Have we got anything from the phone yet?"

"Not much but we're still doing most of the checks. The serial number shows that the phone was stolen five years ago. I'd imagine it's been used with a bastardized SIM card since. The phone's history has been deleted, I'm afraid, and the boys aren't convinced that we'll be able to retrieve it."

"What about prints?"

"Only partials, unfortunately. It's been rubbed down pretty well."

"Shit."

"That said," McAndrew added, "Amy Fawcett's phone was still in her bag and the boys have had more luck there. She sent a text message last night to an unregistered mobile number—07768 038687—asking someone to meet her at her flat. We've looked at the phone contacts of Jake Elder and Max Paine—this is the only number that links all three. We've got Elder and Paine's phone content going back years. The same unregistered user used this number to make appointments with them—just as he or she did with Fawcett."

Now Sanderson smiled—the first time she'd done so in a while.

"Okay, let's run with that. Go back to the phone company—who is it?"

"Lebara—a pay-as-you-go service."

"Go back to them and do a location search. Find out which mobile masts that phone has been pinging over the last few weeks, months. I want to find out where that person has been."

McAndrew nodded and headed off, leaving Sanderson to contemplate her next move. She had already received several phone calls from Emilia asking for progress, but she would have to wait. They didn't yet have the smoking gun, but the case was steadily building, and if they were going to bring Helen in, there was something she needed to do first.

114

"I'm sorry, I just don't believe it."

Charlie tried to keep her voice steady, but there was no hiding the emotion she felt.

"What you *believe* isn't really relevant. We have to be led by the evidence," Sanderson countered.

"DI Grace is a highly decorated officer—she has more commendations to her name than the rest of us put together. Her integrity and professionalism have never been questioned—"

"That's not true. She was nearly kicked out of the force for shooting her own sister."

"She saved my life that day."

"And you've been peas in a pod ever since, haven't you?"

Charlie was about to take Sanderson's head off, but Gardam intervened, holding up his hand to silence her. He had called

Charlie to his office as soon as Sanderson had brought these latest developments to him—Charlie was of equal rank and needed to be included. She was very grateful he had—Sanderson clearly wasn't going to stick up for Helen.

"This is difficult enough as it is," he said calmly. "Let's try to keep personal issues out of it. So what have we got?"

"We have a personal relationship with all of the victims—," Sanderson began.

"According to a journalist," Charlie countered.

"Garanita has a number of photos showing DI Grace visiting Elder's flat, plus I now have the testimony of a neighbor who saw her there on numerous occasions. Max Paine was brutally attacked nine months ago by a female police officer—a client who'd turned on him. Interestingly, Paine left a voice mail for Emilia Garanita hours before he was killed, saying he had important information relating to Jake Elder's murder."

This time Charlie said nothing.

"We can place Grace's bike near the scene of the latest murder at exactly the right time. *And* we believe we can link DI Grace to all the victims via an unregistered mobile phone she attempted to discard on Southampton Common last night."

"Come on, Sanderson, that's speculation and you know it."

"We'll see," Sanderson said confidently. "We also found a partial boot print near the crime scene at Paine's flat. It's a size six—DI Grace is a size six—and the pattern on the bottom is deep, wavy tread, reminiscent of soles you often find on biker boots. As you know, DI Grace—"

"I get the picture. Can we place Grace at the scene of the first murder?"

"Not yet."

"What about Paine's and Fawcett's flats?"

"Still processing the evidence, sir," Sanderson replied, sounding slightly hesitant for the first time. "But the fact remains that DI Grace has been evasive and secretive from the off. She has been behaving erratically and emotionally, making decisions and calls that the evidence just didn't justify. The use of cling film on the third victim can't be a coincidence, given her history. Perhaps she got bored of waiting for us to work it out."

"But why? Why would she do something like this?" Charlie virtually shouted.

"Maybe they blackmailed her and she killed them. Now she's trying to cover her tracks, make it look like a serial killer, when actually she's just covering her arse. Or maybe she's just snapped—she's been doing this stuff for so long and nobody has a closer affinity to this type of killer than her. After all, it runs in the famil—"

At this point, Sanderson's phone rang out, loud and shrill. Apologizing to Gardam, she answered it and retreated. Charlie saw this as her opportunity and leaped in.

"With the greatest of respect to my colleague, I really don't think arresting DI Grace is the right thing to do. We need to evaluate these leads, for sure, but I don't think an arrest—with all the attendant publicity—is a smart move."

Gardam looked at her, but said nothing.

"Look, I know hunches and personal relationships don't count for much," Charlie acknowledged, "but I've known Helen Grace longer than anyone here and she just isn't capable of these crimes. Her first and *only* priority is to save lives, to serve the ends of justice. Whatever may have happened in her personal life, she wouldn't do this. She would never murder someone in cold blood, so for everyone's sake, let's not rush into something we'll regret. She is *innocent*. Please believe me."

Charlie finished her impassioned speech and now became aware of Sanderson standing by her side.

"That was Meredith Walker at the lab," Sanderson said, failing to keep the note of triumph from her voice. "We've got a match, sir. A cigarette butt found in the corridor by the crime scene at the Torture Rooms has DI Grace's DNA on it. She was there that night."

Charlie felt physically winded, stunned by this development. And her discomfort increased still further as Gardam now turned to them both and said:

"Okay. Let's bring her in."

115

Helen checked her mirrors, but the car was still there. She'd first noticed she was being tailed when heading north up Kingsway. She had sped fast round the Charlotte Place roundabout, then forked left up the Avenue. The gray sedan kept pace without ever seeming to speed up or slow down. The tactics she recognized; the car she didn't—which made her very nervous indeed.

It had to be police, but who and why? Helen suddenly had the nasty feeling that she hadn't walked away from Angelique's flat unseen after all. Were they watching her then? If so, they would have photos of her entering and leaving the flat—photos that would look pretty damning if given the right twist. If they were following her from the flat, then had they followed her to the common too?

She could see the large expanse of green to her left now, as she flashed past on her bike, though trees shielded the lake from view.

Were the police there right now? Searching for evidence? There was an alternative scenario—that they had just picked up her tail this morning, following her to Wilkinson's and beyond. But that scarcely made her feel any better. They clearly still had their suspicions about her. In normal circumstances she would have gone straight to her boss to get the lowdown, but how could she do that now? Failing that, she would have gone to the team, to her DSs, but perhaps even they were working against her. Someone must have raised concerns with top brass.

Helen tugged at the throttle, speeding north. The tailing car kept pace. Helen *could* call Charlie to try to get the lie of the land, but it was an inherently risky play. Her communications might be monitored, and even if Charlie *was* onside—as Helen fervently hoped she was—it would put her in a terribly difficult position. Nobody had called her this morning, which was unheard of. They were deliberately giving her a wide berth, which meant that something was up.

There was no one she could turn to, so she would have to handle things herself. Someone was intent on setting her up and it was up to her to resolve the situation. But first she would need to lose her tail.

Highfield Lane was fast approaching. Helen lowered her speed, then suddenly cut hard right, yanking the throttle once more. Her back wheel skidded, screeching loudly; then suddenly she was shooting forward. Moments earlier she'd been heading due north; now she was tearing east, testing the speed limit as she did so. She was expecting the blues and twos to come on, but the gray car remained as unobtrusive—but persistent—as ever. She raised her speed now—forty, then fifty miles per hour. She could get pulled over for speeding, but that was the last thing on anyone's mind at the moment. The fact that they hadn't pulled her in meant either that this was just a surveillance gig or that they wanted to do so discreetly.

They would obviously be radioing her progress in and there was every chance she might be riding into a trap. Cobden Bridge was coming up—this was a good place to trap fleeing suspects, as they generally didn't fancy a swim. It looked clear, but . . . Helen pumped her speed up to seventy miles per hour, overtaking three cars before zooming back into the lane. At any moment she expected unmarked cars to appear, blocking the other end of the bridge. But as she ate up the yards to the end of the bridge, the way remained clear. As she reached the end, she dropped down onto her right knee, biting hard into the tarmac as she spun down Bullar Road. She roared down it, then braked hard, not daring to cross Bitterne Way without looking. It was busy today, vans and lorries speeding along, and as Helen awaited her opportunity, she flashed a look in the rearview mirror.

The gray car was still with her, moving fast down Bullar Road toward her. It was fifty yards away, now forty, now thirty . . . Throwing caution to the wind, Helen tore across the four-lane carriageway, narrowly avoiding another bike, before speeding on. The pursuing car bided its time and Helen now became aware of a red estate car up ahead that seemed to be taking its time to reach Freemantle Common, almost as if it was waiting for someone.

The road was pretty quiet today. It would be a great place to strike and sure enough, the Astra now pulled across the road, blocking her route. The blue light was out now, the doors opening in readiness for an arrest. The gray car was not far behind, so Helen didn't hesitate, lowering her speed, then ramming back the throttle to mount the pavement. The officers were already getting back into their car, so Helen raced down the empty pavement before joining the road and speeding off.

There was no need for stealth—now it was all about speed. She sped through Merry Oak and Itchen, paying heed only to the space in front of her, ignoring the traffic signals that attempted to arrest her progress. And as she reached Weston, Abbey Hill cemetery came into view in the distance.

This had been her destination all along. If she could get there, she had a chance of escape. The pursuing cars were not far behind, their high-powered engines helping them to keep pace with her Kawasaki. Now Helen was leaving the main road, mounting the single-track road to the cemetery. There was no way down now—she was boxed in—so she cut loose, ripping her speed up to the max. Within moments, the cemetery gates appeared in front of her. Jamming the brakes, Helen skidded to a halt in front of them and was off and away before her bike had stopped moving.

As she vaulted the gates, she heard the cars pull up, but Helen didn't hesitate, darting off down the main path toward the far end of the cemetery. This was her terrain and she planned to use her knowledge of it to her advantage, cutting diagonally across the minor paths, making maximum use of the cover the tombs and statues provided. She could hear shouts behind her, but they seemed a ways away—she had a few minutes' grace now, but she would have to use them wisely.

She found herself in the most secluded part of the cemetery. She had bent her path this way partly out of an instinct to stay hidden but also out of habit. This was the location of her sister Marianne's final resting place and as Helen approached her grave, she suddenly slowed her pace dramatically. Not because she thought she was safe, but because of what she now saw in front of her.

Leaning against Marianne's grave was a simple bouquet of flowers. Suddenly Helen knew exactly who wanted to destroy her. And, more important, she knew why.

116

Her heel dug sharply into the turf and the ground seemed to give way beneath her. Hearing her pursuers approaching, Helen had vaulted the railings at the far end of the cemetery and thrown herself down the hill, hoping to disappear from view and confuse her pursuers. But the ground was wet and slippery and she lost her footing almost immediately, careering down the hill on her back, picking up speed as she did so.

For a moment, Helen didn't know which way was up. Then suddenly she came to an abrupt halt, somebody punching her hard in the side. Recovering herself, Helen now realized she was in a thornbush and the sharp pain in her side was a thick branch that had rammed into her ribs. She was winded and muddy but, as she was still wearing her leathers and helmet, was largely unscathed.

Picking herself up, she looked up at the cemetery, now a good seventy or eighty feet above her. She could still hear voices, but no one was peering over the railings in her direction. If she moved swiftly, she had a chance of evading her pursuers completely, so, breaking cover, she ran down the side of the hill. She moved from bush to thicket to bush, occasionally casting a wary look behind her.

Before long she'd made it to the bottom of the hill and, cutting her way along a footpath, made it back to civilization. Hurrying down a side street, she spotted Chamberlayne College, then, heading left, hurried toward Weston. Spotting a bin, she pulled off her helmet and jacket and dumped them. The call would have gone out to uniform as well as other surveillance officers now, so she would have to be careful.

Her side was hurting her now, but she pressed on. She couldn't head home and needed somewhere—a sanctuary—to gather her thoughts. Somewhere public but not too public. Suddenly a Ladbrokes came into view and Helen ducked inside. There was a smattering of punters about, but they were far more interested in the dog racing and the fruit machines than her. Buying a coffee, Helen sat down at the betting bar, a copy of the *Racing Post* open in front of her. She barely took in the text on the page, her brain pulsing with urgent, disquieting thoughts. Why had she been so complacent? Why had she ignored the evidence that was staring her in the face? She had seen someone in the derelict flats opposite her months ago but had dismissed the apparition as a junkie. But the person within had been watching her all the while, waiting for the moment to strike. How long had he been there? How many times had he seen her sitting at her window? How many months had he been inveigling his way into her life?

Since Max Paine's death, she'd feared the murders might be connected to her, but she'd suppressed these thoughts. Her chat with Gardam had reassured her, but how naive and foolish that looked now. The fact that she was summoned to the third murder suggested that she was being set up, and the use of cling film confirmed for her the identity of the perpetrator. Her sister, Marianne, had killed their parents in the same way, securing their limbs, then wrapping their heads in cling film. She too was now dead, but her son, Robert, was alive. Helen had ruined his life by accidentally outing him as the son of a serial killer. He had remained hidden for several years since that devastating moment, but had finally resurfaced. Helen had wanted to be his guardian angel, but her cursed touch had brought him only misery, rejection and pain.

Now he was back for revenge.

117

"Do you have any eyes on her?" Sanderson barked, her stress levels hitting the roof.

"Negative."

"Any idea where she might have gone?"

"She probably hopped the fence and made her way down the hill—but I couldn't tell you in which direction."

Sanderson cursed. Another member of the team looked up, intrigued, so, pushing the door to Helen's office shut, Sanderson lowered her voice.

"Where is the nearest road? If she wanted to head back into town, where would she head to?"

There was silence on the other end, as the surveillance officer conferred with his colleague; then he eventually replied:

"Probably Weston or Newtown."

"Okay, leave one man at the cemetery in case she doubles back for her bike, but the rest of you get to Weston and Newtown and fan out from there. We'll circulate her description to uniform, but keep your eyes peeled. You lost her—you can bloody well find her."

Sanderson clicked off, realizing too late that she had raised her voice once again, to the evident interest of her colleagues. It was not surprising—in spite of everything she'd experienced with this team, she had never felt so stressed as she did right now. Getting Gardam to agree to the arrest had been hard enough, but then to lose her . . . They had got too close, blown their cover, and Helen now knew that she was being pursued. Having been so upbeat earlier, Sanderson suddenly felt deeply anxious. She had no idea where Helen was right now and, more important, no idea of what she might do next.

Her phone rang suddenly and Sanderson glanced down eagerly at the screen. But it was just Emilia Garanita—again. Rejecting it, she marched from Helen's office, slamming the door behind her.

118

What the hell was she playing at?

As her call went to voice mail, Emilia clicked off and threw her phone angrily onto her desk. She and Sanderson had made a pact to keep in touch, but she had the distinct feeling she was being kept at arm's length. Sanderson wouldn't have a case at all if Emilia hadn't given her the story. That whole team—Sanderson included—had been so infatuated with Grace that they'd never stopped to ask any questions of her. She'd had to lead them to Helen's wrongdoing and she was damned if she was going to be shut out at the moment of triumph.

She wanted to wait until they had made an arrest before publishing the story. With a suitable tip-off from Sanderson, Emilia could be in position to get a photo of Grace being marched to the cop car in cuffs or driven through the back door in custody. She'd had a four-word text this afternoon, suggesting an arrest warrant was imminent, but since then nothing from Sanderson.

Suddenly Emilia wondered whether she'd backed the right horse. She couldn't have approached DS Brooks, of course—it was clear where her loyalties lay—and everybody else was too inferior in rank. She'd felt certain that Sanderson was the one—she was suggestible, frustrated and lacking in confidence—but, then again, you never know how people will respond when it comes to the crunch. Perhaps Sanderson was just inexperienced at playing the game or maybe she was a little less innocent than she let on. Could she have taken Emilia for a ride?

She sincerely hoped not. Because Emilia was in a position to do serious damage not only to Sanderson's career but also to the Hampshire Police in general. She needed them and vice versa, yet they had always treated her badly—at best like an irritant, but more often as a necessary evil. Grace had been a particularly bad offender in this regard—her hostility to Emilia very clear. Often Emilia had been on the back foot in their relationship, but now finally she was poised to attack.

And her weapon of choice would be tomorrow's edition with its screaming banner headline:

COP TURNED KILLER

119

Helen walked quickly toward the back of the store, keeping her head down. She was an odd sight for a cold autumn evening— boots and leathers on her bottom half, but only a thin black vest top above. More curious still were the scratches on her face and arms. She looked a little like she had been dragged through a hedge backward, which of course she had.

It was cold in the refrigerated section of the supermarket and Helen didn't linger, marching to the manager's office at the rear and pushing inside. Peter Banyard was still unnerved from their first meeting and looked positively shocked now by her second appearance of the day.

"Are you okay? Can I get you anything?" he eventually said, clocking her strange appearance.

"I'm fine, but I need to ask you another question."

"I haven't got your paperwork ready yet if that's—"

"That's not why I'm here. I want you to look at this picture, tell me if you recognize this man."

Her hand was shaking slightly as she held up her phone for him. On the screen was one of the photos the press had used when they'd "outed" Robert Stonehill several years earlier.

The manager stared at the photo.

"Do you know him?" Helen repeated more loudly.

"Well, yes. That's Aaron West."

"He works for you?" Helen continued, insistent.

"He's one of our temporary workers. We take them on around Halloween, Bonfire Night and so on."

"Does he work the tills?"

"Tills, shelves, wherever we need him. He does a few shifts a week—has been for a few months now."

Just enough time for him to plan Helen's downfall. He had lifted customers' credit card details while working the tills, then used their details to purchase his specialist S&M gear—gear that would eventually lead the police back to her.

"Did you check his credentials? His ID?"

"Yes," Banyard replied, looking unnerved, "although the checks for temporary workers aren't perhaps as rigorous as for our permanent staff."

"I bet they're not," Helen snarled back, just about containing her anger. "Do you have an address for him?"

"We should do," the manager replied, "but I'm not sure that will be necessary."

"What do you mean?"

"I just saw him out the back. In the locker area. I can take you th—"

But he didn't get to finish. Helen was already gone.

120

She sprinted across the store, scattering shoppers in her wake. The Staff Only door was fifty feet away and Helen charged toward it, glancing around for someone to help her open it. But there was no one to hand and she couldn't delay, so she launched herself at it. Her shoulder hit the cheap door hard, wrenching the lock from its socket.

Two alarmed faces stared at her as she hurried inside—two employees who were about to return to work, dumbfounded by Helen's dramatic entrance.

"Where are the lockers?"

For a moment they were speechless.

"The lockers," Helen barked.

One of the workers now pointed to a door on her left. Helen was off again, eating up the yards to the door and pushing through it. To her dismay, the dingy locker room was empty, but Helen sensed movement and now saw the fire exit at the far end of the room swinging gently to a close. Had he heard her coming and taken flight? If so, he was only a few seconds ahead of her.

Helen burst out into the night, scanning desperately left and right for signs of her quarry. And there he was. Not forty yards away from her down a narrow alley, sprinting as if his life depended on it. Helen took off in pursuit, pounding the concrete as she pushed herself to narrow the gap between them.

It looked as though the alleyway would lead them back into the main shopping precinct, where most of the big stores were to be found. Was that Robert's plan? To lose himself in the crowds? Helen couldn't allow that, so even though her lungs were burning, she upped her speed again. The bitter irony of her pursuit wasn't lost on her—she'd been searching for her nephew for so long and now here he was, intent on escaping her.

He had now reached the end of the alleyway and darted round to the left. Helen couldn't afford to let him out of her sight, but she was only fifteen feet behind now. Reaching the end of the alley, she tore around the corner in the same direction as Robert—running smack into a middle-aged man laden with shopping bags. She cannoned off him, falling to the ground, jarring her frame nastily on the concrete floor as she did so. Pain seared through her, but she was already clambering to her feet. Holding her hand up in apology, she sidestepped the concerned shoppers hurrying to help her.

She ran her eye over the sea of shoppers but couldn't see Robert. Had he taken advantage of her accident to disappear into one of the main shops? No, there he was. Helen glimpsed his deep red hoodie, bobbing as he hurried north toward the precinct exit. Shaking herself down, Helen tore off in the same direction.

The chase was on.

121

"We've just had a call from Wilkinson's in Shirley. Apparently, DI Grace just left there in a hurry."

McAndrew's tone was hushed. She clearly felt awkward working against their boss, but orders were orders, so she'd brought her news straight to Sanderson and Charlie.

"This is the address of the store—"

"I know where it is," Sanderson interrupted. "Alert uniform in the area to be on their guard—I want any sightings radioed in immediately."

"I'll advise officers in outlying areas to head toward the precinct—they can form a wider net in case she slips through."

"Was she on foot?"

"I believe so."

"Good, then we've got a good chance of taking her. I'll take the car down there now."

Charlie watched Sanderson head off, her emotions in riot. Since the arrest warrant had been finalized, she had been torn in two. One part of her wanted to do her duty like McAndrew, but the greater part of her wanted to warn Helen of the danger she was now in. She couldn't call or text her as that would be too easily traced back to her, but perhaps there was a pay phone in one of the local pubs? Charlie had the sense that the net was closing on Helen now, and unless she did something to help her, she was doomed.

"DS Brooks is coming with me. You can take point here."

It was said to McAndrew, but was aimed at Charlie. Sanderson was looking at her as if she could read her mind, sensing her disloyalty. The eyes of the room were on her now, so with a heavy heart, Charlie said:

"Sure. Let's go."

There would be no escape for Helen today.

122

Helen grasped the chain-link fence and vaulted it in one easy motion, landing gently on the other side. Her nephew had veered away from the city center as fast as he could, seeking out the footpaths and back alleys that would be deserted as night closed in. Before long he'd reached an allotment and was now cutting across it, heading toward the south of the city. Helen was close behind, running as fast as she could over the hard, rutted ground.

Had Robert always planned this as an escape route? He seemed to know his way without thinking, avoiding public places and possible obstructions. Normally Helen would have called in her pursuit in an attempt to cut him off, but that wasn't an option now.

When they'd first met, Helen would have been confident of winning this contest. Robert was just a young man then—he didn't have her physical training, nor her experience. Now there seemed to be something different about him. He was leaner, fitter, and she could see that his head was shaved. He had a smooth, militaristic look, almost as if he was the one who had now been in training, preparing to avenge himself on the woman who had killed his mother and ruined his life.

Robert was only twenty feet ahead but vaulted the boundary fence without hesitation before sprinting on. His levels of fitness really were impressive and Helen suddenly had the nasty thought that it would be she who'd tire first. Clearing the fence, she touched down hard, narrowly avoiding a tree root, then burst forward once more. If she lost him, who was to say when she would get another chance to confront him? It was now or never.

They had been running for over ten minutes, but Helen knew that Robert's escape options were narrowing. They were nearing the outskirts of the docks. There were many warehouses, in use and derelict, for him to hide in, but the whole of the Western Docks was fenced off and unless Robert had a craft of some kind waiting for him, he couldn't keep heading south.

Up ahead of her, Robert slammed into the dock's perimeter fence, scaling it as he did so. Helen could see he was wearing gloves, but as he reached the top, he yelped in pain, the razor wire clearly doing its work. But he pushed on through, falling to the ground on the other side, obliging Helen to follow him. She scampered up the links, pausing only at the top to maneuver herself through the coiled wires. It would lose her valuable seconds, but it would be disastrous to get caught up in it, and a false move would cut her to ribbons.

The metal teeth of the wire caressed her cheek as she eased her head through, but didn't draw blood. Twisting again, she wiggled her torso through the gap, feeling the back of her vest tear slightly as it snagged on its way through. Now she could grip the fence on the other side and, pulling her legs through, quickly swung down onto the ground—just in time to see Robert disappearing into Quay 42.

Helen stumbled as she moved forward—her legs were growing weary of the pursuit—but she drove herself on. Quay 42 was a derelict outpost of the Western Docks and was a fitting place for this endgame to play out. The last time Helen had visited the mothballed warehouses that littered it was to recover one of Marianne's victims. Perhaps the historic associations were too much to resist—Helen couldn't believe he'd made his way here by chance.

She was entering the dock area now—great, empty warehouses looming up on all sides. Helen hurried toward the old dockside, peering into the shadows on either side, searching for her prey. Was he hiding in the shadows, waiting to attack her from behind, or had he come here to make his escape? Peering over into the water, Helen could see no craft, no signs of movement. Turning, she cast a look farther down the quayside, but it too was deserted. She had been too close behind for Robert to have made it out of the quay completely, so he was here somewhere. Was he watching her right now?

There were four main warehouses on this part of the quay, all in equal states of disrepair, shattered windows giving a fractured view of the darkness within them. If Helen picked wrong, then he would escape. There was no margin for error now. He was unlikely to be hiding in the first, as he had veered round to the left past it when entering the quay. Presuming he hadn't doubled back, this left three more. The next-nearest one was little more than a shell, the roof having collapsed some time ago. There was plenty of detritus within to provide cover, but the moon that now hung overhead was full, lighting up the interior clearly. It would be a gamble to conceal yourself there in plain sight, so Helen moved on to the last two. Both of these were in good repair and would be smart places to hide, the fire escapes that snaked down the sides providing a possible means of escape if need be. If Helen were being pursued, she would have picked one of these two.

Helen wrenched open the door to the nearest one and peered inside. It was one vast hangar, littered with abandoned crates and dead pigeons. Again there was plenty of cover, but there were no internal walls to hide behind, so now Helen's gaze strayed to the last warehouse, which bordered the quayside. This was a two-tier building—a series of offices and small units on top of the main hangar. This seemed much more promising, so, making her choice, Helen hurried toward it.

The main hangar doors lay in front of her, but the fire escape that led up to the second floor intrigued her more, as it would have been out of view when Helen had entered the quay complex. She walked forward confidently, then came to an abrupt halt. A dark spot lay on the ground by the steps and bending down, Helen dipped her finger in it. Holding it up to the light, she could see that it was blood, glistening in the moonlight, fresh and wet.

Now Helen moved quickly up the steps. Reaching the top, she paused. There was every chance that Robert was inside. She was about to face him unarmed, with nothing but her experience and training to protect her. If he meant to do her harm, even kill her, then who would ever know that she'd been down here? That she had solved the case? For the first time since this desperate chase had begun, Helen paused to catch her breath, pulling her mobile from her pocket. She sent a quick text, then, switching the phone to silent, stepped into the darkness within.

Immediately, something came at her. She flung her arm up to

protect herself, then watched in alarm as the startled pigeon flew away, the sound of his flapping wings echoing around the empty rooms. Any element of surprise was gone now, so Helen pressed on, walking swiftly down the corridor that stretched out in front of her the full length of the building. There were small offices off it and Helen checked them over as she walked past. She wasn't keen to get caught in one of these—she wanted him to make the first move, rather than walk into a trap herself.

Her eyes scanned the space ahead of her, looking for signs of movement, and then, in the distance, she saw it. At the very end of the corridor there was a room that was probably the biggest in the building. It overlooked the water, it was the width of the warehouse and all roads led to it. And unlike every other room in this decaying edifice, it was emitting a pale blue light.

Intrigued, Helen crept forward. As she did so, she spotted a few abandoned bits of scaffolding. Bending down, she picked up a short length of pipe and carried on, getting closer and closer to the office ahead. She was fifteen feet from it, now ten, now five. Helen stood on the threshold, then pushed into the room, braced to defend herself.

But no attack came. Was Robert even here? It was hard to make out the outer edges of the room—her eye was drawn to the computer whose weak light she had noticed from the corridor. Next to it on a rickety table was a camping lantern and Helen grabbed it, turning it up. Now the room came into focus—empty coffee cups, an ashtray full of cigarettes, discarded sandwich wrappers, a hoodie hanging over a chair, but also a white iPhone 5 nearby. Helen guessed it was Max Paine's—but time would tell. And flanking all this, pinned up on the walls, were maps of Southampton, picking out Banister Park, Bitterne and the docks.

This, then, was Robert's bolt-hole—a perfect hiding place from which to plot his killing spree. And as Helen took another step forward, turning the lantern to get a better view of the room, she saw him, framed by the large windows behind him. He was silhouetted against the moonlight, but as Helen stepped closer, she took in his face. He looked pale, impassive and oddly effeminate—there didn't seem to be a single trace of hair on his face, head or neck. She hadn't seen him in years, and now as he took *her* in, his blue eyes sparkled malevolently.

"Nice to see you again, Helen. It's been a long time."

123

The unmarked car hurtled down the road, siren blaring and light flashing. Even though she was safely strapped in, Charlie held tight to the armrest. Sanderson was wound tight tonight and driving way too aggressively. She didn't dare say anything, but she didn't want to become a casualty of her colleague's desperation to nail their boss either.

They were heading fast toward Shirley, but as they reached the outskirts, Charlie's phone pinged loudly. Sanderson gave her an accusing look, as if Charlie had deliberately done this to distract her, before returning her attention to the road. Irked, Charlie pulled out her phone. But as she did so, her finger froze, hovering over the Read button. The message was from Helen.

Charlie glanced sideways at Sanderson, then pressed the button. The message was short and sweet.

Western Docks. Quay 42.

It was timed as having been sent three minutes ago. Was Helen in trouble? Did she need help? Was this her covert way of asking for it, by texting instead of calling? Charlie stared at the message, unsure what to do. Should she text back? Probably—that was what a good friend and colleague would do—but if it was later discovered that she had been communicating with a suspect on the run, then that would be her career over. She owed Helen so much—her livelihood, her position, her life even—but there was too much at stake now, and if she was honest, there were too many unanswered questions.

Which was why, with a heavy heart, Charlie turned her phone toward Sanderson and said:

"I think you'd better see this."

124

They stood stock-still, sizing each other up. Robert showed no signs of wanting to attack her, but neither was he preparing to flee. He was boxed in, Helen blocking his route from the room, yet he seemed oddly unconcerned.

"When did you know?" he said suddenly.

His voice was as she remembered it—young and raw—but the warmth he used to possess had vanished. He seemed older, but not happier.

"After Paine, maybe. But I hoped I was wrong."

"Isn't that just like you? Always in denial."

"About what?"

"The harm you do. The pain you cause."

"I've only ever wanted to help people. I spent months looking for you, trying to make amends—"

"But you didn't find me, did you?"

"Not for the want of trying. I know I turned your life upside down—"

"Is that how you'd put it?"

"You were happy—you had nice parents, a good home—but you were my only blood relative. I wanted to look after you, help you make the right choices—"

"Then I guess I'll be another thing on your conscience, won't I?"

This time his tone was gleeful and taunting.

"You did all this because you wanted to," Helen said, gesturing to the maps, the phone. "It's nothing to do with me."

"In some ways I did them a favor. Jake was hopelessly obsessed with you. Paine was eating himself up with bitterness—"

"And Angelique? What the hell had she done?"

"Nothing yet. But you would have harmed her, just as you did the others. Everything you touch dies—don't you know that yet, Helen?"

Helen stared at him. He knew her better than anyone else and was determined to make that count.

"Including yourself?" she said quietly. "Isn't that what all this is about?"

"Well, the last time you faced off with a blood relative, you shot her. So it would be kind of poetic, wouldn't it?"

"I never wanted to kill your mother. She forced me to."

"Isn't it a coincidence that you always end up in a position where you are *forced* to hurt people? Do you never ask yourself if you *like* inflicting pain?"

"That's not true."

"Isn't it? What did you feel when you were beating Paine? Wasn't there a part of you that didn't want to stop?"

Helen wanted to deny it, but couldn't find the words.

"You see, Helen, you're no better than the criminals you chase. Think of me as your subconscious, acting out the fantasies and desires that lie within you."

"Tell that to the judge."

"There's not going to be a trial, Helen. This starts and ends here."

Helen said nothing. She had sent her text over ten minutes ago. She would have expected to hear distant sirens by now, but there was nothing. Robert stood in front of her, framed by the dark sea, looking relaxed and happy. Helen had no idea what he was planning, but his mood made her decidedly nervous.

"How did you know?" she said suddenly, breaking the silence.

"That wasn't hard, Helen. I've been your quiet shadow for nearly a year now. Little boy blue following you around day after day after day. I saw you meet Jake Elder in that city center bar. I heard him arguing with his boyfriend afterward. Did you feel lonely after that exchange, Helen? I saw you sitting in your window looking beautiful and sad—"

"And a day later I visited Max Paine," Helen replied, suddenly realizing how careless she'd been.

"I watched you visit him then and the time after. I saw how agitated you were after you'd come to blows. And the next morning, I saw him. He had a cap on and was covered in makeup, but boy, was he a mess. You must have really gone to town on him."

Helen looked at Robert. The young man who had once cried on her shoulder now stared at her, hateful in his triumph.

"Am I really worth all this?" Helen said finally.

"You have no idea."

"You've been stalking me for months, giving up your own life—"

"I *had* no life thanks to you."

"Bullshit. You don't have to play the cards you're dealt. You can choose a different path, make good choices—"

"You killed my mother. Nobody told me about that—for years I was given half-truths and evasions. Then you came along and told the whole fucking world."

"That was never my intention."

"'Son of a Monster'—that's what they called me. 'The Spawn of a She-devil.' I was a nobody—don't you get that?—and suddenly I was famous."

Helen stared at him. The memory of the press pack descending on his quiet family home in Aldershot still haunted her.

"After that, I couldn't go anywhere. People knew who I was, what she'd done—they wanted nothing to do with me. As if her sins were mine. And yet what had she done? She'd killed to protect you. To save her little sister."

"I know that's what she thought she was doing—"

"I was going to kill myself," Robert interrupted. "I was going to call you up, tell you where I was and then do it, before you could get to me. I'd saved up my pills, found a hotel room, but when it came to it, I couldn't do it."

Helen looked at him as he took a step forward.

"Not because I was scared, but because I was angry. It's my rage that has sustained me all these months. My rage and my hatred of *you*."

Helen stayed where she was, refusing to be intimidated. And in the far distance, she now heard the sound of sirens. Robert seemed oblivious, continuing his rant against her.

"After you shot her, you danced on her grave."

"I loved your mother. I still do. But she was a murderer—"

"You tried to justify your own actions by denigrating her."

"What she did was wrong."

"No, what she did was right," Robert barked back at her. "Which is why it felt right."

Helen suppressed a shudder. Marianne had been utterly unrepentant at her trial, even confessing to enjoying murdering their parents.

"What did she say at her trial? 'I enjoyed watching their faces, knowing they couldn't hurt me anymore.' I read the transcripts—I read everything about her. Her testimony was all I had left of her."

Helen felt the emotion rising in her—Robert had been the innocent in all this, yet he too had been swallowed by the darkness.

"You were never like her."

"But I am now. Thanks to you."

"And does it make you happy?"

Robert looked at her oddly, as if trying to read the trick in the question.

"Yes. I think it does. You see, I could have killed you at any point during the last twelve months, but I wanted you to suffer. To feel the pain that I've endured since you ransacked my life. All your dirty little secrets put on view for the world to enjoy. Jake, Max and poor Angelique . . ."

The sound of the sirens was now unmistakable. Help could be only minutes away. There could be no triumph for Helen, but at least she could bring this thing to an end.

"I contacted my colleagues before I came in here, Robert," she said softly.

"I assumed you would, but I'm glad we've had this time together."

"So what happens now? If you want to hurt me, you've got a couple of minutes to do it."

Robert stared at her, his hands hanging by his side.

"I'm not going to hurt you, Helen. That was never the plan."

Still Helen braced herself, ready to roll with his attack. But Robert simply turned and opened the windows behind him, flinging them back so they crashed loudly on the wall outside, sending glass tumbling downward. A blast of cold air roared in, whipping Helen's hair around her shoulders. Suddenly everything outside seemed amplified—the sound of car doors slamming echoing around the deserted quay.

"Don't be stupid, Robert. You'll break your legs and where are you going to run to? We've boxed ourselves into a corner here."

Robert turned back to her. Illuminated by the full moon behind him, he seemed even more ghostly than before.

"Speak for yourself."

Helen took a step forward, her anxiety spiking. Why was he so calm? What was she missing here? Did he want to be caught? She could hear footsteps climbing the metal fire escape now, hurrying toward them.

"Like I said, this is about you, not about me."

The footsteps were getting closer. It could be only a matter of moments before Robert was apprehended.

"That's why everything in this room is yours, Helen. The coffee cups, old cigarettes, food wrappers. Even an old hoodie you thought you'd lost. Your DNA, your prints. There's nothing of *me* here, I'm afraid."

Now Helen knew exactly what he intended to do and lunged forward, but she was too late. Hopping up onto the lip of the window ledge, Robert leaped out into the night. Helen launched herself at him but was a second too slow. She slammed into the wall—just in time to see Robert land with a splash in the inky water below. Her adversary had chosen his spot well—an old loading bay overhanging the dock.

Now the full extent of her stupidity came crashing home. But she had no time to react as suddenly she felt rough hands upon her, dragging her back from the window. She tried to speak, but her face was pushed hard into the dirt, even as her hands were wrenched backward and cuffed. Now she was being read her rights by breathless officers too drunk on their own success to listen to her pleas.

Robert's victory was complete.

125

Emilia rubbed her hands together in a vain attempt to keep warm. She had lain in wait behind Southampton Central on numerous occasions, but had never found an effective way to keep warm. She was a naturally cold person—however many layers she wore, she could never stop her teeth chattering.

Tonight, though, she didn't mind one bit. Any personal discomfort she felt was forgotten—this night was her night, the crowning achievement of her professional life thus far. She had endured much over the years—parents who maltreated her, an acid attack that had permanently scarred her, endless mockery and abuse—but tonight she would show them all. She was about to break the story of the year—one that would make her career and finish another in the process.

She had made it down to Southampton's main police station in record time. Sanderson's text was to the point—*in custody. back entrance. 20 mins.*—and Emilia had wasted no time, grabbing her camera and heading out of the door. There was a darkened doorway out the back that made perfect cover and she was poised there now, waiting for the telltale sedan. This was supposed to be a discreet, unpublicized entry to the station, but thanks to Sanderson, it would be anything but. Perhaps Emilia had misjudged her—maybe she could be trusted to honor their deal.

Emilia checked her camera again. Battery level high, night exposure set, rapid-fire mode on—then a sound made her look up. It was low but persistent, the sound of a car moving swiftly but quietly along the deserted street. Emilia readied herself.

Now the car swung into the alleyway behind the station and as if by magic, the heavy rear doors started to creak open. The car swung round toward them, slowing slightly to allow a sufficient gap to open up. Emilia now stepped forward, shooting quickly, grabbing as many photos as she could. She had timed it right, for seconds later the car disappeared inside, the doors clanging shut behind it.

Emilia stepped back into the shadows. Her article was ready to print, barring one small addition. Flicking the camera on to viewing mode, Emilia broke out into a smile. She had what she needed, her coup de grâce.

A shot of Helen Grace's ashen face, staring out into the night.

126

"Look at the camera, please."

Helen stared straight ahead as the flash fired—once, twice, three times. It was blinding, disorienting, the pain piercing her brain. But Helen knew it was just the beginning of her torture.

"Now to the left, please."

Flash, flash, flash.

"Now to the right."

Helen knew the drill—had watched this process countless times—but she had to be led through it now by the custody sergeant. She nodded when prompted, but none of it felt real. She was still in shock, her mind turning on the ingenuity of Robert's scheme. He had trailed her patiently, picking up the detritus of her life, carefully assembling the narrative of her destruction. He had selected his victims well—choosing people who were not necessarily close to Helen, but who were nevertheless part of her secret life. Their exposure through death posed the question of who might want to silence them, leading the police straight back to Helen. She had no doubt now that Robert would have planted further DNA evidence at the Torture Rooms and possibly at Paine's too. She had a connection to all the victims, so her only escape route was to establish a bona fide alibi.

With a shudder, Helen realized that this too would be denied her. She had been out running on the night of the first murder—had someone seen her running north, as if heading home from the Torture Rooms? On the night of Paine's murder, she had visited Marianne's grave—her route from Southampton Central would have taken her right past Paine's flat. She was a creature of habit and Robert had taken full advantage of that, knowing all the while that there was no one waiting at home to confirm her version of events.

"Right. Now we're going to strip-search you."

Helen felt hands upon her, and looking up, she saw a female custody officer removing her clothes. Her vest, trousers and boots were removed and bagged. She would be allowed to keep her underwear on, but only after they had been searched. Helen submitted to this indignity, all the while feeling the sergeant's eyes on her. Helen's torso was riddled with scars—evidence of her historic addiction to sadomasochism, which would no doubt strengthen the case against her. Very few people had seen her like this—naked and exposed—and Helen could feel the sergeant's silent judgment.

This was nothing compared with what was to come, however. Helen knew that her life would be pored over now, her every misdemeanor and insecurity exposed as she was hung out to dry. She was at the bottom of the well, with no means or hope of escape.

Standing there half-naked in the weak light of a flickering bulb, Helen was utterly alone.

127

It felt like she was in the middle of a nightmare. Charlie stood still in the middle of the room, making little effort to help the SOCOs who maneuvered around her. Helen was innocent—she *had* to be innocent—and yet she had led them here. The phone looked like it was Paine's, the hoodie was hers and the cigarettes that lay half-smoked in the ashtray were unquestionably Helen's brand. The coffee cups were Costa, not Starbucks; the sandwich wrappers were from the local deli by the station . . . The place even smelled of Helen—her signature Obsession perfume seeming to hang in the room. This was her space, her brain, but still it made no sense.

Sanderson walked swiftly past toward Meredith, brushing against Charlie as she did so. It was a subtle reminder that they were here to do a job, to gather and process the evidence. Charlie had played her part in Helen's capture, but it had been Sanderson's persistence and instincts that had brought them to this place and she clearly felt that she was in charge. Had her colleague been driven by conviction or ambition? It probably didn't matter—either way she was well-placed to step into Helen's shoes if—when—she was charged with triple murder.

Charlie would suffer as a result. Her life would be made as difficult as possible and she had no doubt that, before the end of the year, she would find herself in Gardam's office, asking for a transfer. Perhaps this was no bad thing. How could she carry on now that her mentor had been disgraced? How could she look anyone in the eye when it appeared her faith had been badly misplaced? Tonight was Helen's nadir, but Charlie felt her life unraveling too. They had been so close—Helen was godmother to her only child. Could she really have got it so wrong? Was it possible that Helen's barren life had finally led her to . . . this?

"I'll check the perimeter, see if we have any witnesses."

Sanderson grunted, but didn't look up. They both knew there wouldn't be any witnesses on the deserted quay and that this was just an excuse for Charlie to leave the room. Perhaps she *was* a bad copper—perhaps she was blindly loyal—but she was still a human being. She walked quickly from the room to hide the tears that were threatening. Guilty she might be, but Helen had always been Charlie's friend and confidante and she was damned if she was going to watch Sanderson dance on her grave.

128

Jonathan Gardam watched through the two-way mirror as the questions rained down on Helen. As soon as her arrest had been confirmed, he'd called in officers from Sussex Police to lead the interviews. There was no question of Sanderson or Brooks questioning Helen, given their relationship with her. Gardam could have fielded the interview himself, of course, but he had decided to take a backseat. He would get a much better view of the action that way.

Helen looked pale and weary, but she was not quite beaten yet. She was patiently taking the officers through the events of the evening, trying to convince them that *she* was the victim. But even from here, Gardam could feel their skepticism. Helen's story was coherent and measured, but detectives of this ilk were not prone to flights of fancy—they followed the evidence.

"Listen, we'd like to take you at your word, but there was nobody there. We checked the surrounding buildings, the dockside—"

"He was there."

"Then why can't we find any trace of him?"

"Do you think I made him up? Why would I have called my colleagues to the docks if I was responsible? Why would I do that?"

"You tell us."

Helen was getting angry now, insisting that she had acted properly throughout the investigation. She was telling them that she hadn't kept her connection to the first two victims to herself—she had discussed it with her commanding officer and been asked to continue on the case. They promised to follow this up, before launching into a series of new questions about her relationship to the deceased. Helen brushed these off, urging them to verify what she was saying before they asked her anything else. Again they batted her back and Gardam was surprised to see Helen now turn toward the two-way.

"I'm not saying another word until you get him in here," Helen was saying. "Ask him under caution if I raised the issue."

"With all due respect, you're the only one under caution here and I'd like *you* to answer my questions . . ."

Helen ignored her interrogator, staring straight at Gardam. It was a bold gesture but a pointless one. She would only see her own face staring back, whereas he could see everything. He had the advantage now, which was how he wanted it.

They would come to him, of course, asking if what she claimed was true. He had the opportunity to extend a helping hand to her now . . . but why should he, when she had already sunk her teeth into it? He would dismiss her claims. He would be surprised, bemused, even saddened that she should try to draw a fellow officer into her depravity.

He had been fascinated by her—maybe he was still—but she had poured scorn on him. And for that she was going to pay.

129

The door closed behind her and Helen heard the key turn in the lock. It was strange how different it sounded on the inside. Out there, among colleagues and friends, the turn of the key had always sounded like a job well done. In here, it was like a death knell.

Helen sat down on the bed and stared at the walls. Her mind was turning on a thousand points, searching for the weak spots in Robert's scheme, but she could find none. She knew already that there would be no help coming from Gardam. If he'd wanted to save her, he would have done so by now. No, this was the perfect get-out for him—if she reported his assault now, who would believe her? Still, Helen wondered whether he was enjoying her destruction. Or did it hurt him, knowing that he would never see her again?

She heard footsteps and looked up. The door remained closed, but a newspaper slid under the gap at the bottom. The footsteps moved away and Helen could hear the custody officers laughing. It wasn't hard to see why. Their gift to her was a copy of the *Evening News*. Picking it up, she flicked past the sensational headline to the inner pages. Much of the paper was devoted to the story, but the crowning glory was Emilia Garanita's profile piece of her. It was entitled FALL FROM GRACE.

Helen binned the paper and lay down on the bed. The fight had finally gone out of her. There was nothing to do now but lick her wounds.

Robert had waited for his moment, then struck with devastating effect. He was a man possessed—his loneliness, bitterness and rage altering him beyond all recognition. He had stayed alive purely to gain vengeance for his mother, and Helen had paid dearly for her sins. Robert had taken everything from her. Her reputation, her job, her friends.

And, worst of all, her freedom.

Don't miss the first Detective Helen Grace Thriller,

EENY MEENY

Now available from New American Library

1

Sam is asleep. I could kill him now. His face is turned from me—it wouldn't be hard. Would he stir if I moved? Try to stop me? Or would he just be *glad* that this nightmare was over?

I can't think like that. I must try to remember what is real, what is good. But when you're a prisoner, the days seem endless and hope is the first thing to die.

I rack my brains for happy memories to hold off the dark thoughts, but they are harder and harder to summon.

We've been here only ten days (or is it eleven?), yet normal life already seems a distant memory. We were hitching back from a gig in London when it happened. It was pouring rain and a succession of cars had sailed past without a second look. We were soaked to the skin and about to turn back when finally a van pulled over. Inside, it was warm and dry. We were offered coffee from a flask.

Just the smell of it was enough to cheer us up. The taste was even better. We didn't realize it would be our last taste of freedom.

When I came to, my head was pounding. Blood coated my mouth. I wasn't in the warm van anymore. I was in a cold, dark space. Was I dreaming? A noise behind me made me start. But it was only Sam stumbling to his feet.

We'd been robbed. Robbed and dumped. I scrambled forward, clawing at the walls that enclosed us. Cold, hard tiles. I crashed into Sam and for a brief moment held him, breathing in that smell I love so much. Then the moment passed and we realized the horror of our situation.

We were in a disused diving pool. Derelict, unloved, it had been stripped of the boards, signs and even the steps. Everything that could be salvaged had been. Leaving a deep smooth tank that was impossible to climb out of.

Was that evil shit listening to our screams? Probably. Because when we finally stopped, it happened. We heard a mobile phone ringing and for a brief, glorious moment thought it was someone coming to rescue us. But then we saw the phone's face glowing on the pool floor beside us. Sam didn't move, so I ran. Why did it have to be me? Why does it *always* have to be me?

"Hello, Amy."

The voice on the other end was distorted, inhuman. I wanted to beg for mercy, explain that they'd made a terrible mistake, but the fact that they knew my name seemed to rob me of all conviction. I said nothing, so the voice continued, relentless and dispassionate:

"Do you want to live?"

"Who are you? What have you done to u—?"

"Do you want to live?"

For a minute, I can't reply. My tongue won't move. But then: "Yes."

"On the floor by the phone you'll find a gun. It has one bullet in it. For Sam or for yourself. That is the price of your freedom. You must kill to live. Do you want to live, Amy?"

I can't speak. I want to vomit.

"Well, do you?"

And then the phone goes dead. Which is when Sam asks: "What did they say?"

Sam is asleep beside me. I could do it now.

2

The woman cried out in pain. And then was silent. Across her back, livid lines were forming. Jake raised the crop again and brought it down with a snap. The woman bucked, cried out, then said:

"Again."

She seldom said anything else. She wasn't the talkative type. Not like some of his clients. The administrators, accountants and clerks stuck in sexless relationships were *desperate* to talk—desperate to be liked by the man who beat them up for money. She was different, a closed book. She never mentioned where she'd found him. Or why she'd come. She issued her instructions—her needs—clearly and crisply, then asked him to get on with it.

They always started by securing her wrists. Two studded leather straps pulled taut, so that her arms were tethered to the wall. Iron ankle fetters secured her feet to the floor. Her clothes would be neatly stowed on the chair provided, so there she'd stand, chained, in her underwear, awaiting punishment.

There was no role play. No "Please don't hurt me, Daddy" or "I'm a bad, bad girl." She just wanted him to hurt her. In some ways it was a relief. Every job becomes routine after a while and sometimes it was nice not to have to pander to the fantasies of sad wannabe victims. At the same time it was frustrating, her refusal to strike up a proper relationship with him. The most important element of any S&M encounter is trust. The submissive needs to know that they are in safe hands, that their dominator knows their personality and their needs and can give them a fulfilling experience on terms that are comfortable for both parties. If you don't have that, then it swiftly becomes assault or even abuse—and that was most definitely *not* Jake's bag.

So he chipped away—the odd question here, the odd comment there. And over time he'd divined the basics: that she wasn't from Southampton originally, that she had no family, that she was closing in on forty and didn't mind. He also knew from their sessions together that pain was her thing. Sex didn't come into it. She didn't want to be teased or titillated. She wanted to be punished. The beatings never went too far, but they were hard and unremitting. She had the body to take it—she was tall, muscular and seriously toned—and the traces of ancient scars suggested she was not new to the S&M scene.

And yet for all his probing, all his carefully worded questions, there was only one thing that Jake knew about her for sure. Once, when she was getting dressed, her photo ID slipped from her jacket pocket onto the floor. She snatched it up in a heartbeat—thought he hadn't seen, but he had. He thought he knew a bit about people, but this one had taken him by surprise. If he hadn't seen her ID, he'd never have guessed that she was a policewoman.

Amy is squatting a few feet away from me. There's no awkwardness now and she urinates on the floor without embarrassment. I watch as the thin sliver of piss hits the tiles, tiny droplets of it bouncing back up to settle on her dirty knickers. A few weeks ago I would have turned away at the sight, but not now.

Her urine snakes its way slowly down the slope to join the stagnant puddle of waste that has built up at the deeper end. I'm glued to its progress but finally the last drops disappear and the entertainment is over. She retreats to her corner. No words of apology, no acknowledgment. We have become animals, careless of ourselves and of each other.

It wasn't always like this. At the beginning, we were furious, defiant. We were determined that we would not die here, that together we would survive. Amy stood on my shoulders, her nails cracking as she clawed the tiles, straining to reach the lip of the pool. When that didn't work, she tried jumping up from my shoulders. But the pool is fifteen feet deep, maybe more, and salvation seems forever just out of reach.

We tried the phone but it was PIN-locked and after we'd tried a few combinations it ran out of power. We shouted and screamed until our throats raged. All we heard in response was our echo, mocking us. Sometimes it feels like we are on another planet, with not another human being for miles around. Christmas is approaching. There must be people out looking for us, but it's hard to believe that here, surrounded by this terrible, enduring silence.

Escape is not an option, so now we simply survive. We chewed our nails until our fingers bled, then sucked up the blood greedily. We licked the condensation from the tiles at dawn, but still our stomachs ached. We talked about eating our clothes . . . but thought better of it. It's freezing at night and all that keeps us from dying of hypothermia is our scant clothing and the heat we glean from each other.

Is it my imagination or have our embraces become less warm? Less secure? Since it happened, we have clung to each other day and night, willing each other to survive, desperate not to be left alone in this awful place. We play games to pass the time, imagining what we will do after the cavalry arrives—what we will eat, what we will say to our families, what we will get for Christmas. But slowly these games have tailed off as we realize that we were brought here for a purpose and that there will be no happy ending for us.

"Amy?"

Silence.

"Amy, please say something."

She doesn't look at me. She doesn't talk to me. Have I lost her for good? I try to imagine what she's thinking, but I can't.

Perhaps there is nothing left to say. We have tried everything, explored every inch of our prison, looking for a means of escape. The only thing we haven't touched is the gun. It sits there still, calling to us.

I raise my head and catch Amy looking at it. She meets my eyes and drops hers. Could she pick it up? A fortnight ago, I'd have said no way. But now? Trust is a fragile thing—hard to earn, easy to lose. I'm not sure of anything anymore.

All I do know is that one of us is going to die.

4

Stepping out into the crisp evening air, Helen Grace felt relaxed and happy. Slowing her pace, she savored this moment of peace, casting an amused eye over the throng of shoppers that surrounded her.

She was heading for Southampton's Christmas market. Ranged along the southern flank of the WestQuay shopping center, the market was an annual event—an opportunity to buy original, hand-crafted presents that weren't on any Amazon wish list. Helen hated Christmas, but every year without fail she bought something for Anna and Marie. It was her one festive indulgence and she always made the most of it. She bought jewelry, scented candles and other trinkets but didn't stint on the comestibles either, snapping up dates, chocolates, an obscenely expensive Christmas pudding and a pretty packet of peppermint creams—Marie was particularly partial to those.

She retrieved her Kawasaki from the WestQuay car park and blasted through the city center traffic, heading southeast toward Weston. She was speeding away from excitement and affluence and toward deprivation and despair, drawn inexorably toward the five monolithic tower blocks that dominate the skyline there. For years they've greeted those approaching Southampton by sea and in the past they were worthy of such an honor, being imposing, futuristic and optimistic. But it was a very different story now.

Melbourne Tower was by far the most dilapidated. Four years ago, an illegal drugs factory had exploded on the sixth floor. The damage was extensive, the heart ripped out of the building. The council promised to rebuild it, but the recession put paid to their plans. It was still technically scheduled for renovation but no one believed it would happen now. So the building remained as it was, wounded and unloved, abandoned by the vast majority of the families who used to live there. Now it was the terrain of junkies, squatters and those with nowhere else to go. It was a nasty, forgotten place.

Helen parked her motorbike a safe distance from the towers and continued on foot. Women generally didn't walk the projects alone at night, but Helen never felt concerned for her safety. She was known here and people tended to steer clear, which suited her fine. All was quiet tonight, apart from some dogs sniffing around a burned-out car, so Helen picked her way past the needles and condoms and stepped inside Melbourne Tower.

On the fourth floor, she paused outside flat 408. It had once been a nice, comfortable council flat, but now it looked like Fort Knox. The front door was riddled with dead bolts, but more striking were the metal grilles—padlocked firmly shut—that reinforced the main entrance. The vile graffiti—*flid, retard, mong*—that covered the exterior gave a clue as to why the flat was so protected.

It was the home of Marie and Anna Storey. Anna was severely disabled, unable to speak, feed herself or go to the toilet. Anna, now fourteen, needed her middle-aged mother to do everything for her, so her mum did the best she could. Living on benefits and handouts, buying food from Lidl, being sparing with the heating. They would have been okay like that—these were the cards they'd been dealt and Marie was not one to be bitter—had it not been for the local yobs. The fact that they had nothing to do and were from broken homes was no excuse. These kids were just nasty thugs who enjoyed belittling, bullying and attacking a vulnerable woman and child.

Helen knew all this because she'd taken a special interest in them. One of the scrotes—a vicious, acne-covered dropout called Steven Green—had attempted to burn out their flat. The fire crew had got there in time and the damage was contained to the hallway and front room, but the effect on Marie and Anna had been devastating. They were utterly terrified when Helen interviewed them. This was attempted murder and someone needed to be called to account for it. She did her best, but the case never went to court for lack of witnesses. Helen urged her to move, but Marie was stubborn. The flat was their family home and had been kitted out specially to deal with Anna's mobility limitations. Why should they have to move? Marie sold what valuables she still possessed to fortify the flat. Four years later, the drugs factory blew up. Before that, the lift had worked fine and flat 408 was basically a happy home. Now it was a prison.

Social Services was supposed to call round to keep an eye on them, but they avoided this place like the plague and visits were fleeting at best. And so Helen, who had little to keep her home at night, would pop in. Which was why she'd been there when Steven Green and company returned to finish the job. He was high as usual and clutching a petrol can that he was trying to light with a homemade fuse. He didn't get the chance. Helen's baton caught him on the elbow, then across the neck, sending him sprawling to the floor. The others were caught off guard by the sudden appearance of a copper and dropped their petrol bombs to flee. Some of them made it; some of them didn't. Helen had been well trained in how to take the legs out from under fleeing suspects. She foiled the attack and not long after had the distinct pleasure of watching Steven Green and three of his closest friends get a substantial prison sentence. Some days the job really did give back.

Helen suppressed a shiver. The dingy corridors, the broken lives, the graffiti and filth were too redolent of her own upbringing not to provoke a reaction. It conjured up memories she'd fought hard to suppress and which she forced back down now. She was here for Marie and Anna—she refused to let anything darken her mood today.

She knocked on the door three times—their special code—and after much unlocking, the door swung open.

"Meals on Wheels?" Helen ventured.

"Piss off," came the predictable reply.

Helen smiled as Marie opened the outer grille for her to enter. Already her dark thoughts were receding—Marie's "warm" welcome always had that effect on her. Once inside, Helen doled out her gifts, received hers and felt utterly at peace. For a brief moment, flat 408 was her sanctuary from a dark and violent world.

ABOUT THE AUTHOR

M. J. Arlidge is the international bestselling author of the Detective Helen Grace Thrillers, including *Liar Liar*, *The Doll's House*, *Pop Goes the Weasel*, and his debut, *Eeny Meeny*, which has been sold in twenty-nine countries. He lives in England and has worked in television for the past fifteen years.

CONNECT ONLINE
twitter.com/mjarlidge